HER VIKING HEART

HEIDI HERMAN

This is a work of fiction. All characters, organizations, and events portrayed in this novel are products of the author's imagination and are used fictitiously.

Edited by Word Nerd Copy
Formatting by Polgarus Studio

DepositPhotos: VitalikRadko, chesterf
Shutterstock: Vibrant Image Studio
Bigstock: Maciej Bledowski

First Edition v3.

Hekla Publishing 1603 Capitol Ave.
Suite 310
Cheyenne, WY 82001

"The Bold and the Generous have the best lives."

— ICELANDIC PROVERB

CHAPTER ONE

"You poor dear, first your mother last year and now your father."

"I'm sorry for your loss."

"I'm so sorry."

Anna nodded numbly and willed the pieces of her body to hold together through hug after hug and the occasional iron-grip of hands clasping her forearms as they shook her emphatically.

"Miss Miller, please call if you need anything."

It had been days since she had heard the first of these common phrases directed at her.

"We did everything we could," had been followed by, "The road was wet when he swerved. It was instantaneous. He didn't suffer."

The line of faces stretched down the aisle to her left; so many people still waited. She swayed slightly and refocused on the tall man with thinning hair in front of her. He wore a charcoal gray suit with a shimmery silver tie covered in tiny dots of blood-red diamond shapes, lined up diagonally with military precision. His nose was large for his face, but his eyes were a beautiful amber brown, glinting with unshed tears.

"I'm so sorry. We'll all miss him," the man said as he grasped her shoulders. Anna didn't recognize him, but tears glinted in his eyes and sorrow was evident on his face.

How many times would she hear those words spoken? In some eyes, she saw pity, some compassion, and others were blank. The required words repeated and ran together. They sounded hollow. She struggled to respond with the socially mandated appreciation, mumbling thank yous, and you're-so-kinds.

A vise settled on her chest, squeezing her lungs until no air could escape or enter. A silent sob escaped her.

*

Three weeks had passed since the afternoon she received the call. Anna went through the motions of life's routine in a fog, barely remembering the details of tasks and activities that once seemed so important. She had not been to work, not that it mattered since she worked for a temp agency. Since the funeral, Anna simply didn't bother to call the office to request an assignment. She didn't have the energy. It all seemed so pointless. She gave up her apartment. After packing up a few cherished possessions and donating the larger furniture to charity, she moved back into her parent's house-her house now.

Anna pulled up to her parent's former home and parked her small car in the driveway. She got out and leaned against the car for a moment, looking up at the structure that had been her home for so many years. She had grown up in this house, and she was surrounded now with warm, bittersweet memories. The two-story, three-bedroom house sat back from the street always had an aura of peace, but now it seemed silent and empty.

Reaching into the back seat, Anna wrestled with the large, flat pile of unfolded boxes, twisting and tugging on the ungainly stack that slithered and refused her efforts to extract them through the car door. Frustrated, she yanked them out one at a time, leaning each against the rear quarter panel, where each declined to cooperate and promptly slid to the ground. Tears pricked at her eyes, and she resisted the urge to stomp on the unapologetic pile of cardboard. Biting her lip, she grabbed two edges—one for each hand— and stomped to the front steps, her arm held out awkwardly to keep from tripping herself on the box flaps.

*

Old maple trees graced the front yard, casting chilly shadows across the path. Every summer, they created a privacy screen of leaves between the sidewalk and the home's wide front porch. Anna had spent countless hours on that front porch. Some of her earliest memories were of running up and down the steps, dashing between her parents' cozy spot on the porch swing and the enticing blinking of the numerous lightning bugs around the yard. She crossed the porch and leaned one cardboard square against the doorframe, where it promptly slid to the floor. She rolled her eyes and dug into her pocket for the keys, her slightly shaking hands fumbling as she tried to slide the key into the lock and open the door. She threw one box in and kicked the other from its resting place on the porch floor before turning around and heading back to the car for the others. Successfully managing the remaining four at once, she turned and headed back inside, closing the door behind her.

The light blue house with its gray shutters and shiny black front door had been host to countless barbeques, holiday parties, and birthday festivities. The living room looked nearly as it always had, comfortably casual, but now there was a light coating of dust on the surfaces, highlighted by the weak sunbeam struggling to brighten the room. Years of Christmas celebrations, football game-day gatherings, and lazy Sunday afternoons reading had taken place here. The house was quiet now but filled with memories that soothed her, easing the constant ache of her loss. Anna knew every inch of the house, and it had never seemed too big when the three of them lived here together. It was odd to be here again, in the space so familiar but now so quiet. The home seemed much larger now, each room echoing the smallest movements.

Anna had already spent days organizing and rearranging rooms and was now nearly ready to box up clothing and sort through financial papers. She had gone through the same process after her mother died, although on a much smaller scale. It had been easier then, with her father here to share the sadness and smile over silly memories.

"Remember this hideous scarf? I gave it to her for Mother's Day one year, and she wore it to church to make me happy. I never realized how ugly it was because she smiled and wore it with pride," Anna laughed. "But, now that I think about it, I think that was the only time she ever wore it."

Her father had smiled, running his hand across the silky fabric. "Yeah, I think it was too ugly to wear. But, sweetie, she kept it."

There was no one here now to relive those little moments with her.

She quickly finished the work in the living room. She hadn't changed much or boxed anything up beyond the personal papers. The master suite, which faced her now, was much more difficult. Deciding what to keep, what to give away, and what to toss was tougher with items as personal as clothing. Each item had so many memories attached.

Taking a break for lunch, Anna moved into the kitchen, her favorite room of the house. Like most homes, it was a place of many happy memories. She had always loved this room with its walk-in pantry and small, sunny dining nook. Her mother had often called it the heart of the house. Anna agreed. Making popcorn for movie nights, Saturday afternoons learning how to make cookies, and times of pumpkin carving, Easter egg decorating, and summer lemonade-making. The project of stripping wallpaper and repainting the walls and cabinets had taken days. At the time, it felt like a punishing chore, but now she recalled the silliness and laughter she and her mother had shared. Every visible brushstroke and drip of paint held the memories of those days.

She smiled as she pulled out black forest ham and Swiss cheese from the refrigerator. Slicing sourdough bread left over from the previous night's dinner, she layered it with the meat and cheese. Returning the packages to the refrigerator, she grabbed a handful of green grapes before kicking the door shut with her foot. Reaching into the cookie jar, she added a peanut butter cookie to the plate and headed for the deck.

Early May in Eastern Iowa was a forecast gamble. Some years it would be eighty degrees and sunny, other times it would be windy, cold, and gray. Today was the best kind of day. It felt like a perfect seventy degrees; the warm rays of the sun were a treat to soak up. Anna enjoyed the balmy temperature while the sun played peek-a-boo with the big fluffy white clouds that lazily drifted across the robin's-egg-blue sky.

She snorted at her mind's description. "A little over the top there, dontcha think?" she asked herself, breaking the silence of the day by speaking aloud. Her parents would have enjoyed this day. She missed them both keenly, but today was more of a nostalgic ache than the aching sense of loss. Some days, the pain seemed to ease a little, and right now she allowed herself to enjoy this moment of contentment. She watched the birds as they flew from the feeders to the trees and she worked her way through the ham and cheese sandwich. As she finished the fruit and cookie, Anna stood up, sighing, and headed back into the house.

She doubted anyone would ever know if she had dirty dishes piled in the sink, but she washed up her few items and set them in the dish rack anyway. She looked around the kitchen with a resigned sigh, seeing nothing more to clean up. She couldn't avoid it any longer. It was time to tackle the bedroom. It had been hard enough when she had helped her father, but now it seemed so much more difficult facing the same task alone. She dragged the cardboard wardrobe box near the closet door, next to the smaller ones she had positioned for folded clothes, shoes, and miscellaneous items. She had a plastic bag for trash, a dust rag, and furniture polish piled nearby. She worked mechanically, blinking her eyes to clear the tears that threatened to spill over as she slowly packed up the last of her father's life.

After an hour, she finished emptying the dressers and cleaned each surface inside and out. She knew the exhaustion she felt was more emotional than physical. "Just the closet," she said aloud, "and then we reward ourselves with a pizza tonight." She winked at her parents' photo on the wall.

Anna grabbed two large armfuls of clothes, carried them out, and tossed them on the bed for sorting. She decided to donate the entire pile to the resale shop, save one sweater she wanted to keep. She trudged back to the closet, eyeing the last few boxes lined up against the back wall. The first contained some of her mother's old photos, a few scarves, and mementos her father had kept. The ugly scarf was in the stack. Anna laughed. He must have snuck it back in after she had put it on the toss pile. The second box was full of what appeared to be decades worth of receipts and tax forms.

"Ugh," she said aloud, "there is no way I'm going through those." She shoved the box back into the corner with her foot.

The third box was different. It was not a box but a plastic file storage container. Anna sighed as she dropped to her knees, sliding the box closer and flipping the top open. She smiled, a wash of memories flooding over her. This was a project box. She and her father had created many boxes like this one.

Every box contained the notes, photos, and research data on any number of topics that caught her father's interest. Her favorite father-daughter activity had been research projects.

The distinctive clear lid triggered a memory. Most of their project boxes came with blue lids, or it might have been that Dad always chose blue. This one had a matching milky-white semi-opaque lid that looked familiar. Anna recalled seeing this on the floor of her father's study recently.

Dad had been a huge history buff, and Anna would often get caught up in his enthusiasm. From riverboats to pearl buttons, everything had a story. They both had a love for the Mississippi River and its part in the Quad Cities history, the four towns on either side of the state line: Moline and Rock Island in Illinois and Bettendorf and Davenport in Iowa. They had toured many of the state's Silos & Smokestacks National Heritage Area historic sites and volunteered together for the heritage area at the state fair. Ten years prior, Anna helped her father research the history of the family home. Even her mother had been fascinated with the original owners and the hardship of early life in the area. Anna remembered the long hours of research with fondness.

Somehow, working with her father never felt like work. He made it into an adventure. Using their research, they compiled volumes of information about a person, the details so vivid they would often create stories about daily life. Anna remembered those stories as if they were books she had read. She imagined a family crossing the plains in a wagon train, what their days were like, and how excited they must have been about the trip. Their months and years of work carving out a homestead in the wilderness. Then, the fear and loss they must have felt when tragedy struck. The records only reflected the tragic history of a large family nearly wiped out by an epidemic and their struggle to keep the farm. *There was always so much more to the story*, she thought.

"You would have made a good pioneer, Anna," Dad had said. "You're not afraid to get dirty, and you learn how to do the task that needs to be done. Keep that attitude, and you'll always succeed in life." He was always turning ordinary moments into a basis for sage advice.

Occasionally, they would research a specific person or event in history.

Buffalo Bill had been one of those projects. After they had visited the famous folk hero's local birthplace, Anna and her father spent months learning about his life from the cradle to the grave. That was years ago, but she smiled, remembering how much fun it had been.

Anna wondered what project he had undertaken this time. She found it odd he had never mentioned a new interest.

Opening the box, she tossed the lid aside and saw that the box was half full with notebooks, printouts, and copies of official-looking documents. She grabbed a handful of papers and files from the top, twisted her legs around, and plopped the pile in her lap. A well-folded single page slipped out of the stack. It looked like a copy of a fax, the letters distorted but still readable. Anna read the first line. "The Idaho Voluntary Adoption Registry is a confidential cross-reference." She paused and reread the line, intrigued. Who would her father be doing adoption research for, and why would he not have enlisted her help? She recalled that he had taken a ski trip to Idaho right before Christmas. What resort had that been? At the time, she thought it was unusual for him to take such a trip but had secretly harbored the hope he had taken a lady friend on a romantic weekend getaway. He had been distant afterward, and she had assumed it was either a solo trip or a disappointing rendezvous. Either way, he hadn't offered details, and Anna had not pressured for any beyond the expected "How was your trip?"

She fanned out the papers, stopping at random for a clue. "District of New York Port of New York" read one page, the lines filled with a flowing cursive script indicative of records of decades past. She squinted at the top. 1946. She found similar records for Philadelphia, Boston, and San Francisco. What did New York, Philadelphia, Boston, and San Francisco have to do with Idaho? She didn't see a connection.

Anna continued to flip through the papers. Many were filled with general references to genealogy research. Had he been researching a specific person? Anna thought so from some of the pages, but there weren't any names highlighted. Whenever they created a project box, they always included an elaborately detailed summary page, outlining their project focus and various highlights. Anna suspected her father used these summaries as another learning exercise for her. This box didn't have a detailed summary, so it wasn't clear what the topic or purpose of the project had been.

She found a copy of an Iowa Census from 1952. Now Iowa? She found copies of phone book pages listing hospitals in Sioux City, Cedar Rapids, and Des Moines. Each one had a dark X.

She still searched for a name. Who had her father been researching? How had he managed to keep this a secret? An even better question was why had he kept it a secret? Did he have a new friend after all? Was there a mysterious, troubling stranger whose background he felt compelled to verify? That seemed far-fetched. It was far more likely it was a boring, innocuous project he considered too dull to include her in. She supposed adoption research could be dull, searching through courthouse or online records. She realized she had never actually thought about the process of researching adoptions. How would one go about it? She wished he had included her on this project. It might have been less interesting than their previous ones, but since it turned out to be his last one, she couldn't help feeling cheated.

Now that she thought about it, perhaps he had shared a small piece of it with her. She recalled the memory of a conversation months back. She had come to the house to make dinner, as she did at least two or three times a week back then. She recalled popping her head into the study, and he seemed surprised to see her, as if he had been a thousand miles away in thought and was startled by her appearance. He had dropped some pages into a box with a lid like the one she looked at now.

Their conversation over dinner that night had been a spirited discussion of instinct, personality traits, and the impact of the environment in which a child was raised. She had been surprised at the number of famous orphans and adoptees that he had named at the time. She wondered now if there was a more personal interest in the area or if he had been involved in this project even then. She sat back on her heels as she tried to recall the details of that discussion. She remembered they talked about the concept of nature versus nurture. How much impact a person's genes have on their personality or instinctive actions and whether those inherent characteristics have more weight than how a child was raised. Would the lessons and learned routines shape a person's life path more? Did the parents and the cultural traditions the children learned growing up have more impact? Or, regardless of a child's upbringing, would the instinct and desires show through no matter what?

They recalled watching a historical program on Viking settlements and the culture's outlook. Those ideas entered their conversation. The program indicated that many had been farmers and fishermen, men and women working together equally to survive. They didn't distinguish between women's work or men's jobs. When times were tough, they would "go a-Viking" which meant, according to the program, sailing to explore, plundering food and treasure as they went until eventually they returned home and resumed their previous life. Anna and her father had been amazed at some of the stories of tenacity, the determination to carve out farms and villages in harsh climates while overcoming losses and fatalities in their communities. It reminded Anna of the struggles the settlers faced in the American frontier. She had heard stories from her grandparents of their grandparents' experiences. Lives that required hard work to farm the land, a stubborn refusal to quit, and a commitment to family. The Viking stories were different only in that they seemed to be optimistic that their situation would improve, and they always seemed to have a desire to return home.

"You know, I might have made a good pioneer, but I think I'd have made an even better Viking. Yup, I've got a Viking heart all right. A little stubborn, independent, and ready to tackle what's next."

He had laughed at that. "I must have been a Viking then too because you're a chip off the old block. That has to be a double dose of nature and nurture going on there."

She smiled, recalling the easy banter they had shared. They had always been able to talk about anything. Why wouldn't he mention this project to her? It seemed odd now that this had not come up. Unless that random topic had sparked an interest that led to the research, she reasoned. The history of a celebrity he had been tracking down, perhaps. Anna felt the spark of curiosity increase. Maybe this was a project she could continue. She hoped it would be someone fascinating, someone she had at least heard of, if not liked.

As she studied the pages, she searched for clues. Somewhere around 1952, there had been an adoption her father was either looking for or had found. That would make the child around her father's age. Based on what she had seen so far, the birth was probably in Idaho and the adoption in Idaho or Iowa. The adoption registry was from Idaho, but the census record was from Iowa. Based on their prior research projects, Anna surmised her father had been trying to determine exactly when the adoption had taken place, and which state would be likely to have the record. The next step would be to identify the adoptive parents and where the child had grown up. The census record probably meant he had tracked the records that far. So, a child was born in Idaho, was adopted and grew up in Iowa. Anna sighed. That wasn't much to go on so far.

She reached for another pile. This one seemed to be Internet site screenprints and search results. She removed the paperclip and spread the pages. A small folded slip of paper fell out. Anna reached for it, unfolding it slowly. It was not a printout, but a handwritten note.

Mother requests child's middle name be Lander.

Her heart skipped a beat. Lander had been her father's middle name. A project box with adoption and historical search. A search on *Lander*. It was an uncommon name.

It was her father's name.

Her mind could find no other explanation.

Her father had been adopted.

Thoughts spun through her brain so rapidly she had trouble grasping any of them. She sat up straight as her unfocused eyes stared toward the closet ceiling for a moment. Shaking her head, she rifled through the pages in her hand but realized she had no idea what she was looking for. She had an excitement that she might still be part of a family, a family new to her, but another painful jolt that the family legacy she knew was not hers. She couldn't help but have the sense of another loss, this one the loss of her identity and heritage. The anger that her father didn't share this with her was there too, along with some fear and uncertainty. She often heard of adoptees seeking out birth parents for medical history because of predisposition to disease or being a carrier or something in their DNA. She had never paid close enough attention, but she wondered if that was a concern. Would that make a difference now?

Anna spent over an hour sitting on the floor, surrounded by the mess of paperwork, absorbing the impact of her discovery. Alone, all she had to hold on to was family history and memories. Every story from her grandparents, her father's recollections of growing up, and the entire family history that had been passed down. Never had there been any whisper that he had been made a part of this family legacy through love rather than blood. The Millers had chosen him, but what happened to his birth parents?

Anna searched her memory for any scraps or hints. She had to believe her father had no idea he was adopted. Unless he kept this a well-guarded secret. She wondered. Had he known all along or had the truth of his adoption come as a surprise. *If he had never known before, then how would he have found out?* His parents had passed away when Anna had still been a teenager.

She stared down at the box. He was researching to find out who his birth parents had been. Where he came from. *If his parents had told him he was adopted, they didn't have the details on his birth parents,* she thought. *Otherwise he wouldn't have needed to do all this research.* She faced so many questions. How had Dad found out? Why had he not talked to her about it? How far had his research taken him? Why had her grandparents kept this secret?

Why did his birth parents give him up? Ann couldn't keep the seed of hope from growing. Her father had birth parents somewhere. If either of them had children, they would be Anna's aunt or uncle. Any of their children would be her cousins. Anna considered the possibilities. She might be able to find a family to claim, but she was afraid to hope. Her rational brain insisted there could there be another explanation for the project box. She wasn't sure if she was ready to know.

CHAPTER TWO

She waited until the following day before making the call she hoped would provide answers. Her fingers shook as they dialed the familiar number.

"Hello?" The warm voice at the other end of the line should have comforted Anna immediately but didn't. Her emotions were still raw, and she drew in a ragged breath.

"Anna? Is that you, honey?" The voice was instantly concerned.

"Yes, Margaret, it's me. It is so good to hear your voice. I've missed you," Anna admitted. Margaret had been a part of her life as long as she could remember. The office manager at her father's agency, her mother's best friend, she had been a frequent babysitter when Anna was young and a close confidant as she grew older.

"I miss you too, munchkin. The loss is so very hard, I know. After working for James for over twenty years, I miss him too."

"Yes," Anna responded, and then paused. Silence stretched across the phone line for a long moment.

"Anna?"

"I found something strange that I need to ask you about, but I have no idea how."

"What do you mean, strange? You know you can ask me anything." Confusion was clear in Margaret's voice. "What in the world is it, Anna?"

"I found a box, and at first, I thought it was some research Dad was doing for someone else. But, part of what I saw makes me think it was for himself, but he never said anything, and it's so weird."

Her words came out in a jumble as the thoughts she had so carefully organized before making this call refused to stay in order and flew out of her mouth.

"Ahh. What kind of research?"

"It looks like birth records research, an adoption or something?"

"Uffff," Margaret made a noise like a rubber beach ball deflating suddenly. Anna instantly knew this was not a surprise and obviously a topic Margaret was well acquainted with. "I had hoped he told you about this."

"He didn't, whatever it is." Anna was frustrated. "So just tell me, okay?"

"I'll tell you what I know, and you might be able to fill in the rest with that box you found. He hadn't talked to me about this in a very long time."

Anna couldn't speak. Words would not form.

"After your mother died, he sold the business and was at a loss. He needed something to do with his time. You remember what he was like. Bouncing from one hobby to another, taking random classes at the community college…"

"Yes, I told him to take a cruise or something, I think," Anna said. Memories mixed with overlapping thoughts swirled in her brain.

Margaret sighed. "Yes. He decided to travel, to see the world some, and he applied for a passport. His application was rejected."

"Excuse me? Rejected?"

"Yes, there was a problem with his birth certificate and some of the information on his passport application. He started researching paperwork and somewhere along the way, came across something that led him to think, that uh, well…"

"What? What did he think?"

"He said he found out that he was adopted," Margaret admitted.

"Huh." Anna could not form a single intelligible thought. Before she made this call, she already knew, deep down. This information shouldn't have come as a shock, but having Margaret confirm it removed all possibility of a misunderstanding. It wasn't a mistake, her own misinterpretation of the mysterious box. Her world was already unsettled, and now it had taken a sideways shift.

Her parents were gone, and without any close family, her memories were all she had. The family history, the stories from her grandparents, and the legacy gave her a sense of belonging. Without that, her very identity seemed in question.

Deep breath, she thought. At the center of every project she and her father had worked on was history. History tied each lifetime together. Nothing made sense if every person simply lived their own life unconnected to a past or future generation. What would be the point? Even though she was alone right now, Anna knew who her family was, or at least thought she did up until this point. What if she got married one day and had children? What stories would she tell them about where they came from, what their history was? Would it be enough to take on the history of adoptive grandparents?

"So," she said carefully and deliberately, fighting back the tears welling up, "I have lost every person in my family, everyone I have ever loved, and now I find out part of that family was never mine in the first place?"

"I don't know, sweetie. After he started the research, he didn't tell me any more about it, and I never asked," Margaret admitted. "It's been a while. It was last spring he first mentioned it. I thought he might have dropped the search, or it didn't turn out well, and he didn't want to share what he had found."

"Do you think he found something?"

"He talked about Wyoming once, but I'm not sure that had anything to do with this. At the time, I took it as part of his ski trip research."

"But what if he did find something? I have to know."

"You didn't find anything in the research that would help?"

"I'll have to go through it when I can concentrate a little better. This was the last thing I expected."

"Is there anything I can do?" Margaret asked.

"No," Anna said. Her words halted as she felt deep tiredness set in. "I think I need to process all this. It's so quiet here now. I was starting to accept how things are now, but everything has changed again."

"What do you mean?"

"What if I have another family out there?" Anna dared to hope. "What if I'm not really alone?"

"Do you think so?"

"Maybe. I think I have to find out, Margaret. Thank you for telling me."

"All right then, honey. You go get a good night's sleep. Everything will look better in the morning. It usually happens like that."

After she hung up, she sat for a moment alone with her thoughts, her mind racing through the possibilities. She trudged off to bed, her mind still clouded with confusion.

*

It took two days for Anna to come to terms with the box and its disturbing secret. She couldn't find the motivation to do much of anything. The silence of the house seemed to close in on her, but there was nowhere else she needed to be. She didn't have the energy to shower or mess with her hair. She wore the same jeans and dug out a wrinkled T-shirt from a haphazard pile in her closet. She wandered around the house, stopping now and again to sit and stare out a window or sightlessly at a photo. She felt the sadness growing deeper, sliding into something more profound. It was a lonely ache that had an almost irresistible pull into lethargy. She couldn't cry on Margaret's shoulder every day. Several times she picked up the phone to call one of her friends, but couldn't decide what number to dial. Cindy was pregnant, and Stacy had a two-year-old daughter, a son in kindergarten, and a daughter in first grade. Getting a babysitter was challenging for Stacy, but for Anna to drag herself into the happy zone of a boisterous trio of children was too much to ask. She hadn't been close enough lately with a handful of others to feel comfortable unloading her tears and near depressed frame of mind. She knew she couldn't let herself spiral into depression; she needed to focus on something, anything outside these four walls.

The only glimmer of hope that came to her now was the possibility of finding more family. She could feel the motivation starting, an incentive to search for them that would give her a goal to focus on.

She wished her father had shared this with her. She had so many questions, and now he wasn't here to answer any of them. Dealing with the loss of both parents, she needed to be connected with a larger family. Her grandparents, distant cousins somewhere, the heritage of farmers and stories of frontier survival. Was her mother's history even solid and reliable now? She felt she could no longer claim the heritage of her father. Well, him, but not his parents, nor any history they had shared. She already felt like she had lost everything, but somehow now she'd lost even more. The shock had taken a while to sink in.

Her father was searching for his birth parents. They might even still be alive. Anna herself might have grandparents someone out there. Perhaps an aunt or uncle, even cousins. She might be completely alone in the world or have a large extended family. She tried to reconcile these facts in her mind and was determined to find out the truth. She needed to know every detail of her true history.

Anna pulled the box out of the closet and covered the dining room table with the contents. She looked closely at each document, organizing the pages into piles. She felt a plan forming in the back of her mind but was afraid to examine it. She studied the pages, trying to memorize every line and each nugget of information.

With no other choice, she accepted that the grandparents she had known her entire life were wonderful people that had welcomed her father into their lives, but they were not her bloodline. Neither of them had siblings, nor did her father, so Anna didn't have cousins, aunts or uncles, or any other extended family from that side of the family. There was an estranged stepsister of her mother's and a second cousin of one of her parents who had borrowed money once, but Anna didn't know where either was living.

The idea that there was another family out there was exciting and terrifying. She may not be alone, but what if they had no idea her father had existed? What if they knew, but it was a dirty secret they wouldn't talk about? What if his birth parents had families as small as hers, and there were no relatives to find? What if the birth mother never told the father, or what if she didn't know who he was? Considering it had been the late 1940s, this seemed a bit unlikely, but Anna needed to know. There were too many questions not to try.

She tried to make sense of the geography. The pages were from different states, and some didn't seem to make any sense. She approached it logically and tried to look at it with the analytical detachment she would give any other project.

Iowa was easy. Her grandparents were both born and raised here. Anna herself had always lived in Iowa, even during college, so the connection with the state was natural.

It seemed that the adoption itself was recorded in Idaho. Anna wondered how her father used his birth certificate to find the adoption registry. Would that have been possible? She pulled out a notebook and scribbled the question. She wondered what raised a red flag with his current birth certificate. She would need to investigate how to research adoptions. Anna knew enough not to assume anything. For now, she would go along with it until she could prove or disprove that theory.

The port of entry documents were from various areas and could simply be original background research. There were not any notes that seemed to indicate relevance to anything else. What did a port of entry in Boston or San Francisco have to do with an adoption in Idaho? It made no sense. Anna picked up the closest page. The Port of New York. 1946.

She considered the possibilities. The port of entry might indicate immigration. It was the 40s, and since World War II had just ended, America was experiencing immigration from all over the world. So many possibilities crossed her mind, and she allowed her imagination free rein of the scenarios. What if her grandparents had left war-torn Europe and one didn't survive? Perhaps her grandmother died and her grandfather was too overwhelmed to care for a baby alone and put him up for adoption. What if it was a case of being a single, unwed mother? A night of passion led to regrets? No; Anna refused to believe her father was anything but loved and only insurmountable hardship had led to his adoption. Her romantic fantasies spun another alternative theory.

She imagined perhaps a sleek Parisian artist or exotic and mysterious Italian heiress as her grandmother and an American grandfather as the star-crossed lovers who met by chance in New York. Her chic and independent grandmother fled a war-torn Europe to arrive on the shores of America. They met and fell in love. Her father was evidence of their courtship. So, what happened? Where would she look for answers?

The table before her held pitiful piles of her history. She missed her father keenly at this moment. Anna had so many questions for him, the powerful and unreasonable urge to seek his advice and assistance made her heart ache. He had always been so good at solving mysteries, mostly because his attention to detail was legendary. He could spot an inconsistency or small anomaly that other people missed. He had been equally adept at focusing that skill in business, puzzles, or word games. It was a blessing when Anna was working with him but infuriating when he so easily solved a problem she had fussed over for hours.

Tears welled up in her eyes. She wanted his help, she wanted to know what this all meant, but most of all, she wanted him not to be gone.

*

"Have you really thought this through?" Margaret asked, her voice concerned. "You are like my own niece, girl, and I don't like the idea of you heading off alone."

Anna sat across from her in the living room and could see the uncertainty in the older woman's eyes. Margaret had spent hours there in the Miller's living room, but for the first time it felt odd sitting here, just the two of them, knowing that her father would never be walking through the door. Anna sat on the cozy lady's chair, Margaret on the sofa. They both avoided the recliner, which had been James' favorite spot. The small table that stood next to it was now empty, the evidence of his passions—books, his laptop, and several spiral notebooks filled with scrawled comments, observations, and reminders—now packed up with the other elements of his life.

"Yes, Margaret, this really feels right. I can finally take a breath, like I have something to focus on now." Anna tried to keep her voice firm and sound confident, looking around the room. "Being in this house, at first with all their things, and now even with their things gone; every day it hurts so much. I have nothing left here, no life really."

Margaret followed her gaze to the corner where the Christmas tree had stood every year, the wide front window with the built-in window seat where Anna had sat and read while her mother gardened outside – even the photos and paintings on the wall. The memories, good and bad, seemed to take over the space, crowding out energy for the living.

"I know I have you, Margaret, and my friends, but everyone has their own life. I need something of my own now. You know how many questions there are for me now. I am going to follow this trail. If there's a mystery to be solved, I'm going to try to solve it."

"But Idaho is so far to drive by yourself," Margaret objected. "What if something happens? You will be all alone out there. But I guess that's never bothered you too much. You've always been so independent."

"I'm okay by myself, Margaret, and even here, I'm pretty much alone. If I have family out there somewhere. I want to find them. But maybe I don't have family out there. In that case, I think it will be good to get away and think things through. Either way, I need to decide what's next for me."

"Anna, I will always be your family."

"I know, and I feel the same. But I have to do this. For me and for Dad. I feel closer to him finishing something he started." Anna smiled, blinking quickly to clear the ever-present tears that threatened to spill over as she walked over to Margaret. "Anyway, I won't go all the way to Idaho. I'm going to start in Wyoming, so that's a little closer."

Margaret rolled her eyes. "Huh. Not by much."

Anna smiled. "Stand up and give me a hug," she said.

Margaret complied, folding Anna into a rib-crushing embrace and holding her there tightly.

"Okay, okay," Anna said laughing as she pulled away. "I do love you, you know."

"And I you, Anna-girl."

Anna drew in a deep breath, held it for a moment, and then exhaled quickly and nodded. Focused on the task at hand, she rattled off the practical details. "I've canceled the newspaper delivery and the cable service and the mail is on hold. The mortgage and utilities are on automatic payment from the estate account. Can you call Joe to have him take care of the mowing and anything that comes up? I cannot imagine there would be anything major that needs to be taken care of. Oh, here are the spare keys." Anna spoke rapidly, firing information at Margaret as the tidbits came to mind.

She knew she was on the verge of nonsensical gibberish. What was she thinking? A cross-country trip with no real final destination. She knew her first stop was a small map-dot where she would search out clues to a mystery she barely understood, completely on her own, in hopes that at some point she wouldn't be completely on her own. Did that even make sense? She decided it didn't matter. It was an excellent excuse for a road trip and a distraction she desperately needed right now.

"Breathe, child." Margaret smiled and gently took the keys. "Everything here will be fine. You take care of yourself and check in with me often, okay?"

"Yes, I will. I'll finish closing the house up today and pack the car. I'm having dinner with a couple of girlfriends tonight. I haven't seen either of them in forever, they've both been busy with new babies. But it would feel weird if I didn't say goodbye, so we all made time. I'll leave first thing in the morning, but I'll take my time. I'll stop often along the way and see the sights." Anna grinned and hugged Margaret one final time before they walked to the door.

Margaret left, and the silence of the house closed around Anna.

One more night and I'll start on the next part of my life, she thought.

CHAPTER THREE

Anna pulled out of the driveway just after nine o'clock in the morning. It was an odd feeling not knowing where the journey would take her or how long she would be gone but she started to feel the excitement grow as she drove away. She left the familiar neighborhood and was soon at the edge of town. Gradually, the familiar landscape of Muscatine, Iowa, disappeared behind her. She drove north and easily swung onto Interstate 80, heading west. Her adventure had begun.

Her fingers tapped absently on the edge of the steering wheel along with beat of the music on the radio. The tune changed and the new melody was too slow, so she reached to change the channel. She already carried enough melancholy without a losing-everything love song contributing its mournful story to the load. At least her pre-defined oldies, country, and current hits stations would be in range for a while. She turned to the country station and appreciatively bopped her head to the beat. *That'll work*, she thought.

The interstate across Iowa was a long stretch of straight road with pleasant country scenery of gently rolling hills. A sign proudly proclaimed "Silos & Smokestacks National Heritage Area." The landscape was beautiful here. The hills were interrupted by regular stands of trees grouped around the small streams and waterways that peppered the area. The classic white water towers stood out starkly against the green farm fields. Anna squinted, playing a game with her imagination as she did when she was a child. The water tower with buildings and homes clustered around each one blurred. It now looked like a giant map pushpin put there to signify that a community gathered in that spot.

Her thoughts wandered from communities to families and she wondered how she ended up on this road, heading toward the unknown, and a bit unsure of the results she was hoping to achieve. The exit came and went for the Herbert Hoover Museum. Idly she thought about taking the ramp and visiting the landmark, as she always did when she saw the sign. She passed it by thinking, as she always did, that it would be interesting to stop, but not right now.

She had not planned for things to turn out this way. She was not ready to be alone in the world. She was supposed to have more time. Time to date and find the right man, to get her father's blessing, then start a family of her own. For the past year, Anna had been wrapped up in her own grief over her mother's passing and spent much of her time with her father. She helped him with the house and adjustment to his life as a widower. He had sold his insurance business and occupied himself with various hobbies, one of which seemed to be an endless stream of charitable causes for Anna to pursue. She indulged him, knowing each was not for the reasons he always insisted—that it was good for the community or a worthwhile endeavor for the church. Anna knew her father encouraged the volunteer work to ensure she kept an active social life and increase her chances of meeting single, eligible men. She got involved in the charities, met a few men, and even dated some, but never allowed any of them to move to a relationship status. She wanted a love like her parents had, the connection of two people who had been meant to be together. She felt that anything less than amazing wasn't worth the effort. She indulged her father's efforts, but hadn't put her heart into it. She, like him, was at loose ends after her mother died. Before that, she had a career and a normal routine but when her mother died, everything changed.

Anna had enjoyed her twelve years working as the business manager at her father's insurance agency; more than the job, she treasured the family business and the daily partnership with her father. She joined the company after earning her degree in business administration. When he sold the agency, he had shared some of the proceeds with the employees as severance packages. He had insisted on giving Anna nearly half the money from the sale, knowing it would mean she wouldn't need to settle on a new job. To stay busy, she often worked for a local temp agency, filling in for a few days or a week as general secretarial help for people on vacation or medical leave and the occasional longer stretch when a firm was taking time to interview and hire for a vacancy. The temp work was interesting but challenging. It was all she had wanted, grieving for her mother and spending time with Dad, her only remaining relative.

She had a small apartment a few miles from her parents' home, although since her mom died, she had spent almost as much time at Dad's house as she had her own. But now, those days were gone. She would never again sit down to dinner and roll her eyes as he outlined the newest fundraiser he had signed her up for. Her mother had first started the efforts, and her father continued the frustrating tradition. It was a thinly veiled attempt to get her to date. Her parents thought if she met a nice man, she could settle down and start her own family. She would somehow forget the humiliating experiences and failed relationships that made up her dating history. Her boyfriend during senior year had broken up with her to ask someone else to prom. After being together since the previous summer, getting dumped weeks before the biggest event of her high school experience had been devastating to her teenage heart. Anna realized later that easily finding a replacement date and enjoying the evening finale to that chapter of her life was a good indication her heart had not, in fact, been irreparably broken. Her pride and self-esteem suffered much more. Throughout college, her string of casual dates and short-term boyfriends hadn't worried her parents too much. Anna was fairly sure they were happy she finished college and avoided any serious relationships until after she graduated. She still wanted to find someone to spend her life with, but after her most recent dating disaster, convincing her stubborn heart to trust again would be her biggest challenge.

*

Her thoughts replayed the history like a movie in fast forward. As she headed down this straight stretch of highway, somewhere between Davenport and Omaha, she felt completely alone. She had not made a hotel reservation and wasn't sure where she would stop for the night. She supposed it didn't matter.

No one was waiting for her anywhere. Not on the road ahead and not back where she came from. *Jeez, Anna, that's a depressing thought.* She snorted. Isn't that why she had undertaken this cross-country road trip? To let her mind get through the grieving process, investigate her father's roots, and maybe somewhere along the way find a new purpose in life? *Okay*, she thought, *I can do this, I want to do this, and it's going to be awesome. Whatever "it" is.*

She watched the landscape pass. The interstate was an unrelieved straight line across the plains. Green fields on either side, interrupted by the occasional small town and necessary concrete exit. The larger cluster of Des Moines came and went, but Anna barely noticed, she was so focused on her thoughts. Her father's parents, the Millers, had been wonderful grandparents. She spent many happy hours at their house. She made cookies with Grandma and learned about baking and gardening. Grandpa tolerated her incessant chattering and questions with a patient smile as she perched on a stool while he tinkered in the garage. He tried to teach her about tools and mechanics, but she had not been an adept student. But she loved his stories. He would regale her with the escapades of his youth, growing up on the family farm. He made his childhood seem like a mixture of Tom Sawyer adventures with a bit of Hardy boys mixed in. She had agonized along with her parents when her grandfather passed away and later when her grandmother's dementia required round-the-clock nursing care and she was forced to give up her home.

Looking back, Anna recalled the feeling of losing the childhood connection with her grandparents the last time she saw their home. The couple had spent seventy years in that house, which had belonged to her grandfather's father for fifty years before that. At the time, she felt like they lost the link to the original family homestead, but more than that, she lost the connection with each of them. She loved them both and still missed them. Why was she even concerned about an unknown set of grandparents? What if they hadn't cared about the child they created? They had given him away to be raised by strangers. The Millers were the ones who had taken him in, loved him, and given him their name. Her name. Was it wrong to wonder about her blood relatives, about her original family name? What about a family of her own one day? How would she pass along the legacy to her own children if she didn't know it? *She better not get ahead of herself,* she thought ruefully. A husband would be the first step, then worry about children.

The low fuel light glowed a bright orange-yellow in the center of the dash console, its sudden appearance accompanied by a mellow chime. Catching sight of a billboard sign, she found she was still sixty miles from Omaha and prayed she would find a fuel stop before then. Her eight-year-old Honda Civic was great on gas, but she preferred to keep it above the quarter-tank mark. Her father had been adamant about that. "Just in case," he always said. She assumed he meant in case she could not find a gas station. Anna appreciated that advice as she noticed the exits and available gas stations were getting fewer and farther apart. Ten miles later, she came to an exit with a blue sign that promised fuel. *Cool, maybe I'll meet my Mr. Wonderful at a roadside gas station.*

She flipped on her turn signal and followed the gentle curve toward a town with the unlikely name of Atlantic. As she topped the hill, a single building surrounded by fuel pumps was the only sign of life. The actual town was a few miles from the Interstate, and only a solitary truck stop was near the exit. With a sigh, she pulled up to the gas pump, turned off the engine and opened the door, enjoying the light breeze of fresh air. Anna got out and stretched as she went through the routine of pumping gas, washing the windshield, and cleaning out the trash that invariably piles up, even on the shortest road trips. As she tended to the minor duties, she looked around the empty lot, nodding to the lone attendant inside, who glanced at her with bored disinterest.

No Mr. Wonderful here, she thought. She finished up and was soon back on the interstate, headed for the state line.

She was alone with her thoughts again. It was not the first time she had taken a road trip by herself, but this one was different. She knew it was because there was no one waiting for a call to know she was safe when she stopped for the night. Margaret would want to hear from her at some point but would never expect a daily call. There was no one eagerly awaiting Anna's arrival, and no one waiting for her to come back home. She had always taken for granted the security of having people care about her.

Looking back, her life had been so safe and happy until the last few months. Now that she considered the years of her life experience, she realized that while it was "safe and happy," she had never been truly adventurous. She had never pushed herself out of her comfort zone to try new things or challenge herself. She had always taken the next step that seemed logical and reasonable. She'd never had an amazing success, no great accomplishments, but also no great losses. Except for her parents. It occurred to her that while she knew loneliness now, she had never mourned the loss of a great love—had never experienced a broken heart. Not truly anyway.

Her last serious boyfriend, David, had been several years before. Anna had been content and he seemed like the perfect guy for her. Her parents had even liked him; actually, it was her dad that introduced them. That was probably why he felt so guilty when they broke up. Anna never told her father the details; it was simply another embarrassing "you're not what I'm looking for or maybe I'm not ready to settle down right now." It was painfully obvious that the first part was true, the second, not so much. David announced his engagement to someone else within six months of their breakup. Anna always wondered if he had dated them both at the same time. Not that it mattered; the end result was the same.

She had been hurt, of course, but more than that, she realized it was a deep disappointment. She had planned on getting married and having children. She thought about the house they would have and Sundays at her parents' house, watching while they played with their grandkids. She didn't really have an overwhelming love for the man she had been considering for the role of husband. That really was a lucky break. What had she been thinking? Anna realized now that she wanted more. More love, more passion, just more. Why was it so difficult for her to find the kind of love her parents had for each other? Anna wondered if that kind of thing simply happened, like the bolt of lightning described in a romance novel, or if it was something that started out small and grew over time. Nothing in her experience came close to the sappy love songs or heartfelt longing described in poetry. She didn't know how to find it but hoped she would at least recognize it if it came along.

*

Anna tried unsuccessfully to shield her eyes against the brilliant golden glow that seemed enhanced by every possible reflective surface. Iowa and most of Nebraska were behind her now and the sun was low in the sky. She'd been mulling over her life choices and decisions for hours now, resulting in a touch of melancholy. Catching sight of the distinctive blue rest area sign, she slowed down for the exit. A brisk walk in the fresh air would be a welcome change from the cloistering silence of the car. After a quick stop at the facilities and stretching her legs, she stood to admire the view.

Behind the building, several walkways converged in a patio that boasted a stunning view of the valley. Anna wandered, savoring the light breeze on her skin and breathing in the fresh air. She noticed several large placards and spent the time to read each one. One provided detailed information about the wagon trains and the routes of the early settlers. Another provided insight into the terrain and the geological formation of the distant mountains and valley. The third stirred Anna's interest. It described the early inhabitants of the area, from thousands of years before. Archeologists had found evidence of settlements in the valley that were over a thousand years old. Native American tribes had lived in the area, worked and hunted here, and left evidence of their lives at a time when much of Europe was unpopulated and the Vikings were exploring the seas. Anna considered the tribes, made up of many families working together as one. The support system and sense of community common at that time had not survived in modern society. *What security there must have been to be part of a society that would be around you for your entire life, knowing that each member of the tribe was a part of your own extended family and you would never be alone.* She walked slowly back to the car, aware now of the twilight falling and a chill in the air. She slid back into the driver's seat and continued the journey west. After the day behind the wheel, her shoulders began to ache almost immediately as she continued her trek. North Platte was ahead, and Anna decided it would be a good place to stop for the night. She was not worried about finding a vacancy. It was still a few weeks until Memorial Day, so summer travelers wouldn't flood this area for another four to six weeks.

She found an inexpensive motel right off the interstate exit and soon sprawled out on the bed, enjoying the freedom to stretch her limbs after a long day in the cramped driver's seat. The television was on in the background, providing some distraction from the onslaught of emotions brought on by both memories and the endless grandparent possibilities created by her wild imagination. She tried to focus, sighing as she pulled the project box onto the bed and dumped the paperwork onto the orange bedspread.

She reviewed the facts in her head and focused on her first destination. She would not be going directly to Idaho, even though that was a key part of her investigation. The adoption had taken place in Idaho, but she had another stop to make first. She looked again at the printout in front of her. It was a single page, well worn, its edges curled and dog-eared. It contained search engine results for "Lander" – the list was small. A University in South Carolina, a business name, a town in Wyoming, and something to do with states in German-speaking countries. *What do any of these have to do with my father?* she wondered for the hundredth time.

The handwritten note had read, "Mother requests child's middle name be Lander." Why would she request that? Anna knew her father had wondered the same thing and had searched the Internet for answers. It was the sort of starting point they had done on countless projects together. There were few results from the search engine, but they were broad in topic. She immediately discounted the business connection because the company would have to pre-date 1945, which wasn't the case. The German states might be relevant, but how? Each time she considered it, Anna wondered if she should have a DNA test performed. Perhaps the answers she sought were right there in her blood, but it was unlikely the results would give her any definitive signpost.

The university could have been one that her grandmother or grandfather had attended and the birth mother wanted his name to be a clue. But if there was a connection to South Carolina, why was the adoption recorded in Idaho? That left the town in Wyoming.

Wyoming made the most sense. If the birth record was from Idaho, the closest state was Wyoming. When she had checked a map back in Iowa, her heart had leaped. Lander, Wyoming, was only about two hundred miles from

Idaho. If the birth mother had wanted to leave a clue, the hometown of herself or the father, perhaps even both, would be a good one.

She had searched the history of Lander but hadn't come up with much information. It was a small town in Wyoming incorporated in 1890. Before it was Lander, it went by the names of Pushroot, Fort Brown, and Fort Auger. Mildly interesting, but not much help. It was a small town, less than 7,000 people, but its claim to fame was that it had hosted the first paid rodeo in the West. Every year they had a big rodeo and celebration for Independence Day. *That's only ten weeks from now*, she mused. *I wonder where I'll be for fireworks this year.*

Lander seemed like such a small town, Anna assumed she would find information quickly or know soon enough that it was a dead end. Either way, this would be her first stop before heading to Idaho. She was excited but scared that the small town wouldn't provide any clues. It might only be a small town that had nothing to do with her father or her mysterious grandmother and the request about his middle name. Even if it was important, years had passed. There might not be any way to find clues about one nameless woman from seventy-some years ago.

Anna stared at the ceiling, absently running her tongue along the ridges of her teeth, a habit reflecting deep thought and preoccupation. She allowed herself the selfish luxury of doubt. The entire trip may well be a waste of time and money. She might never find any family. Maybe the family she already had and lost would be the only one she would ever have, and she would be alone now for the rest of her life. The idea of such a terrifying emptiness was overwhelming.

She took a deep, ragged sigh and slowly pulled the papers into a neat pile. She was not going to wallow in self-pity. She tidied up the small room, forcing herself to move and perform mundane tasks to calm her mind. She brushed her teeth, changed into pajamas, and sat down on the floor in the middle of the hotel room. She kept a strict routine of stretching, relaxation, and yoga each night. Tonight was no different. She focused on breathing and continuing her motions until the knot in her chest loosened, and the flood of emotions calmed.

Feeling more relaxed, she crawled into bed. The drive had been long, and her body craved rest. Her jumbled thoughts finally slowed, and she was able to slip into sleep.

CHAPTER FOUR

Anna found it was an easy day's drive from North Platte across Wyoming and north to Lander. The weather was perfect for a drive, and she made good time. The landscape gradually changed from the monotonous interstate to the scrub brush flatlands with a beautiful backdrop of snow-capped mountains, making for a scenic drive. Even with stops every few hours for fuel, food, or to stretch her legs, Anna arrived in the small town by dinnertime. Or, what her Iowa mind thought of as dinner. Here in Wyoming, it seemed the proper term for the evening meal was supper, or so the desk clerk at the Rustic Log Cabin Lodge had informed her when she checked in. The clerk had met her request for a recommendation for dinner with a raised eyebrow.

"The cafe has a good dinner, but it's a little late for that. If supper's what you're wantin', then your best bet's the Bar & Grill." He grinned as he nodded in the general direction that Anna assumed to be the Bar & Grill's location.

"Thanks." She smiled in return before making her way down the short corridor to her assigned room. It was well-kept and tastefully decorated, and she hoped her room would be the same. She had checked in for three days, but depending on the direction and results of her research, this might be a temporary home for much longer.

She was pleased as she stepped into the dim room. It was clean and had a pleasant, fresh scent. It was so much more appealing than the typical bleachy aroma or, worse yet, a heavy flowery perfume masking stale cigarette odor.

The light switches on the wall operated several table lamps and a ceiling light above the entry. The open door to the bath revealed a simple room decorated with earth tones that matched the bedroom area. Anna walked the few steps into the room and heaved her suitcase onto the bed. She plopped down next to it and sighed, staring at the ceiling. She had arrived. Only a few weeks ago, she found the box in her father's bedroom closet and now she was here. The four walls of this hotel room were her home now, temporarily anyway. She had closed up the house in Iowa and no one expected her back there anytime soon. She was excited and terrified, but anxious to get started.

The room contained all the basic furnishings. Bed, nightstands, a dresser, and a small desk with a matching chair. A plush-looking reading chair in the corner by the window was an unexpected and pleasant surprise. Overall, it was simple, but the mellow earth tones and natural-looking fabrics made the room seem cozy. The few pictures on the walls were all landscapes, one depicting a mountain scene with a majestic elk standing proud. Another showed a bear fishing in a wide stream, surrounded by tall trees and snow-capped mountain peaks in the distance. The third, a dilapidated barn in a beautiful green valley. She wondered if they were local scenes. The barn looked nice but she made a mental note to ask about bear spray. Was that a repellant? That would be an important thing to ask.

A sleek, modern, flat-panel TV was mounted to the wall above the dresser, directly across from the bed and easily viewed from that vantage point or the comfy chair. A door on the opposite wall opened to a small concrete patio with two chairs and a small charcoal grill. She stepped outside and settled into one of the chairs. It felt comfortable.

Pulling her phone out of her back pocket, she called to check in with Margaret.

"Honey, it's good to hear your voice." Margaret's love and concern were evident in her tone. "You arrived then, and the drive went well?"

"Yes, it was all fine. I have a nice little hotel room I'll be at for a while, at least a few days. Tomorrow I'll start some research."

"I hope you find what you are looking for, Anna. I hate to see you at such loose ends."

"Thank you, Margaret, but I'm feeling good about this. It is not exactly a fresh start, but it's a change and a break from routine. I guess I haven't had much of a routine lately, but you know what I mean." Anna got up and opened the door to the small patio, stepping inside as she talked. "I think it will be good for me to be away from Iowa and think about what's next."

"I think that is a good idea. This has been a major change in your life, and you need to take more time to process it."

"Knowing that I might have more family out here is a pretty big motivator too. Margaret, you are like an aunt to me, but I still want to find my own family."

"You will, Anna. Keep me up to date and let me know if you need anything."

"I will. Thank you, Margaret," Anna said, disconnecting the call, exhaling with a small sigh.

Anna took her time unpacking, storing her belongings in the dresser, hanging a few items, and arranging her personal items on the counter in the bathroom. The empty suitcase was stowed in the closet next to the ironing board. A bit simple, but she had moved in. She felt settled and suddenly starved.

The small town was beautiful, and she thoroughly enjoyed the brief drive to search out the recommended restaurant. The surrounding mountains seemed majestic compared to the gentle rolling hills of Iowa. She stopped to breathe in the crisp air as she exited the car, a few documents from the project box rolled up in her hand. She wanted to make notes for the research she would start tomorrow. She caught the heady scent of beef, onions, and a whiff of fresh-baked bread. Her stomach growled in response. She realized she felt better than she had for weeks, as if a weight had been lifted somehow. It wasn't gone, but it was decidedly better. The knot that seemed to have taken up residence in her chest had unwound a bit.

Anna headed for the establishment's door and stepped inside. The interior was warm and inviting. Exposed wood ceilings were crisscrossed with huge supporting beams. The wood-paneled walls were dotted with cowboy-themed elements. Small paintings framed in wide wood planking embellished with barbed wire accents hung around the room. Ropes, cowboy hats, saddles, and many items Anna couldn't identify were displayed around the restaurant, creating an attractive and pleasing environment, well-decorated and inviting. Rows of booths lined the wall and ran along the center of the room, dividing the restaurant into smaller areas. Cozy tables with four chairs each, snuggled between the booths, each topped with thick fabric placemats, condiments, spices, and a wine bottle candle. The twilight made a perfect backdrop for the candles on the tables by the windows to sparkle against the glass, creating a casual, romantic feel.

She took in the details as she followed the hostess to a table for four. The hostess offered a menu, then quickly and efficiently removed the additional three place settings as she told Anna the day's soup and specialty pie. Moments later, a waitress appeared at the table and took Anna's order of a ribeye, grilled medium-well, and a baked potato loaded with butter and sour cream.

"I'll have some fresh dinner rolls out to you in a minute and be sure to save room for a slice of pie. It's homemade and you'll love it," the girl promised.

As she waited for her feast to arrive, Anna relaxed. She had made it this far. Now that the drudgery of being in the car was over, she felt better. It had been cathartic to spend hours in review and life assessment. She had relived the embarrassment and pain of failed relationships and realized she was still strong – none of it had broken her. Anna began to look forward to what was next. Whatever that might be, it started here. With this town. She still had no idea why her father's birth mother would want to provide this clue to his parentage. Was her grandmother from here? Anna looked around the restaurant, trying not to stare at anyone too obviously. Was she sitting in the same room as a relative? The man in the corner looked a bit like her father, especially the nose. He might be a cousin. She sighed. He might be a completely unrelated stranger.

She had to find out why Lander had special meaning. She thought of the details on several key documents. The immigration entry from the Port of

New York was dated October 1946 and there were no women with infants listed on the page. If that document contained the name of her grandmother, Anna had to assume her father had not been born yet. There was no way to know if her grandmother had been expecting when she arrived, or whether she met someone after she arrived in America. What if her grandparents had met overseas, fallen in love, and planned a life together in America? Either of them could have been US citizens, or possibly both were immigrants. If they planned a life together, what had happened that kept them from living out that dream? There were so many possibilities for what might have gone wrong. Death, disease, the war, family obligations, or the family would not accept marriage to an immigrant, and for some reason, the two lovers bowed to the family pressure. The adoption made it clear that something had not worked out as they planned.

She looked at the next page. This was fast-forwarded to the new adoptive family, the Millers. The Iowa census was dated 1952 and reflected her grandparents' entry: Miller, John, aged 39 and wife, Ruth, aged 36, son James, aged 5. James would have been born in 1947, or possibly late the year before or early the year after, depending on when exactly the census was completed.

Anna didn't know much about the process of adoption, but she assumed that the date on his birth certificate was accurate. It didn't make sense to her that it would be changed. She hoped that was the case, and she could rely on the date she had always known as Dad's birthday. If not, her search would have to range anywhere from 1946 to 1948. *It was bad enough not knowing who she was looking for or where exactly, but adding an unknown when would make it nearly impossible*, she thought. She wrote her father's birthdate at the top of the page, underlining it heavily. She picked up the page entitled "Idaho Voluntary Adoption Registry." She had made a few telephone calls and read through several websites to find out that in Idaho, adoption records are confidential and sealed after they are filed. The registry was managed by the state and helped adoptees and people doing genealogy research obtain data, so she might be able to find out more in person. However, she wasn't ready to visit Idaho just yet.

The meal arrived, and Anna shoved the paperwork aside, turning her full attention to the perfectly prepared steak, which proved to be delicious. As she enjoyed the meal, she considered her next move. Now that she was here, she wondered if the trip would be worthwhile. It was an excuse to escape and figure out her future, but she was not sure if there was any hope of untangling the mystery of her father's birth. A phrase her father often used popped into her head: "Exercise in futility." *No, this will not be a futile effort*, Anna vowed to herself. *I will find an answer.*

She began by learning how to research a family tree. She had no experience in genealogy and did not know where to start once she had found her father's stash of documents. The Internet recommended looking at birth and death records, census records, land documents, and old newspapers to put together the history in a family tree. Adoptions were trickier. Since many adoptions were closed, or the records sealed, it wouldn't be possible to find the exact record she was trying to find, namely an original birth certificate with the biological father and mother listed.

After looking through more sites dedicated to the topic of researching adoptions, she identified more avenues to try. The recommendations included charity records, baptismal or sacramental records from churches, and birth records for the same time period. If she could find someone who gave birth in the same hospital at the same time, it was possible someone would remember an unwed mother. Even if the records were sealed and no announcement made, the memory of this woman had to exist with someone. Anna needed to dig until she could create a list of people to interview. She might not be able to find a paper trail, but she might be lucky enough to find a human connection.

In the 1940s, polite society frowned upon a pregnant, unmarried female. Many times, a family would send a girl away to a home for unwed mothers. There were places women could go to live and work until their child was born, and somewhere there were records for those birth mothers. Anna planned to check newspapers and historical archives to see if there were any maternity homes in the area, and, if so, determine if any records still existed. She knew not all records were online. She would have to use local resources at the library, historical society, and courthouse, and hopefully find people who might remember details that would help. The task was daunting, and finding even a small clue might take weeks.

Feeling stuffed from her huge meal, she hadn't been able to resist the urge to top it off with dessert, which turned out to be an exceptionally delicious slice of homemade apple pie. Anna headed to the cashier, her rolled-up documents crammed in her back pocket. She stood patiently behind a white-haired couple who were chatting with the cashier.

The door opened and the cashier glanced up at the man who entered.

"Hey, Logan. I think your order is ready. Give me a minute." She looked back at the couple in front of her. "Four twenty-two is your change. You and George have a good night, Edna. See you next week." As the couple shuffled toward the door, she looked at Anna and smiled tiredly, "I'll be right back, hon. I gotta grab some singles."

Anna nodded as she glanced at the man the cashier had called Logan. What started out as a quick, unconscious glance suddenly held her fully focused attention. She felt a physical reaction unlike anything she had ever experienced before. For a second, it was hard to breathe and her mouth was suddenly dry. It was an instant attraction, powerful and completely foreign to Anna. The man was amazing. His presence radiated an aura of strength and confidence. Taller and broader than most men she had known, he was not awkward. She watched as he walked the short distance across the entry, moving with confident ease and fluid motion that was beautiful to see. He leaned against the wall to wait. Thankfully, he was quickly engrossed in reading a paper in his hand and didn't catch her stare. Anna took advantage of this and took her time looking him over. He was gorgeous by her standards, strong jaw darkened by a five o'clock shadow, with the tough, weathered look of a man who worked hard outdoors. This was no pretty boy Ken doll; this was a real man. The epitome of a red-blooded American cowboy, or at least her fantasy image of one.

"It's on your account, Logan. Tell your Dad I said hi." Anna heard the girl's voice and realized the cashier had returned with a wrap of dollar bills in one hand and a takeout bag in the other.

The man stepped forward and took the bag the girl offered, murmuring his thanks. As he started to turn, he paused and, for a moment, locked eyes with Anna. She found herself staring into the deepest blue eyes she had ever seen, like the brilliance of a blue jay's wing.

He nodded at Anna and touched his hat. "Ma'am." His voice was deep with a slight drawl. She wished he would keep talking so she could hear more. He walked toward the door, moving with a self-assurance and a level of masculinity she had never seen before. He seemed strong and capable, comfortable with muscles gained as a result of daily physical labor, the byproduct of hard work, Anna thought, the outdoor labor of a cowboy or a rancher. He had a casual power she imagined had been acquired from a demanding lifestyle, one where a typical day's work involved riding a twelve-hundred-pound horse to rope and control a five-hundred-pound steer. The earthy scent of the Wyoming dust clung to him, blending with the leather, sweat, and smell of outdoors to create an intoxicating male aroma. Anna was overwhelmed by him. The attraction was intense and instantaneous. Anna no longer took notice of anything or anyone else in the room. Her breath caught in her throat. The rugged masculine form held her full attention. She continued to stand there, silent, as he turned and walked out the door.

A slight wave from behind the register broke her stupor. "I'll ring you up," the girl said, hiding a grin.

CHAPTER FIVE

Anna strolled down the sidewalk, enjoying the sunny day, trying to shake off the sluggish fatigue that plagued her this morning. Last night, her thoughts had circled around the Adonis, Logan, for so long she felt like he was a close personal friend. His voice, that one word he had spoken, and the memory of his eyes momentarily locked with hers kept replaying in her mind. Sleep had not come easily. She had never experienced such a preoccupation with a man, especially one she hadn't even actually met. She felt ridiculous for having such a strong reaction. He was probably married. What hunk of a man like that would be single? She had to quit thinking about this complete stranger. *She didn't need the distraction and was hardly in a position to be dating*, she thought. She resolutely pushed the thoughts of the sexy cowboy aside, focusing on her surroundings.

The cool breeze was invigorating after last night's restlessness. Even in the confines of the town, the area felt uncluttered. She liked the open feeling here. The library was only a few blocks from her motel, so she left her old Honda in the parking lot there and explored the town on foot. Lander had been founded in the late 1800s and was laid out like most Western towns. There was a main street with businesses lined up in a row next to each other, all housed in solid brick buildings. The street itself was wide, with angled parking stretching for several blocks on both sides of the street. It was so different from the typical Midwestern town layout of a courthouse building situated as the center and businesses surrounding it on each side forming a square. Nearly all the streets back home had parallel parking, which she despised.

Anna arrived at the library shortly after the doors were unlocked. She had decided to start with old newspapers and then inquire about historical society records. She hoped there would be a local historian she could talk to as well. Since she was not sure what she was looking for, she thought getting acquainted with the area and residents from the time period of her grandparents would be a good place to start.

The interior of the library seemed dark after the bright sunshine. It took a moment for her eyes to adjust before she could see the main desk where a lone figure sat. The whole room was small, with less than a dozen shelves and only three reading tables in view of the front door.

"Good morning!" The loud, friendly greeting surprised Anna, who was more accustomed to being shushed in a library.

She grinned. "Good morning," she responded as she set her small box on the counter.

"How can I help you today?"

"Well, I'm interested in the town's history. I am working on a project and I'd like to know more about the area, the people, and some historical highlights. I thought that reading old newspapers would give me some insight." Anna was not sure if an unwed mother giving up a child for adoption would be common knowledge around town seventy years after the fact. Even if someone did know, Anna doubted the locals would gossip with a stranger. She thought a tactic of working up to her real question might be a wiser approach than a head-on interrogation.

The librarian nodded enthusiastically. "Yup, yup, you're right. I can help you with that. We have newspapers on microfiche going back to the first editions. The Ranger is our current paper; it goes back to the '40s. Before that, there were a few different ones; I can show you where you can read those online." She continued without pausing for a breath. "Let's see, we had The Clipper, the Fremont Clipper, that's different from the original Clipper, of course, and Fremont is the county we're in, you know. Then there's the Lander Eagle, the Evening Post – Lander Evening Post, that is, not the Saturday one. Then there was the Wind River Mountaineer and, of course, the State Journal."

Anna resisted the urge to giggle. She wondered if the woman was so knowledgeable on every topic or if newspaper trivia was just a secret love. The librarian kept talking nonstop as she walked from behind the desk toward a door in the center of the back wall. Anna followed the yellow curly mop of hair that bounced on the sweater-clad shoulders of the middle-aged woman. The librarian was several inches shorter than Anna, petite and full of energy. Her boot cut jeans swished at the ankles as she walked briskly around the tables and cut through the shelves of books. She turned back and flashed an easy smile.

"Anything in particular you're looking for? Do you want to start with the microfiche or the older online editions?"

Anna hesitated. "How about the microfiche? That's going to have the oldest copies of the papers, right?"

"Yup, that's it. Okay, I can get you set up in one of the reading rooms back here." She waved in the general direction they were walking. "We've got one room with a film machine and two others with computers."

"That sounds great."

The librarian showed Anna where the cartridges were stored and how to read the codes that identified each one. She chose the oldest one and took it to the large desk unit. There was a flat panel for the image and a shelf above with cylinders and gears. She explained how to load it into the drive at the top and how to work the controls to scan through the pages.

"If you need anything, you let me know. My name's Katherine, by the way."

"I'm Anna. Thank you so much for all your help. I'm sure this research will take days, so we may be seeing a lot of each other."

"All right then," Katherine said. "I don't get too many people in here during the day since the kids tend to come in the afternoon, so let me know if you need anything. I don't leave for lunch; I'll be here all day if you have questions. But I'll leave you to it for now."

The door closed. Anna leaned back in the chair and took a deep breath, then exhaled in a sigh. Katherine was a wealth of information, but Anna felt like she had been in the path of a tornado. Flipping on the lamp, she pulled the chair in and hunched over the screen. Soon, she was immersed in the front-page news of 1949.

*

Several hours later, Anna stretched her neck, rubbing her shoulder with the base of her hand. Her eyes were bleary, and her legs stiff from the inactivity. The old newspapers were intriguing in a trivial sort of way, but nothing earth-shattering had jumped out yet. There were articles on the aftermath of the war, of course, small mentions of servicemen coming home, honors bestowed, and death announcements. There were also notices of fund drives, product advertisements, and a surprising amount of local gossip. The last item gave Anna hope. Notices of parties, who attended, and visits from out-of-state friends and family members were interspersed with thank yous posted for gifts and condolences received. She had learned quite a bit about the local families and the social circles from that time.

Pushing the chair back, Anna stood and stretched again, deciding a lunch break and quick walk outside was just the thing she needed. She gathered up the morning's notes and added them to the project box. Making her way through the library, she stopped to chat with Katherine.

"Making any progress?" Katherine queried with a quick smile.

"I'm really getting a good feel for the town and the residents, I think. At least the ones that were here sixty or seventy years ago. That's the time period I'm focused on right now."

"Gimme a shout if you need anything. You might be able to find one or two people from back then you could talk to. Get some stories straight from the horse's mouth."

"I would love that, yes." Anna jumped on the idea, hoping Katherine had someone in mind.

"That might be good then, sure. You off to lunch? Yup, it's about that time, it is. The cafe around the corner has a great burger and good salads too. You're so tiny, you probably only eat salad, but you know you could stand a good burger to put some meat on your bones."

Anna laughed. "Okay, I'll go check out the burgers." She wiggled her fingers in a wave to Katherine as she headed out the door.

She pulled a pair of sunglasses from her bag and slipped them on as she stepped outside. She turned to the right, assuming the cafe would be located in that direction. She had walked to the library from the opposite direction and had not seen it that morning. Downtown was busier now, the streets lined with cars and the sidewalks in use by a variety of people, some moving with deliberate focus and others wandering slowly. Several chalkboard signs announced sales or the day's special. One sign proclaimed the best walnut fudge in the county and made a note to stop in and taste some for herself after lunch.

She enjoyed the brisk walk, looking around for signs of the cafe. Too late, she realized someone was exiting a business on her right. She sidestepped awkwardly, trying to avoid a collision with the body that had stepped out from a doorway. She avoided impact, but twisted her foot on its side and stumbled ungracefully.

"Sorry," she murmured automatically.

"Ma'am, sorry, my fault," a deep voice replied.

That voice seemed to rumble right through her. She looked up and felt her eyes lock with two deep blue ones. Of course it was Logan, the sexy man whose eyes she had actually dreamed about.

"Are you okay?" he asked, looking at her oddly.

She nodded, stepping back. "Yeah." Anna smiled ruefully. "Just being a klutz."

"Nah, I was in a hurry. My fault. You sure you're okay?" His voice sounded concerned but there was a hint of a smile that played around his mouth.

Anna was captivated again by those blue eyes. "Yes, thank you. Chivalry is alive and well, as long as you don't start laughing."

"Yes, ma'am." He tipped his hat with a crisp nod and started to turn, but paused. "Do you know where you're going from here?"

"Oh, uh, yes, I'm taking a break from research. History." *Oh, that was lame*, she thought. Try again. "The librarian said there's a cafe with great burgers around here. Am I headed the right way?"

"Yes, ma'am," he said turning to stand next to her. "Straight down there and turn to the right at that green awning. Can't miss it." He touched her shoulder lightly with one hand while pointing with the other. Anna felt the urge to lean closer to him. She shook off the unreasonable impulse. The man would think she was insane. *What is wrong with me?* This total stranger had gotten under her skin until she felt like she was on the edge of some crazy obsession. She reigned in her thoughts before she acted on them and embarrassed herself even more.

She turned to look at him, and it felt like their faces were mere inches apart. "Great, thanks," she said.

"Anytime." His light touch left her shoulder and he briefly touched his hat. With that distinctive cowboy gesture, he turned, walking in the opposite direction of Anna's destination. She wasn't able to resist the urge to glance back as he walked away.

Anna found the cafe with ease, and walked inside to join the lunch crowd. The small restaurant was busy but she found an open stool at the counter. After a quick glance at the menu, she ordered the recommended cheeseburger with homemade potato chips. She nibbled as she tried to focus her thoughts on the morning's research. Logan was making that difficult. Anna had never met anyone who intruded on her thoughts so much in so short a period of time. She barely knew him, but she was cataloging his traits anyway. Handsome, funny, sexy, beautiful blue eyes, an easy smile, patience, kindness. She sighed. He probably had three girlfriends already, not that it mattered. Her home was in Iowa. This was Wyoming, and she seriously doubted she would move here, so becoming interested in the local hunk was probably a waste of time. Probably. He was definitely a distraction from her real purpose here.

She turned to her notes, forcing herself to focus on the pages while finishing lunch. The morning's review of newspapers had been interesting, and Anna felt like she had a good handle on the Lander of seventy years prior. Thankfully, she enjoyed reading and found the endless bits of gossip amusing. The real action in town, she found, was always reported in the Society column. The small town seemed to revolve around the activities of a dozen key families, and after a while, Anna had begun to recognize them. Johnson, Williams, Brown, Bryant, Smythe, Jones, Hamilton, Campbell, Morris, and Stewart. The men were prevalent in the articles about politics and town business while the women held the parties, benefits, fundraisers, and charity events. There was a Widow Bryant, but the rest were married women, and two of the prominent men were either single or their wives were not in the public eye. Anna didn't recall seeing any references to Mrs. Johnson or Mrs. Stewart, so there were few society references with those last names. Most of the Johnson and Stewart mentions had to do with politics and business.

She tapped her pen against her lower lip thoughtfully. The "wide research" approach had proven entertaining but would take a long time to find what she was looking for, and possibly never yield results. She could be on a fruitless search for weeks or even months. She was anxious to move past this research phase into the "finding and meeting" phase. She needed to focus on one idea or potential trail and research until she could not go any further. She had to figure out a strategy on how to approach the possibilities, a single path to follow. If it didn't yield results, then she could always try another tactic. She stared at the pages, shuffling, waiting for inspiration.

"Afternoon, Colonel," the waitress yelled.

Anna looked toward the door, where the tiny tinkling bell signaled the diner's arrivals and departures. An elderly man with surprisingly straight posture strode purposefully toward a booth near the back of the cafe, where a seated couple waved.

"Elsie," he replied. "Looking beautiful as ever, my dear. Coffee when you can, darlin'." Anna's attention caught on the man's hat. It was a black baseball cap emblazoned with bright patches and several metal pins that glinted when they caught the light. The lettering across the front proclaimed WORLD WAR II VETERAN in two rows. Between the rows of letters was a wide rectangle of ribbons, similar to those on a military uniform.

The war ended in September 1945, she thought. Anna recalled several documents, and she shifted quickly through the piles, searching. There. The documents from Port of Entry. The first one read "District of New York –

Port of New York, 1946". She hadn't understood why her father had these documents. They didn't seem to fit in with the other research. But, still, they were here. Something had led him to this. The baseball cap had been like a lightbulb going off, connecting the dots. The newspapers she had been reading were peppered with news of troops coming home. The troops wouldn't be using a port of entry, but an immigrant would. But, why would any immigrant come all the way to Wyoming? The easiest explanation was that an American had been overseas in World War II and met a woman who then came to the States after the war. After she arrived in 1946, they were involved and she became pregnant. Then, for some unknown reason, she gave the child up for adoption in 1949. If all that were true, Anna's grandfather was a soldier. There were so many articles in the newspapers from that time that she realized she could identify those that fit that description. Once she had a list, she might be able to focus on each one to narrow it down. At least it would be a place to start, she reasoned.

Of course, Anna realized it was entirely possible that even if her grandmother had come to America in 1946 after meeting a soldier overseas, it didn't necessarily mean the father of her child was the same man. She may never have found the soldier. She may have followed the soldier to America but met someone else who had nothing to do with the military. It was equally possible that her grandmother was an American and her grandfather was the immigrant, or perhaps even they both were.

Anna knew there was a strong possibility it was a wild goose hunt. But it was a place to start. Being here in Lander was a long shot anyway, and she was going to try. She packed up her pages, left a few bills on the counter with the check, and quickly headed back to the library.

CHAPTER SIX

Logan Harris pulled his hat lower, blocking out the morning sun as he rode, surveying the land with the pride of ownership. He never tired of this view. He knew how fortunate he was to own a ranch like this. Good water, protected pastures, and fertile ground for grass to support summer grazing. The land was perfectly suited for cattle and the business had prospered under generations of good management and hard work. The ranch had not been his birthright, but he had poured his heart and soul into it nonetheless. Today he rode for the solitude. His horse, Domino, pranced and sidestepped, shifting the bit in his mouth and pulling at the reins.

"Okay, buddy, I know you've got a lot of energy." Logan grinned. "I go to town for two days, and you're acting like it was a week." He let the pinto break into a brisk trot as he took a deep breath of the crisp mountain air. He was as anxious for this ride as his mount. He had used the excuse to duck out on his dad's pointed questions over coffee that morning. They typically planned the day over breakfast, discussing priorities and schedules for the ranch work. Today, Roy had been intent on another topic.

"It's gotten pretty quiet around here lately." His father had cleared his throat noisily. Roy Harris was not one to hold back when he wanted to say his piece.

"Uh-huh." Logan resisted the urge to say more, knowing exactly what his father meant.

"You think any more about changing that?"

"Nope, I haven't decided anything," Logan replied. "It's a pretty big thing you're talking about."

"Son, you're not a boy anymore, and I'm not getting any younger."

"Dad—" Logan started to interrupt.

"No, now you're going to hear me out. I was twenty when I married your mom, and we worked here long and hard to make a good life. I was as surprised as anyone when Wyatt left this ranch to me, but I have tried to live up to his confidence in me. One day, this will be all yours and you need a family. You need a son to leave it to." His father looked at him piercingly. "You need to have a woman in your life, someone permanent you can build a life with. Maybe someone you can grow this ranch with."

"Dad, I know. This is a legacy I am fortunate to be a part of and I don't want it to end with me. I want a family, but I want to be sure about who I include in that." He pushed his chair back and shook his head. "Besides, I'm not convinced now's the right time."

"Gimme some more coffee since you're up."

Logan chuckled as he filled his father's mug. "Domino's antsy and needs a ride. I'll be back in a few hours."

"Ha! We'll continue this later, boy." Logan knew his dad was not going to let it go that easily. It was too important to him.

Logan had been born on this land when his father served as the ranch manager. Fresh out of high school, Roy had started working for Wyatt Hamilton as a ranch hand. The ranch had been in Wyatt's family for several generations. Wyatt's great grandfather had first come to the Wyoming Territory in 1870 and started what grew into the ranch that existed today. Wyatt's father had died in an accident the year before Roy came to work there and with no other brothers or sisters, it fell to Wyatt to take care of his mother and the family business. It was a responsibility he took seriously. Logan had heard the story so many times it had become part of his own story. Roy had been loyal and hardworking and in time became Wyatt's right-hand man. Wyatt made him ranch manager when Roy married his high school sweetheart, Beth. The newlyweds moved into the manager's house, where Logan was born. In thirty-three years, Logan had only spent his four years of college away from the ranch. This ranch was the center of his life, like it was for his father, and it had been for Wyatt. Logan and Roy had worked together, managing the business since they had inherited it a few years before when Wyatt died. Logan had never been interested in pursuing anything else, but his father was constantly badgering him to get married and start a family.

Dating was tough for a rancher. The reality was that unless you fell in love with someone who you grew up with, or met someone from college who was willing to move back to a remote area, the possibility of meeting someone was slim. Logan had dated a few local girls in high school, but none of them seriously. He had his heart broken by his college girlfriend when she turned down his proposal. A dozen years later, the memory of that conversation still stung.

He had planned out the perfect romantic evening and as they sat enjoying a dessert at a candlelit table, he'd reached over and taken her hand.

"Lauren, I love you so much. Come to Wyoming with me." He had looked into her beautiful brown eyes earnestly.

"The past two years with you have been so nice, Logan," she'd said, smiling hesitantly.

"We can have the rest of our lives to be happy together." He'd slid out of his chair, smoothly bent on one knee in front of her and opened the small box. "Lauren, will you marry me?"

She had stared at the slim gold band, with its single stone sparkling in the candlelight.

He'd waited.

She'd remained silent, twisting her lower lip in an uncomfortable embarrassment.

His heart had sunk and the proverbial knife twisted in his gut. He'd risen slowly, stepped back and sat down in the chair across from her.

"Logan, I'm sorry." She raised her eyebrows in a questioning gesture, as if unsure of his reaction. "It's not you, really. I do love you. It's that, well, I don't want to be just a rancher's wife living in the middle of nowhere." She'd wrinkled her nose, shaking her head like she was describing something messy and disgusting.

"Are you kidding me with this?" he had asked, confused. "After two years of telling me how much you love me and dropping hints about kids and our future, you've suddenly changed your mind?"

"Well, I always thought you'd give up the idea of ranching. It's not even your ranch, you know. Just someplace where your father has worked his whole life. Don't you even want something of your own?" Her posture had changed then, leaning back with her arms crossed, almost daring him to argue with her. "Wouldn't you rather be in a bigger city, around more people? Lord, I really think I would die of boredom if it were only us except for our big night out at the local bar and grill every Friday night."

In shock, his mind had been a blank as he'd struggled to process her words.

"I have a job offer in Denver," she'd said. "Graduation is only a couple weeks away now and I put out some feelers a while back. I'm a good graphic artist, Logan; I want to pursue the career I came here to learn."

"What about us?" he'd whispered.

"I'm sorry, but I have to think about what I really want. I love you, but not enough to give up my dreams."

She had walked away that night, and they had never spoken again. Logan returned to the ranch after graduation and buried himself in work. His business degree allowed him to take over the ranch management and finances while his father focused on the day-to-day operations. He avoided women for several years, but in time, he turned to someone who understood his lifestyle and dreams. Stormy Adams had been like part of the family as long as Logan could remember. She was three years younger than he was, and in their twenties and thirties, the age difference didn't matter. Growing up, she was the little kid that hung out at their place constantly. She could ride, help out with the chores, and manage to be annoying less than half the time, so Logan thought of her like a cousin or a sister. For the past few years, they had an on-again, off-again relationship that stopped short of a serious commitment. He had to admit, she had grown into a stunningly beautiful woman. At five-foot-nine, she stood nearly eye-to-eye with him, had flawless skin, wide green eyes framed by long thick lashes, a straight nose, and full, lush lips. She walked with a smooth, gliding gait, her blonde hair flowing to the middle of her back, and a commanding presence that demanded attention in any room. She was a goddess, and he should be craving her company.

Logan sighed. Stormy had become more possessive and demanding lately, and he had resisted her efforts for a permanent commitment. She made no secret that she wanted to marry him and join their neighboring ranches into a larger spread. She had a hunger for money and power, and her ambition for success had always been much greater than Logan's. She would be a powerful partner, but Logan knew her desire for status and wealth far outweighed her desire for him. Any man would be a fool to turn her away, though. She was beautiful, intelligent, and driven to succeed. The perfect life partner: committed, focused and loyal. He couldn't help but feel it was checkmarks in boxes, not the friendship and passion he wanted in a wife. He could not bring himself to commit to a life focused on material gain over the warmth of a loving family. He had known Stormy so long that it was difficult for him to see her with the passion of a lover. Thinking of her never caused a shiver to run up his spine, and the sight of her face never made his mouth dry or his hands tremble.

Unlike that cute brunette he had met in town. One brief conversation on the sidewalk and every detail of the exchange had replayed in his mind repeatedly. The sparkle of her warm brown eyes, the adorable pert nose sprinkled with light freckles, and that bright smile that made his heart nearly stop. Those gorgeous brown eyes. They were deep and soulful, almost amber-like in color and glinting with flecks of gold. Her throaty laugh and easy manner captivated him. She seemed more like the kind of woman he could spend a lifetime with, enjoying every day. He wondered if she was the kind of woman that would be happy in a place like this. He thought he needed to find out. Right after he found out her name.

He lifted the reins and encouraged Domino in the direction of the house. They had been out for a few hours and Logan had a pile of paperwork back on his desk that needed his attention.

*

The late afternoon sun slanted through the window, landing on the colorful area rug, the dust motes dancing on the beams of light. Logan leaned back in the leather desk chair, stretching, looking out at the empty yard. The house was silent, except for the distant ticking of the grandfather clock in the front hallway. Normally he enjoyed being alone in the house. Those rare times allowed him time to concentrate on special projects or focus on clearing paperwork. The ranch was often busy with vehicles constantly pulling in or leaving. Mail and package deliveries, feed trucks, hay delivery, the farrier and vet, an occasional contractor, salesmen, and friends. This was an area where many conversations were still held in person rather than by text or telephone. He surveyed the yard from the house to the barn that was visible through his window. His truck, along with his dad's and a couple of the ranch hands' vehicles were parked in uneven rows on the gravel drive between the buildings. A couple of horses stood in the corral, looking over the fence as they swished their tails. A small flock of birds sat on the barn roof while a single barn swallow swooped and fluttered.

Today, he felt nostalgic for the days of family dinners and the aroma of a home-cooked meal that called everyone to the table. Despite being an only child, Logan had always felt like part of a large family. Wyatt had been a confirmed bachelor, but he had always been outgoing and friendly, treating his employees as an extended family. He frequently hosted barbecues with half a dozen neighbors and claimed nearly the whole population of three counties among his friends. The closest neighbor, Jack Adams, had been a classmate, confidant, and business colleague. Jack and his wife Alma were frequent visitors to the Hamilton ranch. When Logan's mother had been alive, she and Alma would often join forces to feed the entire clan, friends and neighbors joining together in as a family by choice, if not by blood.

It was an unusually quiet afternoon, but he knew the crew would be coming in soon for the evening meal. Three of the four hands typically came to the main house for dinner, although each of them had living quarters with their own kitchens. The ranch had a bunkhouse, where the ranch hands stayed, located a quarter of a mile away from the main house. The bunkhouse was made from four small efficiency cabins connected together like two duplexes, constructed in a single L-shape building. Each one of the units contained a small galley kitchen with a hotplate and microwave, table and chairs, a double bed, and a private bath with a small shower. There were four units, all occupied at this time of year. One of the men had started seeing a girl who lived thirty miles away and he tried to head out to her place when work was done for the day. The rest usually gathered in the main house for dinner together rather than cooking for themselves in the bunkhouse.

They took turns making dinners, and this week was Mitchell's turn. Mitchell was a grizzled cowboy of indeterminate age whose culinary skills relied heavily on a slow cooker. Most of his creations came from the slim paperback recipe books he picked up from the supermarket checkout stand. When his week to cook came, he would visit the grocery store using the small booklet as a shopping list. He would stop by in the morning, dump the ingredients into the crockpot and set it on low. From the smell permeating the house, Logan guessed dinner was along the lines of a meat and gravy concoction, most likely beef stew or pot roast. The savory blend of onions and spices with the beef made Logan's stomach growl. He had to admit, whatever Mitchell made, they all usually had seconds.

He headed off to the kitchen to set the table.

CHAPTER SEVEN

Anna leaned back from the library table that was beginning to feel like home, even though it was only her second day there. She rolled her head from side to side, stretching the near-frozen muscles in her neck and shoulders. She sighed contentedly, feeling accomplished with her progress.

The previous day, Anna had returned to the library and begun her new line of research. She was glad she had spent so much time reading the newspapers because now the families seemed quite familiar. She had reviewed the society pages again carefully and made notes on each family, the events, and all the participants that were listed by name or mentioned in passing.

She had been thinking about too many possibilities. Anna decided that she would have the best chance at success if she chose one scenario to research. If it didn't work out, she would create another and follow that to whatever conclusion it might have. For now, she chose to assume her grandfather was in the military. During his deployment in WWII, he'd met a woman who would eventually become Anna's grandmother. This line of research could lead to a dead-end eventually, but at this moment, she was excited about the prospect.

Reviewing the newspapers again, she combed through each, looking for references of soldiers returning from the war. She also looked at the society announcements for mentions of awards, duty stations, and even short visits by servicemen. Jotting names on a notepad, she considered her new parameters. She was looking for those who had joined the military, were deployed overseas, who weren't killed in action, and who had some association with the Lander area. It was still pretty broad, but the community wasn't that large, so it should be a manageable list, though she worried about missing a name or two in the research. What if a family or specific son didn't make the news? It was possible, likely even, but she stubbornly stuck to the idea of one line of investigation. She knew she had to focus on one path, logical or not, or she would never make any progress.

It took the rest of the week, but she eventually developed a potential list of eight men. One of these men might be her grandfather. Her grandfather. Anna managed a wry grin. It was a bittersweet moment. She couldn't help but feel a longing to talk to her father. He had started this process, and now she had actual names to investigate and narrow down to what she hoped would be a single name. Her grandfather. *Dad, one of these names could be your father. I wish we could have done this together.*

Nothing was certain yet, but at least she felt like she was making progress. It seemed a world away, but only a week ago she had been in Iowa, preparing for the trip here. Now, she was in a town that might have been home to one of her biological grandparents, and she might be looking at one of those names right now. She based the list on the premise that her grandfather had met her grandmother overseas during World War II. Anna believed that had been her father's thought as well, which is why he had collected so many records of immigration. It wasn't much help yet, because she didn't know which port might have the record she needed. She was working on the theory that her grandmother had come to America from another county. In 1945, it was reasonable to assume the lady had met a member of the military and they fell in love. Anna rolled her eyes and shook her head at her own romantic fantasy. *Well,* she thought, *it's my working hypothesis until I prove it wrong. I wonder if that's even possible to prove.*

Anna was attempting to tackle the task logically, so she decided to take a scientific approach. With so many variables, she needed to make a few assumptions. If she reached too many dead ends, she could go back, revise an assumption, and start again. For now, Anna had decided on five things.

All right, Dad, let's make this project official now, she thought with a grin as she opened a new file on her computer and started a project summary page.

1. Research birth parents for James Lander Miller.
2. Child's birthdate April 25, 1948.
3. Assume the birth father lived in or around Lander, Wyoming, the year prior to the child's birth.
4. Assume the birth father would not have been married at the time of the baby's conception.
5. Assume the birth mother was from another country.

Anna looked at the list and considered the fourth item. There really was no basis for that assumption. When she thought about it realistically, it was more likely he was married and that would explain the adoption. As she thought, she slowly crossed it out, knowing it was wishful thinking that some other set of circumstances had led to star-crossed lovers being separated. In the late 40s in a small town, a married man meeting up with a single foreigner, however clandestine the meetings might be, would have started gossip. A child that resulted from the affair would certainly be a reason to turn to adoption.

She picked up the results of her research for the past few days – the list of eight potential men who might be her grandfather.

Two were married before they left for the war. One had a wife with two small children at home, the other married mere days before his deployment.

Two had sweethearts whom they married when they returned. Anna had found engagement party notices and wedding announcements for each one.

The fifth spent several years in a military hospital after stepping on a landmine during his tour of duty. It was a miracle he even survived, but he spent the rest of his life as a home-bound invalid.

A sixth possibility was over thirty when he was drafted, and seemed to have made a career in the military. He never returned to live permanently in Lander.

There were two more who never married, from what she could find, making a total of eight possibilities that fit her initial criteria.

The more she considered possible events and circumstances, the more she realized that one of the first four men on her list was the most likely candidate to be the father. These were the men who were already committed to a relationship or marriage. A man who was not free to make a life with a woman and raise an unplanned child.

It didn't make sense that two single people in that time would have an affair, create a child, then not marry and raise him or her together. Anna thought the last two on her list were the least likely to be the biological grandfather she was seeking. Why would two single people expecting a child together not get married? Anna decided that she would put those two men at the bottom of the potential list and track them down if the others didn't pan out.

She also thought it was unlikely that her grandmother would have had the opportunity for a relationship with the injured soldier who never left the house, or the officer who rarely returned to Lander. *It was possible*, she thought, *that if her grandmother was a nurse, she might have had ample opportunity to interact with her lover.* As she considered it, Anna wondered if her grandmother would have followed her love and became a nurse after he was injured in order to care for him after his return home. If that had been the case, why wouldn't she have stayed with him permanently? But there had been no mention of a nurse or sweetheart in anything that Anna had read. She made a note to ask around for some gossip that may have escaped the proper society pages. Without any further information, she moved that name to the bottom of the list and considered the next candidate.

She contemplated the mindset of a career military officer. Would that explain why a marriage didn't result from an unplanned pregnancy? Perhaps he didn't want a wife or family tying him down and limiting his career advancement. Anna pondered that for a moment. She wasn't certain if that would be a viable concern. Many career military officers had families so why would a wife and child be a limitation? She realized she didn't know much about military careers. However, she didn't find any record of him living in Lander again, so any potential affair would have had to occur during brief visits. The small window of opportunity would make it less likely, but Anna realized that didn't lessen the possibility of a relationship, so she left him on the list, but not one of the first she would investigate.

The list of eight was manageable. Based on her thought process, she decided to focus on the first four to begin with, the ones who had been married, as the most likely candidates. It seemed logical that a married man would be more likely to put an illegitimate child up for adoption than a single man. Anna sighed, knowing that it was a pretty big assumption, and there could be any number of scenarios that led to the adoption. But it was a place to start. If none of those four panned out, she would move on to the two single men, Marvin Smythe and Wyatt Hamilton, putting Eugene Morris, the injured soldier, and Clarence Williams, the career military man, at the end of the list. She looked at the first four: Harold Jones, Frank Johnson, Leonard Campbell, and Donald Brown.

If they were still alive and lived in the area, she wanted to meet each and attempt some sort of interview or inquiry. She wasn't sure how to approach the topic. You can't simply ask someone if they fathered an illegitimate child and abandoned the mother and child. There was also the potential that some or all of these men had died, and she would only be able to locate next of kin. In a small town with generations of family history, this first step shouldn't be difficult. If it ended up being next of kin, uncovering any truth about an illegitimate child would likely be quite a challenge. But, one step at a time.

It was barely after twelve o'clock. Anna decided to return to the cafe for lunch and to learn more about the Colonel. There was the possibility she might see him in the cafe again. As casual as the greeting she had heard yesterday had been, Anna guessed the lunchtime stop was a habit. She hoped it had been anyway, and that today would bring a repeat. Walking to her car, she stowed the project box, then headed to the cafe with a small notebook in hand.

The aroma of chargrilled meat, french fries, and the sweet scent of vanilla permeated the diner. Anna thought this must be what heaven smelled like.

"Sit anywhere you like, sweetie," a disembodied voice called out from somewhere in the back of the restaurant. There were more empty seats today, the cafe not nearly as busy as it had been on her previous visit.

Anna followed the directive and slid into a booth by the windows. Grabbing a menu, she scanned the tables but didn't see the older gentleman they called the Colonel. Between glances around the room, she pretended to study the menu.

"Hiya, hon, wha'cha havin to drink?" The cheerful voice startled her.

"Iced tea, please." Anna looked up at the waitress she had seen before. "That would be great, thank you. And, um…" She hesitated, suddenly self-conscious.

The woman cocked her head, looking intently at Anna. She shifted her weight, kicked one leg out, and rested her hand on her hip, getting comfortable in her stance.

"You want to order now or do you need another minute?"

"Oh, yes. No, well, not for the menu. I was wondering about something else. I was in here a few days ago when a man came in as I left. You called him Colonel. I was wondering about him."

"You a private eye or something?"

"What? Jeez, no." Anna laughed. "Nothing like that. More of a historical researcher."

"Huh. What're you researching?" the girl asked, unconvinced.

"I'm trying to find some relatives that might have been in the area in the late 40s. I think one of them might have been in the military, so I thought he might be able to help me out. I wanted to ask him some questions about the town and people around that time."

"Well, he likes to tell his stories. I can ask if he wants to talk ta ya and let you know. He should be in for dinner any time now."

"That would be great, thank you so much," Anna said earnestly.

"You got it. I'll go get your tea. You gonna order food?" she asked.

Anna nodded. "Absolutely. I'll have today's special."

She waited patiently for her lunch as she watched the door, hoping to see the Colonel's black hat appear. The burger arrived and she was halfway through it when she spotted the distinctive cap. He took a seat at the diner's long counter and was drawn into conversation with the pretty waitress. Anna wasn't sure if she should get up and join them, smile and nod from a distance, or act like she was not aware they were talking about her. She was relieved when she saw the Colonel nod, then turn toward her and smile. She quickly stood up and walked over to the counter.

"Hi, I see that – I am so sorry, I don't think I know your name." Embarrassed at her oversight, Anna blushed as she turned to the waitress.

"Kim."

"Kim," Anna repeated. "So, Kim told you about my little request?" She turned to look at the Colonel.

"Yes, she did." He reached over and firmly shook her hand. "I'm Leonard Campbell."

"Colonel Campbell. It is Colonel, correct? It's nice to meet you. Thank you for your service," Anna replied. "May I buy you lunch today? I was finishing up myself at that table over there."

"I don't often get offers from pretty girls anymore. I best not pass one by now," he chortled as he rose and started toward the table Anna had indicated. "Kim, could you send my dinner over when Sam gets it ready?"

"You bet, Colonel." Kim smiled.

Anna followed the old man to the table. Her heart was racing. The hours of research and lists of names jotted down on paper had led her to this moment. The first name on her list now had a face, a voice and a twinkle in his eye.

Leonard Campbell. Potentially her grandfather. Grandpa. She looked furtively at his profile for any family resemblance.

She slid into the booth across from Colonel Campbell and watched as Kim added another placemat, paper napkin wrapped utensils, and a glass of iced water to the table.

"Thank you so much for your time, Colonel Campbell," Anna said.

"Call me Leo, or just Colonel, darlin'. I retired a long time ago, so there's no need for the formality."

"Leo, then, thank you. I'm Anna Miller."

"So, Anna, what is it you're researching? Kim said you might have family you're looking up?

"I think so, yes," Anna said slowly. "I'm not certain, but I believe I may have relatives in this area." She lowered her voice to a conspiratorial whisper. "It's a bit of a mystery and it might be digging up an old scandal, or uncovering one that no one ever knew."

"Huh. I see. Sounds intriguing. Fill me in," Leo said, leaning in.

"I came across some puzzling documents recently when I was packing up my parent's home. My mother passed last year and I lost my father recently," she explained. "There were papers about adoption, some immigration and census printouts, and a few other things." She shook her head. "Three months ago, I would have said there was no way either of my parents was adopted. That's something I would have known, right? At first, when I looked through the papers, I thought my father was doing research for someone else, that he was helping out a friend or something."

Leo nodded, his face attentive as he focused on her story.

"He also did a search on the word Lander. There were only a few items on his list, but one of them was this town." Anna paused for effect, enjoying sharing this full story with someone.

"Lander was my father's middle name."

Leo raised his eyebrows but didn't comment.

"I don't know how he found out some of the information he did, but I'm trying to research based on the records he left. I believe one of his birth parents had a connection here and I'm trying to verify if that's true."

Kim slid a bowl of broccoli soup and a club sandwich onto the table and, after a nod from Leo, moved on to check on other patrons of the cafe.

Anna sipped on her tea and nibbled at the french fries remaining from her meal. Leo took several bites, and Anna could tell from his expression he was mulling over her story.

"So it would be your grandparents you are looking for then," he stated. "From what you have, do you think it's your grandmother's or grandfather's family that is local?"

"Truthfully, it could be either. I'm going to assume for now it would be my grandfather's family. I am basing that on some of the paperwork I found and, honestly, a lot of guesswork. My father had several pages of immigration records from 1946. New York, Boston, San Francisco. For that year, it made sense that an American who served in the war met someone in a foreign country and then came back home. I'm thinking grandfather was American and grandmother the immigrant," Anna said. "I know it's a big leap, but I thought I'd try one avenue of research, and if it's a dead-end, I'll start over and see if there's a Lander connection on the other side." She shrugged and continued. "My current hypothesis is that my grandfather was an American soldier who returned home here, and my grandmother followed him from some foreign county."

"It would be possible that an American woman was traveling abroad or even served as a nurse in the military and met a man during that time. America was seeing a lot of immigration from many countries," Leo mused.

"Maybe. I wondered that myself. I read many of the society columns but I didn't see anything like that mentioned. I would have thought that a young woman serving as a nurse in the war would be news. I guess since I was looking at newspapers from 1946 forward it would be right after all the World War II news. More like people returning from the war," Anna corrected herself. "Even traveling abroad would likely have been mentioned; it wasn't all that common then and it seemed like pretty much everything made the news. For certain, a visitor from a foreign country seems like something that would be reported on. I read more than one item that made mention of someone visiting family from two counties over," she laughed.

Leo nodded. "Those were the days when life was simpler."

"You know, I recognize your name from some of those news clippings," Anna said. "Mrs. Campbell was quite the hostess. I saw her name often. Let's see, I believe you were in the army and married your high school sweetheart when you returned."

He smiled. "Yes, mother loved to be in the center of the Lander society, and I recall many a garden party. That engagement party was really something too. My Mildred was the love of my life. Those years that I was away made it sweeter when I got back. We started our life and never looked back. She's been gone three years, and I still miss her every day."

"I love to hear stories like that. It's nice you were so happy. It seems as if that kind of love doesn't come around very often." He nodded, and Anna continued. "So, you made the rank of Colonel and chose to not make the military a career? You returned here?"

"During the war, promotions were common in the toughest times. I made lieutenant colonel when I was twenty-five." Leo stopped speaking, and Anna felt that the war was not a subject he wanted to delve into.

"And then you came back home," she said hesitantly. "If you're up for it, that's what I would like to talk to you about a bit more."

He nodded briskly and shook his head as if to sweep away the more unpleasant memories, but as he looked her in the eye, he seemed agreeable to answer questions.

Anna opened her notebook and pulled out the list she had prepared, holding it as she explained. "I know this is a long shot, but I guess I felt like I had to start somewhere. I made a list of men who might potentially be my grandfather. Men who were the right age and had spent time in the military, then came back what would have been the year before my father was born. I know it's a lot of assumptions and guessing, but if there's even a possibility…" Her voice trailed off as she looked at Leo expectantly.

He nodded. Anna slid the unfolded the page across the table.

Leo looked down and read the lines. He frowned. As he read further, he raised his eyebrows and pursed his lips.

"Well, young lady, this is quite fascinating. I see we have several things to discuss." He waved to Kim, who breezed to their table.

"Darlin', we're going to need a couple slices of pie and some coffee."

When Kim had left, he looked at Anna, "My name's on this list. You think I might be your grandfather?"

Anna had anticipated and dreaded this moment of awkwardness. "Well, I'm not saying you are, but you fit into the general parameters I set up. I told myself if I'm going to do this, I have to be comfortable with asking the question, so here goes." Anna took a deep breath and smiled, "Mr. Campbell, sir, is it possible you had a liaison in the summer of 1947 with a woman who was not your wife? An association that may have resulted in a child that you were or perhaps were not aware of?" She watched his face for signs of guilt, anger, annoyance, or any other clues. "I know it's an indelicate and an extremely personal question, but it's important to me to find my history, my father's birth parents. Finding his birth parents would mean finding my grandparents, and getting to know my family, if they are willing to meet me."

"Anna, you seem like a sweet young lady, and as much as I would like to say it's possible, I'm afraid not. I had a few dalliances abroad, but once I got married, I never strayed. We never had any children of our own, and now that she's gone, a granddaughter like you would be a welcome surprise. I may not be the grandfather you're looking for, but I can still help you, perhaps."

An hour and a half later, after hugging Leo warmly and promising to get together again, Anna felt like skipping down the sidewalk as she headed back to her car. She was excited and pleased with the results of her lunch meeting. Filled with new information, her head was spinning as she sorted through the details. She did her best thinking while driving or hiking. She'd had enough of the car from the drive out here and opted for a hike. It was a perfect afternoon to explore the trails she had read about in a brochure from the lobby at the lodge. The Popo Agie trail in Sinks Canyon would suit her mood. A challenging grade, a little tree coverage, part along the water, and some open sunshine. The brochure promised a gorgeous view at the end, so Anna was looking forward to it. After a quick stop in her room to change into jeans and the heavy-soled boots she favored for hiking, she grabbed a trail guide and jumped in the car.

Anna pulled into the convenience store on the edge of town to pick up a few bottles of water and an energy bar for an afternoon snack. As she cashed out, her mind played over the details Leo had provided to her earlier. She nodded distractedly to the clerk and started to turn, her items clutched in a small bag when she was startled by a voice directly behind her.

"We meet again."

Without looking, knew the owner of the voice, his image filling her mind, and her previous train of thought evaporated. She had successfully ignored the thought of this sexy guy, who likely had an equally impressive woman in his life. She had focused on other things, but memories of him, of his eyes, his voice, and that lazy grin had a way of popping in and out of her head. She had, for the most part, ignored the tempting distraction, and had been rewarded with progress on her research. The whole point of being in this town, this place, was her family, not this hunky cowboy.

She glanced back. The man was divine. She smiled, "Small town. Guess it was only a matter of time."

"If we're going to keep meeting, we might as well have a proper introduction. I'm Logan."

"Logan. I'm Anna. Nice to see you again." Anna groaned inwardly.

Like she had any doubt whatsoever about his name.

"You too. How's the research coming, Anna?" Her name rolled off his tongue as he nodded. She liked how it sounded when he pronounced it in his slow, deliberate manner.

"Fantastic. I've been getting so much done I'm taking the afternoon off to enjoy some outdoor time."

"It must be kismet, running into you again," Logan said. "It means you must have dinner with me."

"You think that's what it means, do you?" she said thoughtfully. "Well, who am I to question kismet? Sounds like I really have no choice."

"None. I think if we're going to keep crossing paths, we should get to know each other. More than that, you are a beautiful lady, and your smile is like pure sunshine."

Anna rolled her eyes and laughed. "Now how can I resist an invitation like that? I think you're right. At this rate, it is likely I will keep running into you, and I guess I need to know more about you besides the fact you are a shameless flirt and a passably handsome man."

"See? That's the spirit," he said enthusiastically. "But we'll have to work on your compliments. That was pretty shabby."

"Huh. I think your ego can probably handle it." She loved this banter and his sense of humor. She was surprised at the comfort level she had with him, considering how crazy he made her. She was not suffering from any sudden bouts of stupidity or a blank mind. She felt like she was actually witty.

"You wound me, but you can make it up to me at dinner. Tomorrow night?"

"Tomorrow night." Anna nodded. Maybe he didn't have a wife or girlfriend after all. "I don't have a pen, but I'm staying at the lodge on the hill, do you want to call me there later?"

"You got it."

"I look forward to it." She smiled and touched his shoulder as she passed. "But now, I'm headed out for a hike. Enjoy the day, Logan." She worked to stay nonchalant and flirty, trying not to let her hand slide across his bicep as she walked. It was challenging. This man captured her attention like no one had before and playing it cool took effort. It was destined to be a short-term thing, but she couldn't resist the invitation.

CHAPTER EIGHT

"I'm feeling a bit out of my element," Anna said, shaking her head. "I don't think I've ever done this before."

"Done what? Gone on a date?" Logan grinned.

"Smart aleck. Usually, I know a little something about a guy before I go out on a date," she replied. "This feels a little odd, being here and knowing so little about you. But, then, I guess we shouldn't worry about not having enough to talk about."

"I wasn't worried." He leaned in across the table, clasping her fingers in his warm hand. His physical presence was overpowering and he was still several feet away.

"Are you always so confident?"

He laughed. "No, honestly. You have an effect on me. I don't know what it is but I am completely taken with you." He leaned back, away from the table to allow the server to refill their drinks.

"Your order'll be out soon, guys."

They were seated in a cozy booth at the same restaurant that Anna had first seen Logan. It seemed unreal to Anna how many changes had come to her life in such a short amount of time. Only a week ago she had first glimpsed this man who took her breath away and tonight he had knocked on her door, picking her up for their first date. She had dressed in a simple sundress and sandals, pleased he was also casual in jeans and a crisp white button-down shirt. His sleeves were rolled up, revealing tan, well-muscled forearms. His hand had brushed her lower back as he led her to his truck, and she had felt a shiver of electricity run through her body.

The night was living up to the level of any young girl's fantasy as she looked across the table at this gorgeous man who had admitted to being attracted to her. Her, Anna, the one who had always been pretty, but never pretty enough, or clever enough to be any man's first choice. It was intoxicating.

"So, tell me something about you," Anna said. "Have you always lived here?"

"Yes, born and raised right here. I left for college but came back to run the ranch with my dad."

"Has it always been in your family?"

"No, but we were as close as family. Mr. Hamilton was like a grandfather to me. His family had owned the ranch for several generations; one of his grandparents settled the land in the 1800s. He never married and didn't have any children, so he left the ranch to my dad. One day it will be mine."

"You raise cattle?" Anna asked, trying to focus on his words.

Watching his lips was distracting.

"Yup, we have a few hundred head, farm a little, and work with horses. How about you?"

"Me?" Anna laughed. "No, I don't know much about cattle and I don't really work with horses."

Logan flashed a quick smile and cocked his head at her teasing, but waited expectantly. He seemed to want to hear about her life.

"My story is pretty boring," she said. "I was born and raised in Iowa. Went to college and got a degree in business management. Came back and worked with my father at his insurance agency."

"So what brings you to this part of Wyoming? I thought you were new in town, so I was surprised when you said you were at the lodge. Are you here on vacation?"

"No, I guess I'm sort of on a quest." She paused, hesitant to share her real motivations. Would he think she was crazy for leaving her home and everything familiar to drive hundreds of miles on what was basically a wild goose chase? He might not appreciate why it was so important for her to find out who her true grandparents were. She knew that finding out the Millers weren't blood relatives didn't take away any of the memories. Logan might not understand this search, but she didn't know what else to do. She wasn't sure how much she wanted to unload on him until she knew him better, but he was so easy to be with that she found herself wanting to confide in him. "I guess I'm considering what the next chapter in my life will be."

"Really? What does that mean?"

"I was the only child of parents who were both only children, so my family circle started out pretty small. The past few years, it was just me and my parents. I lost my mom last year and Dad a few months ago. I'm pretty much on my own now."

"I'm sorry," he said sincerely. "So why come to Wyoming? Why not stay in your hometown where your friends are? Not that I'm not very glad that you're here and would like to see you stay for a while." Logan winked, lightening the mood.

Anna chuckled. "I appreciate the warm welcome. But I'm here following some clues, and I'm trying to research some family history."

The server reappeared, bearing a large tray filled with plates of steaming food. He served Anna a grilled chicken with potatoes and broccoli, then placed a large steak and baked potato in front of Logan. Small dishes of spiced apples, gravy, and a plate of biscuits followed.

"How's that look, guys? Everything okay?"

"Yes, this looks great," Anna said, smiling at the teenager. "Thank you."

As they dug into the meal, Logan asked curiously, "So tell me more about this quest you're on. How did it bring you to Lander?"

"I suppose that is a very medieval term, isn't it? But it does feel like a quest. Something life-changing."

"Really? I definitely need the details now."

As they worked through the dinner, Anna shared her discovery of her father's adoption record and brought Logan up to speed on her research.

"Anna, that's fascinating," Logan said. "I mean, wow, you don't hear a story like this every day."

"I'm not sure how it's going to end up. I can't wait to look into some of what Leo told me. I'm hoping I can identify at least one grandparent in the next couple of weeks. It would be wonderful if at least one of them were still alive and willing to talk to me."

"So, what's next? You have a list, and the Colonel filled in some blanks for you. Do you head back to the library now or search public records?" Logan seemed genuinely interested, and Anna was grateful to have another person to talk to about the process.

"I think more research would be dragging my feet. I feel like I need to reach out to the names on my list and see if any of the details match. What do you think? Is that too direct?"

"No, I don't think so. Even if someone considered an unwed mother a family scandal in 1948, I don't know if it would still be an issue today. I don't think talking about it would be too embarrassing," Logan said.

"I hope not."

"You could run into some problems, though. If the two involved have both died, I doubt either would have told anyone, so you might not find out anything. But then, if you're looking for a man who messed around and had an illegitimate child, I doubt you're going to get him to admit it now."

"I know. I've been trying to come up with a strategy for that," Anna admitted.

"But some of the older folks around here are particular about appearances, so you might meet with some brick walls even if you get a chance to talk to them. Have you thought about how you're going to bring the subject up?"

"Not exactly," Anna said honestly. "I'm still giving that part some thought."

"May I see your list?" he asked. "Maybe I can help you with the approach. I know most everyone around here."

"Oh, Logan, that would be fantastic. I hate to impose on your time, but would appreciate the help." Anna stopped short of gushing.

"And I'm not offering based on any ulterior motive to spend more time with you," he said with a grin that told Anna that was precisely why he was offering.

"I'll take any help I can get."

Logan smiled and set to work answering as many questions as he asked.

The conversation flowed, and they talked as if they had been friends for years.

They finished dinner and walked the short distance through town to a small park, enjoying the pleasant evening. The quiet was interrupted only by the hushed buzzing and chirping of insects. The park was dimly-lit with rows of old-fashioned lanterns on tall posts. As they walked, Logan easily slid his hand around hers, and she felt a warm tingle spread from where their bodies joined in the innocent touch. The overwhelming sensation of being close to him was making it difficult for her to concentrate. She had never felt such a connection with another person.

"It's beautiful here," she said, looking up at the dark shadows of the mountain peaks above the town.

"Yup," he said nodding. "I bet it's pretty different from Iowa."

"It is, but I like it."

"Are you getting homesick?" Logan asked.

"I'm not sure. No, not exactly. Can you be homesick for a time instead of a place?"

"I never thought about it. I think that would be more nostalgia than homesickness, though. I guess that's more of what you're feeling. Still adjusting to being alone?"

"I suppose. There isn't much left for me there. It's a lot of memories, but I'll keep those no matter what. I'm not sure if I'll go back or start fresh somewhere else. That could be part of why I wanted to do this research. It gave me an excuse to get away and put off a decision for a while."

"Wyoming is nice," Logan said, moving his arm around her shoulder. "You might think about relocating your warm smile here permanently."

Anna leaned in and sighed. "I'll keep that in mind. I'm starting to feel comfortable here."

"Do you have any idea how much longer you'll stay? How much more do you think you have to do?"

"I'm not sure. I guess some of that depends on you. And whether I uncover anything from talking to folks around here." She sighed. "I know I'm probably wasting my time, and I won't find anything, but it's like doing one last project with Dad, you know?"

"I'll do what I can, but it's good you know it might not go anywhere."

"It's not like I'm in a hurry to get back." Anna squeezed his hand. "It's pretty nice right here."

"I like the sound of that." Logan stopped and turned to face her. "Anna, I've enjoyed spending time with you."

She smiled. "It's a little corny, but this has been the best first date I've ever had."

"I like to hear that." He looked at her for a moment, then slowly moved closer. "Girl, you are beautiful."

Anna anticipated the energy of the kiss. It had been over a year since she had been on a date and even longer since a first kiss. The magical first kiss was a moment she always anticipated and always found disappointing. But then, she had never experienced the level of attraction she had with Logan. His kiss was everything she imagined and more. He pulled her closer into his embrace. His left hand clasped her waist, and the other gently on the side of her neck, his thumb against her cheek. Anna felt a shiver run through her, although the night was warm. She had never experienced a sensation equal to that kiss. Logan was a man like none she had ever known, and a far better kisser than she had known. She savored the moment.

They were in no hurry, enjoying the evening and each other. They strolled the park hand-in-hand, talking, stopping now and again to kiss, and gradually working their way back to Logan's truck.

As he drove the short distance back to the lodge, Anna wondered which she was looking forward to more: Logan's help with the introductions or simply seeing him again. Either way, she was pleased with the prospect. "If you have time later this week, or this weekend, I would love to find out what families are still in the area," she said.

"Let me know what the names are, and I'll help you reach out to the ones I can. If I think the Colonel would be better help, I'll let you know that too."

"The funny thing was Leonard Campbell was one of the names on the list, but there are three I'd like to start with."

"That's it? Just three?" Logan sounded surprised.

"Well, I'm starting with the ones that were married about that time. I'm thinking if a married man were the father, it would be more likely for the baby to be put up for adoption." Anna explained. "Leo was one of those four, so there are three more I'd like to find and talk to if I can. If none of them pan out, I'll go to the other four, who were single. If none of them turn out to be my grandfather, I go back to researching again and come up with a new list."

"Okay, let's see how these turn out first and then worry about the next step."

"That was my thought exactly," Anna said, smiling. "I can't thank you enough for the help. Everyone here has been so nice – first Katherine over at the library, then Kim at the cafe introducing me to Colonel Campbell. And Leo himself being so nice. It has all been so great."

Logan was quiet as he pulled into the lodge parking lot. He cut the engine and turned to look at her. He leaned over and placed his hand against her cheek. "It's easy to be nice to you, Anna. I find you fascinating and beautiful and good company. I enjoyed tonight."

He rounded the truck, opened her door, and, with an arm around her shoulders, walked her to the door of her room.

"Until next time, sweet Anna," he said, leaning in for one last kiss.

CHAPTER NINE

"Okay, sounds good. I'll see you at the cafe. I shouldn't be long." Stormy Adams watched as Logan ended his call and slipped his phone into his pocket.

"Hi, hon, I have those papers for you right here," she said and, with a practiced gesture, reached out to touch his arm.

He smiled as he stepped away and nodded. "Thanks, Stormy. I knew you would have this all together for me. I can't believe he finally agreed to sell that pasture land, but I'm sure glad you called me first when you found out."

"Of course, Logan. I know how much it means to you, and we couldn't have someone else buying up that stretch. If you didn't add it to your spread, Dad and I would have added it to ours. One of us had to have it, and your herd is bigger than ours right now."

"Well, I'm lucky to have you looking out for me."

"Of course, babe. You know you can always count on me." Stormy leaned in to hug him, then tucked her hand into the crook of his elbow and led him to her desk. The offer documents were laid out and ready for his signature. As he sat, Stormy thought he deliberately moved his chair further away. Sliding the stack closer, he scribbled his name on the required lines and quickly finished the pile.

"All right, that's it then. I'll get these over to him, and we'll be all set." Stormy said as Logan stood and replaced his hat. She wasn't ready for him to leave yet. "Wait for just a sec. I'll walk with you. You're going to the café, right? I was heading there for lunch myself."

Logan nodded noncommittally and waited as Stormy gathered the papers into a portfolio, then picked up her keys and purse. They stepped out into the bright sunshine. Locking the door of the real estate office behind them, Stormy tucked her hand back under Logan's arm as they walked the few blocks to the cafe.

Stormy could sense something different in Logan's demeanor. She had always been more invested in their relationship than he was, but she was fine with that. She had no great passion for him, but they were the perfect match. Everyone knew it, but still Logan delayed an actual proposal. Stormy had rarely been able to rouse any jealousy from him and was not prone to public displays of affection, but she always considered them a couple. She still had been able to count on him to take her to lunch or dinner and be her obligatory escort to events. He had been the perfect boyfriend for her and would be the perfect husband. Today something was very different and she needed to find out what that was.

Stormy had natural beauty and was comfortable using it to her advantage; it often came in handy in her line of work. She carefully crafted a persona of professionalism and casual elegance. She liked to hint at a willingness to drive a truck through the mud or welcome a wet doggy kiss, but honestly hoped no one would take her up on the offer. She shuddered at the thought. She liked her rhinestone and lace style and indulged in a large wardrobe complete with cowboy boots, hats, and accessories. It didn't blend well with mud and slobber. There were times she tolerated or even enjoyed getting a little dirty, but those were limited and specific circumstances. Her teenage rodeo days and barrel racing had been an integral part of her social life and most of her friends were ones she'd first met in those days. She had always been a fierce and skilled competitor and enjoyed the reputation she earned.

She enjoyed the leadership role she had, both in business and in the community. When the other women were laid back or timid, it was easy to step in and organize. Between the real estate business and a leadership role in the community, she stayed busy. But not too busy. She made sure to pitch in when Logan needed the help. Logan was the key to achieving her life plan.

His ranch bordered her family's property, and combining the two would make them one of the largest enterprises around. If they married, Stormy would quit her real estate job and live the life of leisure she had been born to live. She could manage the help that would take care of the house, leaving her with time to pursue hobbies and travel. Logan wouldn't be a demanding husband, and that suited her plans exactly.

They entered the cafe together, Logan holding the door for her, but she saw his eyes scan the small room. A smile crossed his lips as his gaze stopped at a table in the back. Stormy followed his view and evaluated the table where the Colonel was sitting with a dark-haired girl. In Stormy's estimation, the girl was attractive enough to bear watching.

"Okay, thanks again, Stormy. I'll see you later." Logan didn't wait for her response before moving toward that table that still held his attention.

She had never worried before about his casual approach to their relationship. They had grown up as friends, drifted apart, got closer, drifted again, but always reconnected. She took for granted that eventually, they would end up together and never put much effort into ensuring the outcome. Today was the first time she questioned that approach.

Stormy watched, her eyes narrowing as she took note of Logan's body language. She had never seen him so focused on another woman. She knew he'd had girlfriends in college, and had probably dated since then, but not that she had seen. She felt he had been more distant lately but hadn't thought it was because someone else had caught his attention. *There is no way that brunette waltzes into my territory*, she thought. *I've got too much invested in this; no way I lose it now.*

She needed to know what was going on and whether or not this was a problem she needed to handle.

Anna tried to focus on her conversation with Leo but found her attention repeatedly drawn to the door of the cafe. When Logan entered, she felt her heart jump in her chest, and she fought the urge to wave.

"Well, now that he's here, mebbe you can focus, and we can have a conversation," Leo said wryly.

"Anna! Colonel," Logan said with a nod, leaning over the table to shake Leo's hand. "How are you, sir? You're looking good."

"Yes, yes, I'm feeling good these days. Of course, having lunch with a pretty young girl will put a little pep in any man's step, am I right?"

Logan laughed and slid into the booth next to Leo. "Yes, that will do it. And you sure are keeping company with the prettiest one I've seen in a long time."

Anna resisted the urge to groan at the excessive compliments of the two men. She rolled her eyes and cleared her throat loudly.

She was rescued by Kim, who had seen Logan enter and came to take their order.

"So, where are you on the research?" Leo asked.

"Well, as I shared before, I've narrowed it to Harold Jones, Frank Johnson, and Donald Brown to start. Eugene Morris and Clarence Williams are two more, but right now, I'm considering them to be less likely. Eugene was seriously injured during the war, and it seems he returned here and lived out his life confined mostly to his house. I would think that any affair he had would have been more difficult to cover up. And, in his condition, why would he not want to marry and claim his child?"

"Those are good points, Anna," Logan said thoughtfully.

"I remember Mrs. Morris, though," Leo said. "She was a real patriot, that one. She was so proud to have a son in the Army, and when he was injured, everyone knew what a hero he was. That time was a bit different, you have to understand. The 'bring us your poor huddled masses' wasn't really the song we were singing then. It was more American flags everywhere and support for the war and the American way of life. 'Foreigners' weren't as welcomed as you might think. I'm not sure ole' Mrs. Morris would have welcomed a war bride into her home with open arms." Leo leaned back. "But, in theory, I agree with you and doubt that Eugene would be the one you are looking for."

"I don't think I remember Clarence Williams, Colonel. Do you know who that is?" Logan asked.

"He was ten, twelve years older. I remember his younger sisters more since they were closer to my age. I don't remember much about him, but he made a career of the military. He came back for visits a few times, but I think he lived mostly in California. We would have to check on that if the other names don't pan out," the Colonel replied.

"There are a couple more, but since they were single at the time, I thought they would be less likely candidates." Anna felt a nervous excitement. They were following her line of reasoning without poking holes in her theories. For the first time, she thought that her research might not be based on wishful thinking, but a logical evaluation of facts and reasonable assumptions. These few names may not be the only ones who lived here at the right time to father a child, but since they were the ones she could find in the newspapers, it was a place to start. And maybe through these personal contacts, she would identify other men who weren't on the list yet. Anna was starting to feel like she might find her blood grandparents and connect with a family of her own.

Leo drew her attention back. "So, I looked into the other three names, Anna. Harold Jones passed away about ten years ago. His widow, poor thing, is in a nursing home up near Idaho Falls and she has pretty advanced dementia from what I hear. Most days, she wouldn't be able to remember much. They had two girls, one lives in Idaho Falls, but the other is around here. They're both real nice girls, so I think they would talk to you."

"Hmmppp," Anna let out a noisy sigh as she set her pen down. The page she had been taking notes on showed the proof of her shaky hand. "I didn't expect this to feel so real. I'm nervous just thinking about talking to…who? My aunt? I'm not sure I know how to start the conversation to find out."

Logan reached over and took her hand between his own, squeezing gently. "Anna, it's okay. It will all be okay. I'm here for you. You don't have to do this alone, and you don't even have to do it right away. Give yourself some time to adjust to this. Hey, here's Kim with our lunch. Let's table this for a while," he said, tapping the wood surface and grinning.

"Table it, really?" Anna groaned.

"Not punny, Logan," Leo chortled as he winked at Kim.

The two obviously traded jokes and puns regularly. Anna focused on her lunch as the men shifted their conversation to the weather, cattle prices, feed, and some new bovine vitamin products a local rep had been touting. Anna was happy to listen to them discussing ordinary life while she worked at processing her current situation. A few weeks ago, she had been alone in the world with no idea even what her desires were for the future. Now, she was in a new town, making friends, and possibly on the verge of finding a new family.

She looked around the small diner. It was homey and friendly, with bright reds and yellows over the background of crisp white and stainless steel. The clatter of the lunchtime diners filled the air with flatware scraping against dishes, ice clinking against glasses, and the constant murmur of conversation. The scent of burgers mixed with the comforting smell of vanilla and cinnamon from the famous apple pie. Any one of the people surrounding her in the room might be family. Anna continued listening to Logan and Leo as she finished her lunch, observing the other diners as the crowd gradually thinned out.

Kim stopped by to check on them a few times, eventually clearing the empty dishes. They declined dessert, but all accepted drink refills. Anna took a deep breath.

"Okay, so if Harold Jones passed away, let's talk about the other two," she said. "Are either one still…living? Living here?" She was still uncomfortable with the words "died" or "dead" and avoided using those terms if she could.

"Frank Johnson and Donald Brown," Leo said, grinning, looking at Logan. "Well, yes, Frank is here."

"Yes," Logan said, his eyes glinting with mischief. "I think Frank would be pretty easy to get in touch with."

"What is it? I think you two are up to something. Tell me," Anna demanded.

Leo said, "That's easy. Kim is married to Frank's grandson. He lives with them. He goes to the Methodist church every Sunday, and most Friday nights he still goes to the VFW to play cards."

"Wow. That's amazing. But I should have expected to have come across a connection. I mean it's reasonable in a small town that there would be, of course." Anna's voice trailed off as she became aware of her rambling.

"Then Donald Brown, he is still here too. He and his wife both. They have an apartment at the assisted living complex. They are both just the nicest people you would ever want to meet," Leo said. "I've been friends with Don since we went to school together. I don't think he's your grandfather, but I will go with you and introduce you to him and his wife, Donna. I'm sure they will tell you whatever they can remember from that time.”

“That would be wonderful. Thank you so much,” Anna said gratefully. “I think they might be the easiest ones to start with to explain my situation.”

“I would agree,” Logan said, nodding.

“So, why do you think Donald is unlikely?” Anna asked, looking at Leo.

“Honestly, I came back maybe a week or two before he did. I know I got back in town first. But we spent a lot of time fishing and down at the VFW. Donna is a pretty outspoken woman, and if Donald was spending any time elsewhere, I think I would’a heard about it. But, I guess when a man is running around, it would be in his best interest to keep it a secret.”

“Well, he might be an easy one to either confirm or cross off the list. I guess we’ll know after we go for a visit,” Anna replied.

“You two can do that, and I’ll talk to Kim about arranging a visit at her house,” Logan said. “You seem pretty comfortable with her, and I think you will have an easy time talking with Frank. I know him, and actually know Kim and her husband Carl pretty well, so I can go with you.”

“That sounds good to me. Then I think I could use the first couple of visits to work up to talking to those sisters. It’s tough to wrap my head around the idea they might be my aunts,” Anna said with a shaky laugh.

Logan slid the lunch check off the table and crossed the small room, catching Kim’s attention. As he dug into his pocket for cash, Anna could see an animated conversation between the two of them. From the bantering and laughter, she knew they were good friends. She immediately felt better about Logan arranging the meeting with Kim’s family. She had already taken a liking to Kim, and the thought of the five of them having an evening together actually sounded like fun.

She looked at Leo and smiled. Relief and optimism filled her. He chuckled and shook his head, reaching over to pat her hand.

“Why don’t you and I go over and see the Browns this afternoon? That way, you won’t have time to fret about it,” Leo suggested.

Anna kicked back in the Adirondack chair on the small patio of her room at the lodge. The sun had set and the twilight had the trees shrouded in shadow.

She had called Margaret, spending nearly an hour sharing stories of the trip and updating her on the progress of the search. Anna shared that she had talked with the first two prospects on her list and had six others she had started to track down. No, she had not found her answer yet, but she felt peace from the progress she had made. The town was nice-very friendly. Yes, she was making friends, and yes, she was taking care of herself.

Anna leaned back in the chair and realized she did feel at peace. The wind gently hissing through the trees, crickets chirping, and frogs croaking all blended together like a soothing jazz soundtrack. She closed her eyes and let relaxation sweep over her. Peace. After so many weeks of dealing with pain, sorrow, life questions, her own insecurity, and a general feeling of being unsettled, at this moment, she felt peace.

Tomorrow would be soon enough to review her notes and absorb the details from the afternoon's visit with Donald Brown. For now, she could relax.

And then there was Logan. Logan, who was like no other man she had ever met and pretty much the embodiment of her fantasy man. Her cell phone buzzed. She picked it up and checked the display. Speak of the devil.

"Hi, gorgeous. How was your day?"

"Hey there. Really good! How was yours?"

"Great. Things went smoothly today, and I've got a cold drink, a comfortable chair, and a pretty girl on the phone."

"Sound like you've got it made." Anna laughed. "What more could you possibly want?"

"Oh, I can think of a few things, and I'm working on 'em, trust me." Anna loved the slow drawl of his words, the combination of his playful tone and suggestiveness.

"Hmm, that sounds interesting," she said, grinning. "Care to elaborate?"

"Most definitely," he said smoothly, "but it would require more in-person sort of details. Why don't you come out to the ranch soon and I'll share my thoughts with you."

"We can arrange that," she said, unable to keep the smile from growing. "I would love to hear what's on your mind."

"Right now, I'm thinking you're a pretty special lady, and I want to get to know you a lot better. I'm hoping you'll be sticking around here for a while."

"I'd like that. I can't promise anything, but we'll see how it goes. I might find roots here or even family."

You made some progress then? Any exciting news to share?"

"No, not in the sense that I found out anything solid, but it really felt like I was doing something to make progress."

"Progress in what way?"

"I don't know. It's silly I think. Maybe it doesn't make sense, but it felt good to go from looking at old newspaper articles making lists of names to actually talking to a live person with one of those names. It made this process more solid somehow like I'm actually moving toward accomplishing something."

"That's great. You sound excited about it," he said encouragingly.

"I know that sounds weird, but yeah, I am I guess," Anna said. She had been hesitant to share some of her thoughts with Margaret but felt comfortable enough with Logan to open up. "I've been thinking about it a lot and this whole process is strange, but it feels right. Not to be too deep or philosophical, but it's more like I'm discovering myself more than researching my past."

"Discovering yourself?" he asked. "That does sound pretty deep."

She laughed. "Well, not so earth-shattering I guess. No soul-searching kind of stuff. I really enjoyed the conversation and companionship with Leo and the Browns. I was thinking that even if none of them were family, or even if I never found blood relatives, I would be happy with finding purpose in my own life. Listening to their life stories, it was good. Their lives have been good, surrounded by people they love, who love them. Having a history like that with someone who chooses to be with you, not bound by blood, but by love. That's pretty awesome."

"That sounds like a pretty good life goal to me too," Logan said. "Maybe I can talk you into working on that together."

Anna laughed. "You are persistent. That is an admirable quality. I tell you what, I'll keep looking into my roots and you keep helping me figure things out. In between, we can work on getting to know each other. You do have my attention." What was it about this guy that made her feel so flirty? Conversation with him was so easy, she felt as comfortable with silly flirting as she did with deeper, more personal thoughts. She didn't know where it was going, or even if as a relationship it could go anywhere, but she didn't want it to stop. She had thought her time here would eventually end and she would go back to Iowa, but that thought was becoming less appealing.

"Your attention is a good start," he said confidently. "I can work with that. I'd like to see you, but I've got a busy few days ahead of me. Will you be free later this week?"

"I'd like to see you. Sometime later this week, sure."

"Perfect. I'll call you later then. Sweet dreams beautiful."

"Sweet dreams."

CHAPTER TEN

She awoke the next morning with nervous energy, hoping to have another opportunity to talk with a potential grandfather. She grabbed coffee and a Danish from the lobby, then returned to her room and updated her notes with the detail of Donald Brown's history. Anna had been disappointed that Logan had not accompanied them, but Leo kept his word and had taken Anna to meet the couple the previous day. Don and Donna had been gracious hosts. Anna had an instant reaction upon meeting Don Brown that he was a warm, sweet person, but definitely not a blood relative. He was small and spry, moving quickly about as he fussed with drinks and refreshments, reminding Anna of a barn swallow, swooping and flittering. Donna was ensconced in a plush chair, her legs covered with a light blanket. Don moved from the kitchen to the living room, providing snacks as Donna kept up a steady stream of conversation. It was obvious to Anna that Don doted on his wife, watching as he stopped to touch Donna's arm in passing or tuck in the blanket a little tighter around her legs.

Don was a few inches shorter than Anna; she gauged him to be about five-foot-four with a slight build. He had bright blue eyes, a round face, and wide smile. He didn't physically resemble Anna or her father James. As they talked, Anna learned that Don and Donna had been childhood sweethearts, engaged from their junior year in high school. After his time in the military, where he had been deployed to the South Pacific, he returned just before Christmas in 1945. He and Donna married, and Don started working with Donna's parents at the car dealership they had owned. He eventually took over the business and now his two sons and grandson ran a conglomerate of three dealerships. Anna could hear the pride in his voice as he talked about the family, the business, and the life they had led. Anna took some notes of events as they recalled highlights from the annual rodeo from the Fourth of July. Don and Donna each recalled friends and mentioned a few names Anna had not heard before, so she jotted those down as well.

She had asked many questions about the time period Anna's father would have been conceived and born, but Don didn't seem to be hiding anything and the life stories didn't give her the feeling he had carried on an affair. She wasn't much of an expert but had done a little research to know what to look for when someone was hiding the truth. During the conversation, Anna hadn't noticed any nervousness, or what the articles said were classic giveaways: covering the mouth while talking or looking away to avoid eye contact. She also hadn't observed any stuttering, conflicting details in the stories, or any unease at all. As far as she could tell, Don enjoyed the visit thoroughly and relished the opportunity to share his memories. Anna watched Donna as well, and she remained smiling, nodding and adding to stories as they shared the family memories.

Anna enjoyed the visit as well, but in the end, agreed with Leo that it was unlikely Donald Brown was her grandfather. She was as certain of that as she could be, short of a DNA test. After writing down the details of the visit, her thoughts turned to the next names on the list. The nervousness and uncertainty built as she considered how to approach the next conversation. Harold Jones was deceased and his widow may not have known about an affair. Anna had no idea how she would even approach that question; how could she be delicate in the inquiry? But there were two women, Harold's daughters, who might be her aunts, and Anna's stomach did flip-flops as she thought about the possibility. She couldn't wait to talk to them but at the same time dreaded doing so. Frank Johnson might be a much easier conversation. How cool would it be if she ended up related to Kim? The thought of true family ties here in Lander was exciting. She might consider moving here to get better acquainted and being close to Logan would be a bonus.

Finishing the updates to her notes, she donned jeans and her hiking boots and headed off to Sinks Canyon and one of her favorite nature trails. The trails had such varied landscapes in a small area that each visit revealed a new scene. The views were breathtaking. There was a river that cut through the canyon and she found several small but beautiful areas of rapids and waterfalls. She sat and watched the water, enjoying the gentle sounds and hypnotic flow. It seemed impossible to hold on to any stress in this environment. She lost track of time as she sat and allowed the calm to soak into her spirit. Finally aware of the chill seeping into her legs and backside, Anna got up and continued her walk. She took one of the thicker forest paths, surrounding herself with the life and vitality of the animals she heard all around her. She found rejuvenation in the morning hours at the canyon.

The serenity of the forest always brought her peace. She had experienced more excitement and anticipation in the past couple of weeks than she had in the past few years combined. The time alone here on the trails had become a necessity to think through everything that was happening and sort out her feelings. She wasn't sure why this grandparent search was so important. Perhaps it was about finishing her dad's last project, finding the closure that everyone always talked about. Maybe by solving the mystery of his parents, she would feel like they'd completed one more project together and she could say goodbye. She knew that there was a significant appeal to finding more family. When she thought about it logically, she wasn't sure it was realistic. It had been difficult enough talking with Leo and Donald Brown. What if each one from here on out were more difficult than the last?

As she walked the trail, she considered how things might go. Obviously, she might never figure out who Dad's real parents had been. But, if she did, would they really be open to welcoming her into their family? Anna tied to imagine it and wasn't certain that would be her goal. If they lived in another state, like Idaho, would she really want to move there to be close to them? That would be too weird. Even if they were blood, they would still be total strangers. *I can't simply move to a new town because I found long-lost family there – that would be stalkerish, or lame,* she thought. *Here I am, sad lonely Anna with no home and no family – I'm just going to horn in on yours, okay?*

No, definitely not. If there's something I'm not, it's sad and lonely. As the thought came to her, she realized it was true. The past few weeks had changed her. She felt stronger and freer. She enjoyed the flirtation with Logan but had grown to love the town of Lander and some of its residents. It felt like home, and she was far from lonely. She was taking more chances, letting people get closer to her, and becoming involved in their lives. Looking back, she realized after she and David had broken up a couple years ago, she had used that as a reason to avoid relationships. She told herself she stayed close to home due to her mother's illness, and later as emotional support for her dad, but that was an excuse. She loved her parents, but neither one had needed her to give up her life. She had chosen to be with them and taken advantage of the benefit of avoiding romantic relationships. She could thank her Viking heart for being tough, independent, and resilient. She could survive just fine on her own, but it was clear now she had been missing out on a lot. Her heart was capable of much more than surviving. She owed it to herself to find out how much more.

By the time she returned, it was mid-morning, and the town's business activity was in full swing. It seemed odd, now that her research was on hold, to have no real purpose or activity for the day. She wasn't sure how to pursue any additional research without a name or something more concrete. As she showered and dressed for the day, she realized there was nowhere she needed to be. For the first time in a long time, it didn't feel right. She was frustrated and needed an activity to focus her mind on. While she was waiting for the opportunity to follow up on her research, she needed to find something productive to do with her time. She also needed to find a new place to stay. Today was Tuesday, less than a week before Memorial Day. She had been fortunate the lodge had a last-minute cancellation for the holiday and she was able to extend her stay until the following Friday. After that, it seemed the official start of summer would begin and the lodge was booked solid.

She needed to stay busy. She was starting to miss the activity of an office and the satisfaction of work. Anna checked the local phone book and was happy to find a local employment agency where she could sign on for temporary work assignments as she had done in Iowa. She headed downtown to visit the agency and stop by the cafe to talk with Kim. A few blocks from the lodge, she noticed the County Community Center marquee had a "Volunteers Needed" message on the last line of their sign. She immediately changed her course and entered the building. She was informed the volunteer coordinator was out, but she left her name and then headed over to the cafe.

"Hey, Kim," Anna called in greeting and settled into a table for two in the middle of the empty restaurant.

"Anna. Girlfriend, you're early today. It's barely ten-thirty," Kim said, grinning. "But since you stopped by smack in the middle of breakfast and lunch, I can sit with ya."

"Perfect, because I've been hoping to have a chat with you."

"Logan told me you had something you wanted to talk about and he mentioned Frank, but he didn't go into any details."

"It's a little personal, and I'm still not sure how to share it, but here goes," she said, taking a deep breath before continuing:

"I lost my mom a little over a year ago, and my father passed unexpectedly earlier this year. When I was packing up their house, I found some papers of my father's that indicated he was adopted. I had no idea, and from what I've found, he didn't know until about a year ago."

"And no one else in your family knew?" Kim asked, her eyes wide.

"I guess not. At least I had never heard anything about it. I guess that's the kind of thing that doesn't really come up in conversation unless you know to ask."

"No whispered secrets of skeletons in the family closet, huh?"

"Well, I didn't really have any aunts or uncles on my father's side. Let's see, my grandmother had one sister that died when she was a baby. My other grandfather had two brothers, but neither one had children. They all died probably fifteen years ago. Anyway, by the time I was in my teens, it was just me and my parents."

"That means you don't have any other family now," Kim said sympathetically.

Anna nodded. "I followed the research my father started and it led me to Lander. The Colonel has been helping me, and I have a list of a few men who might be my grandfather." She exhaled. "Your husband's grandfather, Frank Johnson, is on that list." Anna watched Kim's face for a change in expression as she made the comment.

"Really? That's kind of cool. Huh. I wonder, hmmm." Kim seemed to run out of words as her comments trailed off.

"I know. I'm sorry, there's no good way to ask these kinds of questions. 'Excuse me, do you think you may have a child you lost track of like, oh, seventy years or so ago' doesn't really roll off the tongue." Anna laughed nervously.

"Well, I don't know. Carl never said anything, but it's not the sort of thing that would come up in conversation, I suppose. It's not like Frank would have said much even if he had known, so I guess it's not likely Carl would have known either. Interesting," Kim said thoughtfully. "What do you want to do?"

"I was hoping it might be all right to come over and talk to Frank. I don't want to upset him or anything, but if I could ask a few questions and see if there's a possibility..."

"Yes," she said suddenly, "let's do that. I'm off at two o'clock today. Meet me here then, and I'll introduce you. I would love to know more about this, if it's okay with you that I listen in."

"Yes, absolutely. I can't tell you what this means to me."

Anna met up with Kim and rode with her to the small farm at the edge of town. Her nervousness quickly disappeared, thanks to Kim's easy manner. As they walked through the front door, Kim led her to a sunny atrium at the back of the house.

"I brought you a visitor, Frank. This is Anna – she thinks you might be her granddad, you sly old goat." Anna was shocked at Kim's casual bomb-dropping and watched as she strode up to a man who was busily digging in a flowerpot and lightly touched his shoulder.

Frank Johnson was a good-hearted prankster, according to what Kim had told Anna on the way over. He assumed Kim's comment was a practical joke, and he responded with a fit of laughter that ended in a coughing spell.

Pushing to his feet, he grinned at Anna as his sharp eyes took in her details, head to toe.

"Well, if you were my granddaughter, I'd say I did well. You are a pretty one for sure." He winked and slapped his hands together briskly.

"She's not kidding Frank." Kim said laughing. "I guess you need to have a sit down with her and figure out some details."

Frank looked from Kim to Anna and back again. "Well, then, wha'da you know about that? Kim, you go get us some drinks and I'll get cleaned up and meet you two in the front room then." He left the atrium, shaking his head and mumbling to himself. Anna and Kim exchanged looks and burst out laughing.

Minutes later, he joined them and settled in a chair across from the couch where Anna had sat. "So, you think you may be one of my wild oats, do you?"

Anna choked back a laugh as she heard a fit of giggles come from Kim, who had entered the room.

"Well, sir, I…" Anna stopped for a moment. "Well, yes, I suppose so. Not to be too blunt, but I thought I might ask you some questions to find out."

"Well, okay, then, shoot," Frank said, eyes twinkling.

Anna was delighted by his refreshing directness. She decided to be equally direct. "My father was born in 1948 and given up for adoption in Idaho. There was a note in the records he found that his birth mother requested his middle name remain Lander. I also found records on immigration in 1946 that he had collected. Unfortunately, they are pretty generic and I don't even know the name of the birth mother. I'm making a lot of assumptions and, I guess, at this point, poking around at some theories. Right now, I'm looking for a man that might have met a woman during the war, and the two might have had a liaison that led to a child."

"My, my, that simple tale has quite an air of mystery to it." He took a sip from the glass Kim had set on the table beside him. "Thanks, hon, that's good," he said to Kim.

"Do you think there's any truth to it?"

"There could be, Anna dear, but not for me," he replied almost sadly. "There were foreign beauties that pledged their love, and I will admit to some flirting, but my heart belonged to Edith."

Kim had shared that Carl's grandmother had died of cancer ten years previous. As he spoke, Frank's love for his wife was apparent, even after all the years that had passed.

"Yes, I remember the war. It was a terrible time. My sweet Edith was an angel, and she was all I thought of when I was over there. We married just two days before my deployment. I wanted to make her mine and make sure she knew I was coming home to her." He motioned to a grouping of pictures on the wall.

Anna looked at the wood-framed black and white photo of a smiling couple. The dark-haired girl had a wide-shouldered, tight waisted dress and short, tightly curled hair topped with a small hat. Her lips tipped up on one side as if she worked to hold back a smile that couldn't be contained. The man was a much younger version of Frank, looking proud and laughing, standing behind his girl with his arms wrapped around her, his hands resting possessively on her forearms.

Anna felt a longing inside as she watched Frank's expression soften as he gazed at his beloved. Was it a longing for family lost or a desire to experience the depth of love that spanned beyond one lifetime?

They finished their visit talking about Anna's time in Lander and Frank invited her back to visit anytime. She hugged him tightly and thanked him for sharing his memories. She said goodbye to Kim and waved off her offer for a ride back to the lodge, choosing to walk back and spend time with her thoughts instead. She had some decisions to make about a roof over her head and how to spend her time, but thoughts of love and life-long companionship kept intruding.

Logan called early the next morning. After a quick conversation, Anna agreed to drive out to the ranch for the afternoon and stay for dinner. Logan insisted she didn't have to bring anything, but she stopped at the small downtown bakery for an apple pie. Her mother had taught her never to arrive at someone's home for dinner empty-handed.

She headed out of town, noticing how different this direction seemed than her normal route into the state park for hiking. This area was flatter, the land on either side of the roadway covered in vegetation of green and gold, dotted with grazing cattle. A short distance away on either side, Anna could see small hills, and taller mountains in the distance. Wood fence posts with wire fencing lined many properties. As she passed by, she was surprised at how close some of the homes seemed to be. She had expected that ranches would be larger, sprawling properties. These seemed to be small homesteads, with twenty or thirty head of cattle, or in some cases, a small herd of goats or sheep.

It took her less than thirty minutes to find her destination. Logan's directions had been easy to follow, and Anna was relieved to arrive without a single wrong turn. Fortunately, he had described the turn with details of the fence, mailbox, and shrubbery. Anna was sure that she hadn't seen an actual address since she had passed the town limits. As she turned in the drive, a long white fence flanked the lane on each side, leading up to the house. From her vantage point, the property was beautiful. The wide expanse of green wasn't a lawn like she was used to in Iowa, but pasture. On the right, cattle were grazing, and on the left, she could see several horses. The drive led between the pastures and ended in a T-shape. To the right, a two-story white farmhouse stood, surrounded by a lush green lawn. On the left, several trees grew along the pasture fence line, providing shade up toward the barn. Several other smaller outbuildings stood behind the barn. Anna pulled up and parked under the tree closest the barn. As she cut the engine and got out, Logan appeared in the open doorway.

"You found it," he called.

"No problem. Your directions were perfect," she said, walking up to him. "You're sure I'm not interrupting your work?"

"No, I wouldn't have invited you up if it were a problem. You look great." He moved closer and wrapped her in a friendly hug, kissing the top of her head quickly before grabbing her hand and pulling her toward the barn.

"Well, you said jeans for riding, so that was pretty easy to comply with. I did tell you I haven't ridden much, right?"

"You've been on a horse before, though? You've done some riding?"

"When I was much younger, group trail rides."

"Don't worry, you'll do fine. I have a good horse for you, steady and good-natured." Logan stopped in front of a pretty horse, light brown with a chocolate-colored mane and tail. She had dainty feet and large expressive eyes.

"Anna, this is Jelly. Jelly, this is Anna," he said to the horse, patting her on the neck. "Anna's a little nervous, so you be nice to her," he admonished the animal. "I need to finish a few things then we can head out," he said as he picked up some odd-looking tools and straps of leather and headed toward an open stall.

As she watched, Anna realized it was more of an equipment room than a stall. She followed and looked at the small space. There were long poles that held horse blankets that looked like they folded or swung out so that the blankets could be folded over the pole and stacked vertically. There was another section of poles or pegs where saddles rested and unfamiliar gadgets that looked like belt organizers, except the leather hanging on them looked to be complicated gear with extra parts. Some were ornate with metal fittings and some had curved sections. Logan moved among the complicated array, hanging items up, taking others down and examining them before replacing them. Random names picked up from books and movies flitted through her brain—stirrup, bit, rein, halter—and she unsuccessfully tried to match a word with the equipment.

Turning away, she visually explored the rest of the barn. Looking around, she noted that the barn was well-organized and clean. The smell was not unpleasant, rather it was a heady mix of wood, hay, horses, and leather. She could detect an undercurrent of an unpleasant scent, but it was minimal, and she was surprised that it didn't disgust her. Light streamed in from the open door and seemed to come from above her somewhere. Dust motes danced in the sunbeams. She looked up and saw electric lights but no windows. The wide central area of the barn looked like it had recently been swept clean, and inside the stalls, she could see piles of straw, or hay perhaps, piled in each. She realized she didn't know the difference between hay and straw enough to recognize one from the other.

I might be a little too much of a city girl to date a cowboy. The thought was odd because she had always considered herself to be more country than city.

There's a world of difference between country and cowgirl, I guess.

"Okay, Anna, we're all set."

As Anna approached the horse, Logan made a last-minute adjustment to a strap, then ran from one side to the other, under the horse's belly.

He turned and handed the reins to Anna. "Do you know how to mount up?"

Anna looked from the ground to the stirrups and back to Logan. She gauged the height and tried to visualize how to get on top of the horse, but could not remember the process. It had been years, after all. Anna could see Logan watching her mental struggle and heard him chuckle.

He moved behind her, and Anna fought the urge to step back, closing the gap between them and feel his arms wrap around her. She had been disappointed he hadn't given her a real kiss when she arrived. The ones they'd shared already had replayed a hundred times over in her mind, and she had anticipated more today. She couldn't contain the little shiver that ran up the back of her neck as she felt his warmth behind her but worked to remain nonchalant. Their first date had ended in what she thought were passionate kisses, but he seemed offhanded in his affection today. She wondered if something had changed since their first date. Anna had noticed he maintained polite distance during the lunch with Leo. At the time, she thought he wasn't comfortable with public displays of affection. When he had called today, she was excited at the prospect of seeing him again but didn't want to appear too eager. Logan affected her like no other man ever had and it was playing havoc with her senses.

"I'll give you a boost," he said, tapping her left leg. "This one in the stirrup, and swing the other one over."

She struggled to breathe normally but felt her heart beat faster as he boosted her up. Chuckling nervously and at her own awkwardness, Anna fidgeted in the saddle, trying to settle her legs and feet into the positions she had learned years before. Jelly craned her neck back as if protesting the human shifting uncomfortably on her back.

Logan laughed and patted Jelly's neck. "It's okay, girl. She'll get settled."

He leaned down and adjusted the stirrups, his hands sending warm sparks up Anna's leg from where he grasped her ankle. She grit her teeth, well aware she seemed to have no impact on him even though his presence was reducing her to the level of a giddy schoolgirl.

Anna was thankful that he seemed satisfied and moved away. He mounted the tall black and white horse that stood patiently nearby. Looking back, he nodded and nudged his horse toward the door. Anna was pleased to discover that Jelly followed Logan's mount with little encouragement. She tried to remember the basics of how to control the animal but came up blank.

Hoping for the best, she held loosely to the reins and took the opportunity to look around the property as the horses plodded along, tail to nose. The land around the house was flat, and behind the structure, the area gradually gave way to gentle rolling hills, seemingly in mounded layers as far as her eye could see. Some of the distant peaks were still snow-covered from the winter. The grass in the pastures around the buildings was lush and green, very different from the scrubby-looking growth she had seen on her drive through the eastern part of the state. As they rode, she peppered Logan with questions about the land, the history, and the ranching lifestyle. She already knew from their conversation over dinner during their first date that he had been raised on the ranch.

"It's not the biggest ranch by far, but it's more than average for this area of Wyoming. I'm working on purchasing more that will expand our property further to the north."

He explained he also leased grazing land from the BLM, the Bureau of Land Management. Just one head of cattle needed about seven acres of grazing land, so it took a lot of land to support the herd, much more than his acreage, so the leased grazing land was critical. He pointed out the land to the east and told her that was BLM, federal land. He explained that not all the acreage had good grass for feed, some was rocky and in the summer it could be very dry.

"We call it the average cow days per acre."

Logan told Anna the spring calving season was done, so they would be checking on the calves. As they rode near the herd, Anna couldn't resist cooing over the adorable little animals that ranged from a few weeks to a few months old. Logan showed her the water troughs and feeding areas. He explained the calves would stay with the cows for about eight months. To build a herd, they would average about one bull for every fifteen or twenty cows, and their whole herd was several hundred head.

"We have a couple ranch hands that help with all the work. We move the cattle around to make sure they stay in the good grasses. I have a few other business interests, so I can't handle all this myself. We also raise and train horses," Logan explained, "so we stay pretty busy."

"This is so much more than I realized. It's quite an operation."

"This time of year, the calving is done and we have to do the vaccinations and tagging. We move the herd from pasture to pasture so they don't overgraze the land. And, of course, constantly checking the fence lines." Logan nodded to the barrier Anna could see in the distance. The vertical fence posts were barely visible from where she sat on Jelly.

Anna wasn't sure what Logan was doing, but she admired the way his body moved as he went about his tasks. The sun was warm, and Jelly regularly flicked her ears and tail, swatting at flies. Logan strode back from the water trough he had been checking. He easily swung up on his horse and nudged the animal next to Anna's.

"I want to show you one of my favorite spots," Logan said with a wink.

They cut across the pasture, headed for the tree line where the ground started to swell into a gentle hill. Anna could see a faint path that cut between the thicker underbrush. She followed Logan's lead and soon they were on a secluded trail under a cool canopy of trees. She could hear water gurgling in the distance and the air around them was filled with the sounds of insects and the occasional bird call. They rode a short distance and a small stream appeared. It was clear and fast-running. The air around it seemed many degrees cooler, and Anna thought the water must originate from the melting snowcapped mountains.

"It's beautiful," she breathed.

"Another time, we'll come up here and I'll show you the pool that's perfect for swimming."

Anna grinned. "It's a date. It's too shallow here, that's for sure. Maybe we can wade a little, but that's about it."

"We can let the horses graze if you'd like to get down and rest your backside," Logan teased.

"You don't have to make that offer twice." Anna was eager to be back on solid ground. "But I think you'll have to help me. I'm not sure that part of my anatomy can move by itself right now."

She awkwardly slid off Jelly's back with Logan's assistance. She groaned as her feet hit the ground and her legs nearly buckled. Laughing at her own inelegance, she rubbed her legs and rear end to get the blood flowing again.

"Your legs must be rock-hard to do that every day," she said, then almost blushed when she heard the words out loud.

Logan shook his head and laughed. "I suppose riding every day is a good workout. You have to have some strength in this line of work. It's not that easy to control a twelve-hundred-pound animal, and even tougher when you're trying to rope an uncooperative thousand-pound cow."

Anna walked gingerly down the bank to the water's edge. She stood, waiting for the feeling to fully return to her lower extremities before she sat down to pull off her boots, shed her socks, and stick her toes in the cool water. She heard Logan behind her and happily kicked her feet as she leaned her head back and looked at him. Even upside down, his smile was heart-stopping. She righted her head just before dizziness set in. Anna felt his body behind her and his legs appeared on either side of hers. His arms wrapped around her waist and without thinking, she leaned back into his chest. His warmth surrounded her and she felt the shiver of excitement from his physical presence. She closed her eyes and savored the feel of him. She smiled. This was one of the moments she had been looking forward to ever since she received his call this morning.

"Thank you for coming here today, Anna." She could feel his breath on her neck and his voice rumbled, vibrating through her skin.

"I should be thanking you. It is so beautiful and peaceful here. I really do feel bad that I'm keeping you from work."

"Don't worry about that, I can handle it. I wanted to spend time with you, to get to know you better."

"I hope that's working out for you. I know I am really getting to know more about ranching and cattle than I ever thought I would."

"I'm sorry, that's probably pretty boring for you I suppose. You're used to the city life," he said.

"No, not at all. It was fascinating. I had no idea what all was involved. It did help me get to know you as well. It's so evident that you love the land and the work. I can see why you're so happy here."

"And how about you, Anna? Are you happy with your life in Iowa?"

"I'm not sure what my life in Iowa really is now. Things changed so much for my dad and me when we lost Mom, and now with him gone too, I'm not sure what's left for me. I guess I'll see what happens from this summer."

"To the summer then." Logan kissed her neck and held her as they watched the water. He continued to hold her, kissing and nuzzling her neck, causing cascades of shivers down her spine. She turned and without thinking, drew him close and kissed him. He deepened the kiss, taking her breath away. She felt a level of passion for him that was beyond anything she had experienced before.

He pulled back, brushing her hair from her eyes. He took her face gently between his hands and began lightly kissing and nibbling at her lips. She felt his thumb rub gently behind her ear and his fingers massaging her scalp to the top of her neck. Another delicious shiver ran down her spine. There was a sense of rightness with him.

Anna moved her head, ending the kiss to catch her breath. Logan leaned his forehead against hers and made no effort to move away.

Suddenly, Domino sneezed, spraying them with a fine wet shower. Anna squealed and jumped, nearly sliding down the embankment into the creek. She would have, if Logan had not grabbed her arm, hauling her up against him. Their eyes locked for a moment before they both burst into laughter.

"You, um, you have a little snot on you, sir," Anna said with an uncharacteristic giggle.

"Well, I didn't want to tell you, but there's some grassy spit in your hair."

"Ewwww!"

The horses shuffled and sniffed, letting Logan know they thought it was time to head for the barn.

"All right, Domino, Jelly, settle down you two. We'll go."

He waited as Anna pulled on her socks and put her boots on, then helped her to her feet and they settled back on their mounts. The horses' hooves thudded dully on the dirt-packed path as they headed back the way they had come. The occasional birdsong cut through the air. Logan suddenly stopped short ahead of her. He dismounted and walked a short way up the incline on their left.

Anna held her breath. She hoped he had not spotted an animal in distress or, worse yet, a snake. She nervously looked around at Jelly's feet. In response to her agitation, Jelly pranced and threw her head. Anna watched as Logan bent down and seemed to study something on the ground. Logan moved calmly, and Anna saw Domino stood still, showing no signs of agitation, so Anna felt reassured there was no danger. She was curious why Logan had stopped. He spent a moment crouched down, then stood and walked toward her with a smile. Stopping next to her mount, he laid his left hand on her thigh, offering her a small bunch of wildflowers with his right. As she accepted the blooms, Logan winked. Without a word, he turned away, remounted, and continued down the trail. Anna couldn't keep the grin off her face. This man was like none she had met before, and she enjoyed his romantic gestures.

She stared at the small orange blooms. Tiny enough to fit in the palm of her hand, they looked like miniature versions of the lilies from her garden at home. She felt homesick and an unfamiliar longing.

As they arrived back at the cluster of buildings, the barn seemed to be full of activity. Jelly took off at nearly a run, with Anna desperately hanging on, her legs and rear end flopping loosely in the saddle. Jelly slowed to a trot as she neared the barn. Anna felt her face turn beet red when she realized a small group of men was standing at the entrance, with broad smiles and making no effort to hide their laughter.

"Looks like Jelly's controlling you there, missy," the oldest one said, stepping forward and slowing Jelly's progress. "Logan should have warned you to hold on as you get close to home. This one's always first for the dinner bell."

Anna nodded gratefully and accepted his help sliding out of the saddle. She refused to look at Logan as he rode up behind her but had a smile on her face.

"I'm Roy, Logan's dad. You must be Miss Anna."

"Yes, thank you. It's nice to meet you," she said, laughing. "And I appreciate the timely meeting." She tucked Logan's flowers in her shirt pocket, then reached to shake Roy's hand.

"Well, what say you and I go up to the house and let Logan and the boys take care of the chores out here? They'll come up for supper when they're done."

"I would love to, Roy. Lead the way."

The house was a beautiful white two-story frame structure with a wide porch wrapping from the front around to one side with broad stairs for both directions. The side entrance led into a small mudroom that seemed to double as a pantry with a cheery large country kitchen beyond. She felt a pang of nostalgia as it reminded her of the one back home in Iowa. The enticing smells wafting from this kitchen immediately set Anna's stomach to growling, bringing her back to the present.

"I guess you're hungry," Roy observed. "Let's get to setting the table, and we'll get to eating before too long. It's Bo's turn to cook, and you're lucky. He's pretty good in the kitchen, so you'll no doubt enjoy it."

"I'll just take a minute to wash up," she said, pausing to kick off her boots where the small throw rugs had been lined up and were already home to several pairs of shoes and boots. The flowers slid out of her pocket as she bent over so she tucked the small blooms inside her cell phone case and tossed it in her boot. They would wilt quickly, but she couldn't bring herself to throw them away.

She joined Roy in the kitchen and they worked together to set the table with plates, flatware, and glasses along with a varied assortment of condiments. They would wait to put the hot food out until Logan and the ranch hands had finished the evening chores.

Roy gave her a tour of the house while they waited for the others to come inside. Logan had already told her the house was the original ranch house and over a hundred years old. Anna was surprised that the oldest part was actually over a hundred and forty years old. Roy told her it was built in the 1870s when the land was first settled. Roy had inherited the ranch from the great-grandson of the man that started it all. Anna looked around and was impressed with the preservation of the history. Roy seemed to care about the legacy, and the memories of the former owners seemed to linger.

"That's Wyatt Hamilton, there," he said, pointing to a black and white portrait. "That one there, on the right, that's his parents, Ernest and Alice Ann. Wyatt's great grandfather, Samuel, started the ranch. That's him in that picture over there with his wife and their three children. And this one is Samuel's only son, Jacob. Jacob was Ernest's daddy. The two girls, Jacob's girl's that is, and their families are over here on this wall."

Anna was overwhelmed with the number of people. "You keep all of these up even though it's not your family?"

"It is part of my family," Roy said sincerely, tapping his chest. "They're my family in here. Sure, Logan is my blood, but when I came here I worked with Ernest and Wyatt. I learned the ranching business from them. Wyatt was the boss, and I started as a hired hand, but they became family."

Anna studied the photographs and tried to imagine the people that they had each been. She was captivated by Roy's friend Wyatt, his broad smile and piercing eyes. A sense of déjà vu came over her and she studied the photos. She looked at the family history lining the walls and understood. She saw the history of the people, the lives, and the land.

"C'mon, now, I hear the boys coming in. Let's help Bo get that supper on the table." Roy draped his arm around her shoulders and led her back to the kitchen.

CHAPTER ELEVEN

"Dad, Anna is here researching some of the history in Lander, especially the World War II era," Logan said as they passed around the platters of creamy chicken and dumplings, carrots, and fresh asparagus. Anna and Roy had filled glasses with sweet tea, leaving the pitcher at the end of the table.

"Really, Lander didn't have much of a war effort. I'm guessing your research might be a little fast," Roy joked.

Mitchell and the other two ranch hands, Casey and Bo, nodded in agreement. Casey scooped a huge portion of the chicken onto his plate before passing the platter.

"It's pretty specific research. I'm looking into the lives of men from the area who served in World War II, specifically focusing on the ones that returned and lived here in 1947."

"Then you know Wyatt Hamilton served," Roy said as he focused on his plate, stabbing at the smaller bits, filling up his fork.

"Yes," Anna said eagerly. "He is one I don't know too many details about. I would love to know more about him and any of his family that you knew."

"Well, I met the Hamiltons when I was fresh out of high school. This was my first real ranching job and I was seventeen and came up to Lander from Denver. Wyatt's daddy, Ernest, hired me as a ranch hand. That was back in '54."

"Could I get a refill on the sweet tea, there, Roy?" Bo interjected, holding out his empty glass.

"Yes, me too since you've started," Anna said. "So, you met Wyatt after he came back from the war, of course."

"Oh my, yes. He had been back for a while, eight, ten years prob'ly. I guess he came home right after the war ended in '45, or '46. His mama must have been so happy to have him back. When I came to work for them, she still doted on him like he was just a boy."

"What was his father like?"

Roy finished sopping up the gravy on his plate with a biscuit and popped it in his mouth. He chewed thoughtfully then responded, "Mr. Hamilton, he was a real straight shooter. He was cautious and deliberate with the ranch, the animals, and he was frugal. But, those were still some tough times back then. He taught me the value of hard work and everything he knew about cattle. He maintained a strong herd and the bloodlines we have today go back to the stock he and his grandfather bred. I respected him as a man and as a rancher. He was a good man and he raised Wyatt to be a good man as well. That's why Wyatt and I were friends for so many years. I don't think I ever met a man I felt I could trust more than Wyatt. I only worked here a couple years before the older Mr. Hamilton had his accident."

"What happened?"

"It was a freak accident, equipment rolled on him, and he was killed. Really tough time for Wyatt and his mama. Alice Ann, Mrs. Hamilton, that is. I don't think she ever recovered."

"And, Logan, you knew Wyatt also? Oh, sorry," Anna said, realizing Logan had been having a side conversation with Bo and Mitchell.

"It's fine. We're setting some plans for that horse auction next week. Yes, I knew Wyatt, but it was different for me. I grew up here, and by then we were all family. I didn't work for him as much as I looked at him as a grandfather. I followed him everywhere. He let me trail along and help. Looking back, I probably cost him hours of extra work, but he was patient with me and always made me feel like my help meant something." Logan smiled at the memory. "I don't think I could have asked for a better grandfather if I had one that was a blood relative. He knew me from the time I was born, so he was always there."

"And how about his mother, did you know her as well, Roy?" Anna asked.

"Yes, like I said, she doted on Wyatt, but she was strong and tough. She didn't let anybody get by with anything. I think she may have had some strong opinions about Wyatt and his marital situation."

"Really?" Anna said, leaning forward. This sounded like it might be a tidbit of interesting old gossip. "I thought Wyatt was a bachelor. He never married, did he?"

"No, he never did. I know Alice Ann, that was Wyatt's mama you know, had her sights set on him marrying to build a dynasty for the ranch. I recall conversations I overheard before Mr. Hamilton died. They got right heated a few times, the mister and missus; Wyatt too had some heated discussions with his parents. I don't know that I ever heard who they were talking about in those family discussions, but Alice Ann had some friends she would have over for hen sessions. Now in those talks it was real clear who the topic was."

Anna laughed. "Hen sessions?"

"You know, the womenfolk sit around and gossip about everyone and everything in town, tossing advice and opinions about everything." Mitchell piped up, "You know it. Ev'ry man knows better than to walk in on a hen session. The beaks are sharp and they're ready to peck."

Logan, Casey, and Bo all nodded and laughed, but Logan had the good grace not to look her in the eye.

"So, do you think any of Alice Ann's old friends are still around? I would love to know what that old gossip was about," Anna said eagerly.

"Bo, does your grandma go to the Center? Do you know if Hazel is still there?" Roy asked.

"Yea, Hazel plays cards with Gram most afternoons. You know, I just saw Hazel last week," Bo replied.

Anna looked from one to another in amazement. She could not get used to the intertwining life connections in the town. She wondered if things were like that in Iowa and she didn't realize it or whether the Midwest versus West region made a difference. It seemed like an endless string of coincidences that everyone around her took for granted. "All right!" she said enthusiastically. "Bo, would you introduce me to your grandmother's friend Hazel sometime?"

"Yes, ma'am," he said seriously and finished off his chicken and biscuits.

They polished off the last of the meal, then Mitchell and Casey cleared the table. Anna insisted on cleaning up the kitchen and washing dishes. She wiped down the counters and retrieved her boots from the mudroom, tucking her cell phone with the flowers into her back pocket.

After she had finished, Logan walked Anna to her car, grabbing her hand as if it were the most natural thing in the world. She felt the now-familiar current of energy from where their skin touched. They walked in silence, and when they reached her car, she hesitated. He turned her until her back was against the driver's side door and leaned in for a kiss, his hands braced on either side of her shoulders. She rested her hands lightly on his hips, and felt the heavy leather of his belt against her fingers. His lips brushed hers playfully before he pulled back and rested his forehead against hers.

"I'm really glad we were able to do this," he said.

"Thank you for the invitation, and thank you for a beautiful day," she replied.

"I have to leave tomorrow. I've got some horses to pick up in Denver and some business I need to do, so I'll be gone until next weekend. It's too bad because it would have been fun to take you to the rodeo over in Ten Sleep. They have it every year for Memorial Day weekend and it's only a few hours' drive. Have you ever been to Thermopolis? That's another fun place to visit."

Anna laughed. "You'd better be careful, you're starting to sound like a Wyoming travel brochure."

"Can I help it if I love my home state and want to share it?"

"Not at all," she said, leaning in to kiss him lightly. "It makes me feel very special that you want to share this with me. We'll keep Thermopolis in mind for a road trip another time."

"Deal," he said, reaching behind her and pulling open the door.

Smiling, she touched his cheek and slid into the car. "See ya later, cowboy."

The next morning, Anna sat sipping her tea when her phone buzzed on the table. Glancing at the screen, a smile spread across her face as she read a text from Logan.

Good Morning Beautiful

Eager to strike up a conversation, she replied: *Good Morning Cowboy. How's your morning?*

Thinking about you gorgeous so it's starting out good. How's yours?

Fantastic. I'm still wearing the smile you gave me last night.

Glad I could help. I'll see about giving you a new one every day then.

Anna couldn't hold back the grin as she tapped out a response: *I have no doubt you can. I'm getting pretty fond of you.*

Ah, then my plan is working out perfectly.

Anna laughed. Why did it seem so easy to flirt in a text? Face-to-face conversation with Logan flowed but it wasn't nearly this flirty. She loved how easily it flowed. Her phone buzzed again.

I gave Bo your number. He's gonna call about taking you to see his grandma.

Anna sent a quick reply. *Thank You! :-)* She couldn't resist adding the happy face emoji.

Ok I gotta get to work. have a great day beautiful.

You too cowboy. I'll give you a proper thank you later!

LOL. I'll hold you to that!

After a quick phone call to make arrangements, Anna met Bo that afternoon at the Senior Center. She suspected Logan had given Bo a few hours off to arrange the meeting. She was touched Logan would go to such lengths to help her and that Bo was nice enough to meet her here.

"Thank you so much for the introduction," she squeezed his arm in excitement.

He gave her a strange look. "No problem." She realized few people would be excited over the prospect of meeting an eighty-something-year-old woman just to hear sixty-year-old gossip. She tried to curb her enthusiasm as they walked into the activity room.

Bo walked to the corner where a bird-like woman in a bright yellow sweater shuffled cards with amazing agility. "Grammy," he said, leaning down to hug her gently. "You look beautiful as ever."

"You're a good boy, Bo," she replied, beaming. Anna watched the old woman's quick movements, sparkling eyes, and bright smile and saw how much love she had for her grandson.

"Grammy, this is Anna. She came with me today to talk to Hazel."

"Girl, aren't you a pretty one." Grammy chortled and she glanced slyly at Bo. "Is this a new lady friend of yours?"

"No, Grammy, Anna's Logan's lady friend. You remember my boss, Logan?"

"Fiddlie-fie." Grammy laughed and waved her hand as if shooing away an annoying insect. "Fine, fine, we'll find you the right girl soon. You have faith, Bo."

Anna felt sorry for the cowhand as a blush crept up his neck at his Grammy's blunt words. "Yeah, well, whatever. Have you seen Hazel? I gotta get back to the ranch, so would you make sure Anna meets Hazel?" Barely taking time to gain his Grammy's agreement, Bo disappeared.

"I think you embarrassed your grandson," Anna said, trying to hold back a grin. "He was really very sweet to come introduce me to you."

Grammy laughed delightedly. "You know, I do that on purpose. He needs a stronger spine, and if I can still embarrass him, my job's not done yet. And he didn't properly introduce us, hon. Call me Gladys."

"Gladys, I like your style," Anna whispered conspiratorially. "Hazel," Gladys called, "come here. We have a visitor that came to talk to you."

Anna thoroughly enjoyed the remainder of the afternoon. She understood the appeal of the many socials, afternoon teas, and fundraisers she had read about in the newspaper archives. She could not recall when she had enjoyed such entertaining storytelling. Once Hazel knew she had an interested audience, she had no qualms about sharing all the juicy gossip she had held onto for nearly seventy years.

"Well, let me tell you this, that Alice Ann was quite high and mighty. She didn't think any woman around here was good enough for her Wyatt. If it weren't for the benefit to the ranch, I don't think that she would have joined up with that Bessie Bellamy. There is no way Alice Ann thought that Grace

Bellamy was good enough for Wyatt. And, no one around here believed Bessie's stories about the Bellamy family. It wasn't just Alice Ann. Bessie would tell anyone who would listen that she was a shoestring relative of Mary Bellamy. The Mary Bellamy, the first woman elected to the Wyoming legislature, you know. Not that it did her any good. Well, the Lander Bellamys never made it into the inner circle of society, so Bessie set her sights on having her daughter Grace join the Hamilton family. Alice Ann saw the benefit of increasing the size of the ranch, especially with the additional water access the Bellamy land would provide. Those two mamas worked to fix it so their children would make their dreams come true. The mamas' dreams, anyway."

"Really? So why didn't they marry?"

"Grace wasn't interested in Wyatt. That is, until she saw him in his uniform. After he enlisted in the army and she saw him as a hero, she stopped playing around with those other boys and worked to get his attention. Of course, by that time, he was shipping out and no one knew if he would ever come home from that terrible war."

"But he did," Anna prompted.

"Oh, yes, he did come home, and Grace was still waiting for him. But he wasn't having any of it. He seemed real polite and friendly, but distant. Gladys, remember Alice Ann was fit to be tied!" Hazel exclaimed.

"Oh, yes, she was furious Wyatt wouldn't toe the line on that one. But we all found out why soon enough."

"Really? Why? What was it?" Anna was completely pulled into the story.

"Well…" Hazel took a deep breath and paused for dramatic effect.

"Oh, for pity sakes, Hazel" Gladys nearly shouted, throwing her hands up in the air.

Hazel winked at Anna. "Alice Ann was real stubborn about getting her way. She never intended to be mean-spirited, but she would get carried away sometimes. Something happened and things with Wyatt were never the same after that."

"What do you mean? What did she do?" Anna asked.

"That's my point, I don't think anyone ever knew. They patched things up in time, but for a while they were pretty stiff and formal with each other. Oh, my just like old Simon and his niece Betty. Gladys, do you remember the spat they had about them cows? Lordy, but that battle went on for months."

Anna laughed as she listened to the amusing stories of family life in a small town and surrounding ranches. After an hour, she felt like she had grown up in Lander and each of the family stories as vivid as if they were her own memories. She felt comfortable enough to ask her true question.

"So, I'm wondering if either of you might remember someone. I've been working on my family tree and have somewhat of a missing relative that I think may have lived around here for a while. Would either of you recall a newcomer in town after the war, a woman, around 1947? She probably would have been traveling alone and was an immigrant from another country." Anna asked hesitantly. She had spent so much time thinking about her potential grandfather, she wasn't sure how to inquire about her grandmother. She wasn't sure she wanted to hear the commentary if she asked about an unwed pregnant woman who lived in the area back then.

"Well, let's see." Gladys pursed her lips thoughtfully. "Sometimes the years run together, and there was so much coming and going around then. We were all so young, starting out in life and the whole world was changing."

"Yes, that whole time we were getting married and having babies." Hazel chimed in. "Not long after, they built new rail lines coming in and all sorts of business came here. There were all sorts of new folks moving in, but a single foreign lady is what you're interested in."

"I thought perhaps there might have been something memorable, or if she lived here long enough you might have met." Anna looked from Gladys to Hazel questioning.

"Well, I don't quite remember exactly when, but there was one girl I recall being around for a spell." Hazel said. "Quiet, but a pretty little thing. I was living at the boarding house then and she took a room there too. That likely would have been in '47 or '48 I suppose. We got to be friendly some. She was a sweet thing. Went to the Lutheran church real regular every Sunday." Hazel paused, sipping from her water glass as she searched her memory for more details.

"You know, I recall she was foreign, with one of those last names that had the funny letters. I only heard her say it once or twice, but she went by Sunny. I remember thinking that name suited her, always seemed happy and smiling. She never said what brought her to Lander. I always thought it was a young man, but when I tried to ask, she acted like it was a secret. She took in sewing there at the boarding house. She did beautiful work and was always coming and going to pick up and deliver what she was working on. Had herself a secondhand bike and she rode that contraption everywhere. Big old basket on the front for her sewing." She grinned suddenly at the memory. Anna could almost see the spectacle of a young girl on a bicycle, probably weaving as she went, with a huge pile of clothing obstructing her view. She grinned at Hazel as the amusing image came into her head.

"Now, most people wouldn't probably remember her, but I do because of what happened and I was there at the boarding house. I haven't thought of that in years." She sighed

"I remember that bicycle." Gladys chimed in. "I saw her around town some. I remember the bicycle but I can't recall the girl."

Hazel nodded and continued her story. "Sunny went out one day, just like most times except when she came back, it looked like she had been crying. Wouldn't say what was wrong. It was a little while after that she asked me about other towns in America. How far things were and such. Right after that, she packed up her things and the Reverend came by to pick her up. Said she had a new job up in Idaho Falls."

She stopped, squinting as she looked across the room, and then raised her hand in a half-hearted wave to someone. Anna looked in the direction of Hazel's glance and saw someone at a desk waving a telephone receiver with one hand and pointing to it with the other. "Excuse me, let me see what that ruckus is all about."

Anna felt a thrill of excitement. Idaho Falls. The same town where Harold Jones had moved his family. This had to be the connection she was looking for. Leo had said Harold's widow was in a nursing home there, and the daughter might talk with her. Anna quickly said her goodbyes to Gladys and asked her to thank Hazel for the story. She promised to come back soon for another visit, and quickly headed for the door. As she left, she dialed Leo's number. She needed to make arrangements for a trip to Idaho Falls and talk to Harold's daughter, who might be her aunt.

Anna sat with a paper cup of wine, enjoying the slight breeze on the small hotel patio. It was nearly nine o'clock and she checked to see if Logan was free.

Hey cowboy, you busy? Time to talk? she texted.

Her phone rang in response. "Hi, babe."

"Well, hey there. That was fast."

"My girl has a minute to talk to me, I'm gonna take advantage of it."

"Sweet talker."

Logan laughed, "What's up?"

"I wanted to thank you for letting Bo take some time to do the introduction today. It was fantastic."

"Really? Glad it went well. Tell me about it."

"Hazel had so many stories about Lander and everyone here in the late 40s. All those articles and people I've read about, she knew nearly all of them."

"Did she know your grandmother or who your grandfather might be?"

"Well, I didn't ask her exactly, I wasn't sure how to really ask, but she did tell me about a young girl, a foreigner who lived here for a while then moved to Idaho Falls. And Leo said that Harold Jones moved his family to Idaho Falls, so I'm thinking that it might be the connection I'm looking for."

"Wow, Anna, that does sound promising. You must be pretty excited about it."

"I can't even tell you how much. I wanted so much to just jump in the car and drive over there to see."

Logan laughed, "Well, it's a good thing you waited. It's about five hours over some pretty winding mountain roads. It's a tough drive in the dark, especially if you're not familiar with it."

"That's what I thought too, when I checked a map," Anna said with a sigh. "Plus it's a holiday weekend, so I thought it would be better to go over there on Tuesday maybe."

"That sounds like a good idea. Speaking of the holiday weekend, what are you doing?"

"Kim invited me over on Monday for a cookout. I guess it's a Memorial Day tradition for her," she said.

"I'm sorry I couldn't be there to go with you," he said. "Darlin', I wish I didn't have this trip, miss you already. It's nice to hear your voice."

"You too, cowboy. Your trip going well so far?"

"Everything's going smoothly so far. It should be pretty straightforward." He filled her in on the details of his schedule. "I'm already looking forward to being done and seeing you next week."

"Me too." Anna stifled a yawn. "I am so sorry. It's not you. It's been a long few days," she said with a laugh.

"I know. You've got a lot going on. Okay, angel. I'll let you get some sleep."

"Thanks. I'm glad you had some time to talk," she said. "I really do love talking to you, Logan."

"You too, babe. Sweet dreams."

"Sweet dreams to you too, cowboy."

Anna arrived at Kim's to find the yard full of people, many of whom she had never met before. Anna was introduced to Kim's husband, Carl, two of Carl's brothers, a cousin, and several of Kim's friends, or possibly cousins, before she lost track. Many of them worked on local farms and ranches, usually coming into town only for supplies or weekend entertainment. Kim, having grown up in the area and having the social-centric job at the cafe, knew nearly everyone in the county. Anna made small talk easily and found everyone to be very friendly and welcoming. After a large plate of potato salad, the adventurous choice of a veggie burger, and a surprisingly good gelatinous lime-green fruit salad, Anna wandered toward the corner of the yard where a game of horseshoes was set up.

"Heads up!" Anna heard a shouted warning and looked around. She watched as several Frisbee games threatened to collide with each other. Kim's body came flying toward her and Anna narrowly jumped out of the way before being flattened by her friend.

"Hi," Kim said, slightly out of breath from the exertion. "Are you having fun? Whew, I need a break. Let's sit and watch these clowns huh?"

Anna grinned, helping Kim up and impulsively hugging her shoulder. "You got it."

They settled in a couple of lawn chairs situated between the patio and the lawn, where they could watch the games in progress. "Thank you so much for the invitation today. Everyone is so nice and your house is really beautiful."

"I'm glad you came. You are a welcome addition to our little circle. Speaking of that, are you staying around for a while longer?"

"Yes, what's that expression, 'for the foreseeable future', I think it is."

Kim grinned. "A little vague but answers the question."

"Yeah, I'm starting to feel like I need to find something productive to do with my time, a job or something, and I really need to find somewhere to stay. I only have two more nights at the lodge, then they won't have a room for me anymore."

Kim looked around the room, assessing the crowd that was gathered. She stood up and grabbed Anna's hand. "All right then," she said, grinning. "Let's get you connected up with some folks I think can help." Kim pulled Anna toward a small group, like a woman suddenly on a critical mission.

Within an hour, Kim had, as she put it, secured "a couple of gigs" for Anna. One office required filing, the school library needed a few volunteer hours for a special project, and the committee for the Fourth of July celebration immediately claimed as many hours as Anna would offer.

More importantly, she found out about the aunt of someone's work friend who had a room to rent. It was actually a small summerhouse behind their house, complete with a kitchenette and small bathroom. It sounded perfect. She took down the phone number and immediately made arrangements to secure the little cottage. She was excited to make the move, then make the arrangements to visit Idaho Falls.

CHAPTER TWELVE

Certain there must be a clue, perhaps even the final answer, in Idaho Falls, Anna packed a few toiletries and a change of clothes when she got home. She had a couple days before Friday and the first of the month, a convenient coincidence since she had to check out of the lodge and the cottage lease started the same day. She planned to start the drive early in the morning, remembering Logan had said it was close to a five-hour drive. She called Logan to update him. The call went to voicemail, so she left a brief message. A moment later, she heard a text notification chime.

Hey Babe. Business dinner. Can't talk.
Is OK. Left voicemail.
Call you later? Couple hours?
Can't :-(Early day, gonna zzzzzzz.
K. Sweet Dreams angel.
Sweet dreams cowboy.

She put the phone down and realized she had a big sappy grin on her face. Jeez, I'm crazy about him.

After packing, she tried to make notes and considered how to approach the conversation the next day. Leo had given her the name of the nursing home where Harold Jones's widow lived, as well as the name of his eldest daughter: Elaine Jones Schuyetzf. Fortunately, the name was unique enough that Anna was able to find it in the local online phone book.

Uncertain how to have such a personal conversation on the phone, she took a deep breath and dialed, hoping the right words would come.

"Hello?"

"Hi, is this Elaine Jones um…Schuyetzf? I hope I'm pronouncing that right," Anna started.

A pleasant, but tired-sounding laugh drifted over the line. "I have heard much worse. All things considered, you did fine."

"Oh, good. I would rather not start out on the wrong foot."

"Start out…" the woman prompted with more of a statement than a question.

Anna took another deep breath. "I'm researching my family history from Lander, Wyoming."

"Oh, yes, my father was from Lander."

"Yes, someone who knew him here gave me your number. There were several men here that went to school together and joined the military around the same time. I believe my grandfather may have known one or more of that group."

"I see. That sounds interesting," she said cautiously. "How is it I can help you?"

"Well, to be honest, I was hoping I might meet and speak with your mother. I understand she was from this area as well and might remember a few details."

Anna could almost feel the pain in the woman's heavy sigh. "Mom does not have too many good days anymore. But one thing that does make her happy is to talk about the glory days. I can take you to meet her, but I'll stay the entire time. I can't let you tire her out."

"Oh, of course, I understand," Anna said quickly. "I appreciate the opportunity and I would love to hear any stories you have of your father as well. You may have information that could be helpful to me."

"Well, I'll do what I can, but it was so long ago; please don't get your hopes up," Elaine said.

Anna set out just after sunrise, too excited to sleep. The route took her through the Grand Teton National Park. The landscape was breathtaking and she enjoyed the drive immensely. After crossing into Idaho, she drove through the Caribou-Targhee National Forest before the road flattened out just before Idaho Falls. As much as she would have liked to spend more time in each of the areas, she didn't take time for any stops. She was anxious to arrive and was looking forward to her visit with Elaine. They had made arrangements to meet in the family day room at the center where Mrs. Jones lived.

Anna tried to keep her nerves in check, but she could not shake the feeling that very soon she would be meeting her aunt. After grabbing a quick lunch from the drive-thru of a fast-food restaurant, Anna found the nursing home without difficulty and left her car in the parking structure. She grabbed the bag stuffed with her wallet and piles of notepaper, threw her key inside, and strode toward the entrance.

Once inside, she followed the signs to the family day room. There was only one occupant in the room, a pleasant-looking woman standing by the window, pensively watching the squirrels run through the yard outside. Anna approached the woman, dropping her bag on a table she passed.

"Elaine?"

The woman turned, and Anna immediately felt comfortable. Elaine was a few inches taller than she was, about forty pounds heavier, with short white-blond hair that curled crazily around her head. She was older than Anna had imagined, the lines of life etched deeply around her eyes and mouth. A pair of bright red glasses were stuck in her hair, conveniently pushed up and ready to be pulled into service when needed. She carried her weight easily, turning around with the grace of a dancer. Her bright hibiscus flower-covered blouse swirled around her thighs over tight denim leggings. Anna's gaze was drawn to Elaine's tiny feet clad in plain white tennis shoes, which seemed to emphasize their petiteness. Anna smiled, and Elaine returned the greeting.

"Anna, it's nice to meet you." The cheery greeting and the bright outfit seemed at odds with the tired sadness around her eyes.

"Thank you so much for agreeing to meet and talk with me. I can't tell you how much it means," Anna said earnestly.

"I'm happy to help, if I can. To be honest, I have found myself a little out of sorts since I retired. I thought I would have so much to keep me busy, but some days I'm at loose ends. It's only been a few months. I suppose an adjustment is to be expected."

Surprised at this unexpected positivity, Anna nodded. "I have felt the same way myself the past few months. My circumstances are a little different, but I understand the loose ends."

Elaine nodded. "Let's sit."

Anna felt completely at ease with Elaine and confided all the details of her story and everything she had discovered about her mysterious grandparents.

As Anna reached the end of her tale, she watched Elaine's face as the would-be aunt struggled to process the information.

"Anna, my goodness… I… I don't know what to say," she stammered.

"I know it's a lot to process and I'm sure you have questions for me."

"So, you think that my father is your grandfather? That you are my niece? Or half-niece, as it were?"

Anna could not tell if Elaine was coming to terms with the possibility or if righteous indignation was building to an explosive denial. She remained quiet and waited.

Elaine got up from the table and paced the small room. It was a typical dayroom. Roughly twenty by thirty feet, with beige walls and a tiled floor. In one corner, a grouping of cheap couches and chairs stood on a dull throw rug along with a few side tables piled with dog-eared old magazines. Several round tables, each with four upholstered chairs were scattered around for eating, talking, and game-playing. A long bookshelf against one wall held an assortment of books, games, and puzzles. The decor was in tones of beige and brown with yellow accents. The end result was an ugly room, uncomfortable and depressing.

Elaine returned to her previous spot by the window. Anna could tell she was not focused on the scene outside, but rather lost in thought, in reliving old memories.

"My father had a difficult time after the war," Elaine said slowly. "Mother used to tell us about him, about them, from before. He was fun and loving, and he knew how to laugh. Growing up, I saw glimpses of that sometimes, but I knew an entirely different man. I just wanted to tell you."

Anna nodded, unsure how to respond.

"The man I knew as my father was quiet, sometimes almost withdrawn, and he was very strict. He had specific ideas about how everything must be done and we learned early on not to deviate from his rules. Looking back, I see so much now. In today's world, we would have known that he suffered flashbacks from the war and struggled with depression and alcoholism. He was abusive, both emotionally and physically, and very controlling."

Anna walked over and gently rubbed her shoulder, at a loss of how to comfort a wound so deep but so old.

"My mother doesn't remember things that way. After she was diagnosed a couple years ago, I noticed over time that her memories changed. She remembers only the man he was before the war, when he was happier. She will tell you what a good man he was, and so giving. Some things she says I don't think actually happened."

Elaine reached over and grasped Anna's hand. "Please don't misunderstand. I loved my father very much. My entire childhood, I tried so hard to please him, and the smallest bit of attention or praise from him brightened my whole day. I didn't know to be upset about the difficult times, I was just happy for the good times. I rebelled as a teenager and he yelled." She snickered and shook her head. "Oh, good lord, how he yelled. He didn't approve of my boyfriends, or my choices, but I knew he loved me. He was always, always there for me if I really needed him. To this day, I miss that difficult, obstinate man." She rubbed away the sudden tears that filled her eyes before they spilled over, then sniffed and exhaled sharply.

"Enough of that," she said emphatically. "I will say that he often surprised me. If there were a dalliance in his past, either before or after he and Mom were married, I'm not sure I would be surprised. And, I would agree that if he had an indiscretion after they were married, and if there were a child involved, it wouldn't be terribly unbelievable that he would deny responsibility. He would have not have wanted to embarrass himself or his family. Although," she continued thoughtfully, "I wonder if that might be why they moved to Idaho Falls."

"You don't think there would have been a job or other family that led to the decision to move?" Anna asked.

"I never really thought about it before, I assumed it was a job, larger town, more opportunity and all that," Elaine said. "We can try to ask Mother, or perhaps my sister may know of some other family history. We can ask her." Anna realized that Elaine spoke almost as if she considered Anna part of their family, as if she had accepted the possibility. A shiver of excitement ran through her that she might actually be standing here with her aunt.

"I can't thank you enough, Elaine. I know sharing some of this has been difficult."

"It's okay, really. I think it's better to accept things head-on rather than delude ourselves about reality. We end up happier in the end, I think. Just look at us. Accepting the possibility that my father was human and made mistakes might lead to having a new member of the family. I never had children of my own and Emma has two boys, so I think adding a niece would be nice."

Anna's heart jumped at that thought as well.

With that, Elaine locked her arm through Anna's and started toward the door. "Grab your bag. Let's go introduce you to my mother."

Geraldine Pratt-Jones was having one of her good days. Anna stayed in the hallway while Elaine entered the room to greet her mother. Anna could hear snippets of their conversation, and Geraldine seemed lucid and alert. Anna was relieved, but her nervousness increased. The knots in her stomach contracted painfully and she suddenly felt lightheaded. *Is this what a panic attack feels like?* she wondered. This is not my grandmother, she reminded herself. *This could be my grandfather's wife, who would have every reason to hate me.* The realization did little to calm her nerves.

Elaine stuck her head into the hallway and waved, motioning Anna inside. Her feet felt leaden as she moved toward the open door. The pressure in her chest made it difficult to breathe. She felt more nervous than she ever had in her life, and that included her recent first date with Logan. She suddenly latched on to the thought of him. As strange as it was, he seemed to bring her peace. She took a deep breath and entered the room.

"Mom, this is my friend Anna," Elaine said carefully to a frail-looking woman with sparse fluffs of snow-white hair. She was wearing pale blue slacks and a white shirt, layered with a pink bed jacket covered in blue flowers. Huge fluffy pink slippers hid her feet and reached above her ankles to the hem of her slacks, filling the gap with a wide band of pink fur.

"It's nice to meet you, Mrs. Jones," Anna said, clasping the thin, shaking hand the old woman offered.

She followed the direction of Elaine's motioning hand and pulled a chair close to Geraldine's rocker.

"Mom, Anna came up from Lander to visit. She has been talking with some of your and Dad's old friends down there."

"Oh, yes, Lander is such a pretty little town, isn't it? I do miss it there."

"You grew up there?" Anna was willing to follow whatever train of thought Geraldine started, and guide the conversation later if needed. Since she wasn't sure what Geraldine knew, any fragment of a memory might prove important later.

"Well, I wasn't born there, but yes, my mother took me there when I was about eight to stay with my aunt and uncle."

"Did they live in town or in the country?"

"We were in town. My aunt was a schoolteacher and my uncle worked for a local mine. I liked it there, it was a nice town."

"Do you remember Leonard Campbell?"

"Who, now? Was that Daisy's brother? I'm...I'm not sure." Geraldine looked confused.

"Maybe not. Did you meet your husband when you lived there?" Anna prompted, knowing that thinking about Harold would likely calm her.

"Yes, yes. My, he was handsome in those days. So sweet. We had so much fun. We were married the week after our graduation in 1940, you know. I was a June bride."

"How romantic that must have been," Anna breathed.

"We were so happy, had our Elaine here right away, and had a little house in Lander right down the road from his parents. Harold got a job as a salesman with that new automobile dealership," Geraldine said, her pride evident.

"How nice it must have been for you to be near family."

"Yes; we didn't know then, but I was very happy about that later. I remember I was six months along when we heard about Pearl Harbor. Harold was called up, and just like that it seems, he was gone. I had my Emma about a month after Harold left. I didn't know if he would ever come back or if he would ever know her."

"Those were very difficult times for you, I'm sure," Anna said soothingly, looking anxiously at Elaine. She wanted desperately for Geraldine to talk about the time when Harold returned, but had promised Elaine she would not stress the elderly woman. Elaine gave a slight, tight smile and nodded briefly. They would continue, for now.

"But, now, Harold did come back to you, didn't he?" Anna said brightly.

"He did at that," she replied

"And you two lived in Lander still?"

"Well, we didn't stay long. We moved to Idaho Falls for the medical facilities and because Harold didn't want to be close to family."

"Why was that?" Anna instantly regretted her abruptness but had gotten caught up in the story and blurted out the question without thinking.

"He hated talking about the war, and the condolences and pitying looks were more than he could take. He was bitter, but it was the pity more than anything that made him angry."

"I don't understand."

"Harold contracted malaria when he was stationed in the South Seas, and as a side effect, he was sterile. We couldn't have any more children."

CHAPTER THIRTEEN

Anna's head still throbbed.

In one moment, one word, Geraldine had taken away Anna's certainty that she had found her family. Sterile. Even if Harold Jones had an affair, he couldn't have fathered a child. How could she have been so sure, yet so wrong? She felt the loss intensely, and she was once again very aware of how alone she was in the world.

Her research would get more difficult now, with the remaining four potential grandfathers on her list either dead or living in areas unknown. She sighed. She had known this undertaking would not be easy, and that there would be some wrong turns along the way. But she had not expected it to be so painful. How could she feel like she lost something she never had? She had really wanted Elaine to be her aunt. After Geraldine's revelation, she and Elaine had been shocked, neither knowing what to say. Geraldine prattled on, not realizing the bombshell she had dropped on her daughter and a total stranger.

Anna had suddenly felt awkward and uncomfortable, and Elaine seemed equally ill at ease. They both stood. Elaine shrugged, and they hugged briefly. Anna had headed straight for the closest hotel and checked in for the night.

She needed to plan her next step. Where was she going to go from here? She knew this journey was not at an end and it was not time to return to Iowa. Of that she was certain. *When you don't know what else to do, dinner is always a good idea*, she thought.

Grabbing the room key and her wallet, she left the hotel and hiked over to the strip mall she had seen when she drove in. Her stop in the small grocery at the top of the hill stocked her room with wheat crackers, roasted garlic hummus, and a four-pack of little thirty-ounce bottles of wine. She briefly considered but then rejected takeout from the Chinese restaurant next door. She wasn't hungry, but the snacking and wine would help her think, she reasoned. That and a good soak in the hot tub. She was quickly back in the room and setting up her indulgence for the evening. After turning on the tub, she opened the crackers and hummus and bottle of wine, setting them on a chair she pulled over to use as a table. When the tub was full, she gratefully sank in.

The water surrounding her was warm, almost too hot. She felt the stress and tension gradually leaving her body as she relaxed into the soothing bubbles. The powerful jets of the Jacuzzi gave her a hydro-massage, but Anna had to work hard to block out the droning rumble of the motor. *Was it a motor?* she wondered, taking a sip from the mini bottle of wine.

The sweet alcohol was doing its part to soften the hard edges of the day. The television was tuned to a sitcom rerun, but the volume was turned low. Anna had only turned the set on to stave off the silence of the room and had no desire to actually watch the program. At least the familiar voices of the popular show's cast and the regular bursts of laughter were preferable to a news report or reality show.

She let her thoughts wander and not surprisingly, those thoughts landed on Logan. There was something about that man that had a hold on her on a deep level. Even when she wasn't actually thinking about him, she could feel him, there, just beneath the surface. It was disturbing and exhilarating, and yet comforting and exciting all at once. She felt like she was going crazy, but that suddenly every love song made sense. It was ridiculously sappy and she felt like a love-sick teenager. Which was even worse because she barely knew the man. She felt like she had known him forever.

Without much consideration, she reached over and grabbed her phone. The carefully pressed flowers fell out. They looked more like dead stalks of grass at this point but still made her smile as she gently picked them up. Knowing it was silly, Anna wound a dollar bill around them and slipped them back into the credit card sleeve of her cell phone holder. Grinning, she hit his number, looking forward to hearing his voice.

His voice came on the line and, uncontrollably, her heart leapt. Then she realized the stilted words were not live, but the prerecorded message of his voicemail.

"Hi, Logan, it's Anna. I was calling to say hi and give you an update. It didn't pan out, so I can cross Harold Jones off the list. I decided to stay the night and see if I can come up with anything researching birth records tomorrow. Maybe I can get lucky. I'll call you when I'm back in town. Bye."

She glanced at the clock. Just after eight. She hoped he would call back and they could talk. She felt like she needed a friend and valued his advice. Without anything else to keep her mind occupied, she exited the tub, donned sweats, and then thumbed through the movie selection with the remote. Making a selection, she fell asleep before the plot unfolded.

The next day, Anna easily found the large courthouse for Idaho Falls, which, unfortunately, was the last easy part of her day. She drove around for nearly twenty minutes before finding a parking space six blocks from the building. The day was unusually warm, and she was sweating by the time she arrived at the doors, the back of her hair sticking to her neck and itching uncomfortably under the collar of her shirt. There was no elevator, and the birth records were housed on the fourth floor. She sighed.

After climbing four flights of stairs, taking a number, and waiting her turn, she was given forms to fill out with a set of instructions and acceptable forms of identification to provide her relationship to the subject of the birth certificate. She discovered that Idaho considered birth certificates to be confidential for a hundred years. Since she could not prove she was a direct relative, Anna was denied a copy. She was frustrated because she needed the record to know what birth name was given. Unfortunately, Anna needed to know the birth name to fill out the forms and confirm her identity. At this point, all she had was a date of birth, the baby's sex, and the nickname of the potential mother, not even the full actual name. She wasn't even sure the Sunny Hazel told her about was even her grandmother. None of that was solid enough for a valid search. Which left her right back at square one.

She felt certain her father had gotten this far, but from a different angle. Where had the handwritten note come from? It was obviously from someone who had some connection with the mother and most likely would have been a note from an adoption file. But it made no sense that he would have come across the note and not the birth certificate with at least his birth mother's name. Unless he had acquired the original birth certificate along with the note. But then why wouldn't he have kept the two documents together? Anna felt the beginnings of a throbbing headache.

Returning to her car, she was greeted with a parking ticket fluttering in the light breeze. Great. Thoroughly disgusted with the results of the trip, she grabbed another fast-food lunch and took the road east to Wyoming. The scenery was just as beautiful heading back, but to Anna it had lost some of its allure. She had no desire to pull off and explore any of the trails like she had planned. She drove straight to Lander and back to the welcoming comfort of her new pseudo-home summerhouse cottage.

*

After a restless night, Anna found her mental outlook had not improved since the previous day. She felt at odds, out-of-sorts, and in general, unneeded. Her grand adventure and research had yielded nothing and she was still in a town with no job, no family, and no real purpose. The only bright spots she could cling to were her new friends and, of course, Logan. At least she hoped he was a bright spot. After their first couple of dates, when she thought about him she felt a measure of peace and definite excitement, but now she felt a prickling of doubt about his feelings toward her. He had not returned her phone call from two nights before. After the lousy day she had, she wanted to call him but didn't want the disappointment of another voicemail. Had he changed his mind about her? Perhaps she had built it up and was far more attracted to him than he was to her. Or it was completely innocent and he was just busy. Anna realized she had become unreasonably upset he hadn't called. *I am acting like a sixteen-year-old girl, freaking out because some guy I'm crushing on doesn't like me back.*

It was such a strange emotion for her, but Anna again realized she had never been affected by a man before in the way Logan affected her. She knew if she allowed it, he would consume her every thought and action. For the first time, she thought she understood what a compulsion or addiction must feel like. Logan was either the best thing to ever come into her life or the most devastating. Only time would tell.

She dressed in jeans and a tank top, donned her hiking boots, and set off for her favorite trail in Sinks Canyon. It wasn't possible for her to stay in a gloomy mood when surrounded by the bright sunshine and vibrant life of nature. She hiked along the moderate trail, breathing in the heady scent of pine and catching the occasional whiff of the musky-woody-moldy-dirt mixture of the underbrush. Her boots made little noise on the hard-packed trail. The blanket of last year's leaves had been blown under trees and bushes and gathered up by small rodents to line their winter nests. The path was clear of the debris and lined with the healthy early summer growth of grass, weeds, and wildflowers.

She let her thoughts wander, allowing the flood of feelings as her mind jumped from topic to topic. She always felt better after letting her emotions run free. Her disappointment in the grandparent search was understandable; anyone would think so. Dad would understand. She felt the familiar sense of loss thinking about him, wishing she could discuss all this with him.

When she stopped to listen, the forest was alive with activity and animal kingdom conversation. Birdsong, whistles, chattering, and squeaking surrounded her, improving her mood to the point a smile crossed her lips. She was alive, she was healthy, and if she were truly honest, she was attractive, financially secure, and had no limitations of any kind. Anyone would be thrilled to have her life.

She perched on a rock overlooking a stream that cut through the valley. Tall mountains loomed on each side, casting the wide crevasse in shadow.

She was starting to realize, also, that spending time alone had benefits. She had spent so many hours over the past few weeks of this journey reviewing her life, her choices, and thinking about how she felt toward each decision. Anna had discovered quite a few things about herself that she never realized before. She enjoyed the outdoors. In college, and her life in Iowa, she had not thought about going to a national park, camping, or even hiking. Now that she had time, there was a continual desire to be in nature.

She didn't have a passion for business. Anna had worked at her father's business after college because it was expected and, while she enjoyed the routine and the clients, she had no passion or desire to continue in the field of insurance.

One thing she had learned from the recent research and interview process she had undertaken was that she enjoyed working with the elderly. Anna recalled her conversations with Leo, Hazel and Gladys, the Browns, Frank Johnson, and Geraldine. Each visit had been delightful, and she had felt good after spending time with each of them. *And their vocabulary must be rubbing off*, she thought. Delightful?

She resolved to go back to the Senior Center and follow up to join the volunteer program. There must be some good she could do while deciding her next move. Feeling rejuvenated, Anna made the trek back to the cottage to shower and change into a clean pair of jeans and a lightweight shirt. It was barely nine o'clock in the morning and the day promised to be warm. Since she had no schedule to keep, she walked through town instead of driving. The exercise would be enjoyable, and she could see the shops and businesses she had not run across yet. The cottage was in a residential area on the opposite side of downtown from the motel she had stayed at, so the route was still unfamiliar. The walk took less than thirty minutes, and Anna was pleased to find a nail salon, dry cleaner, and a small second-hand bookstore she promised herself she would spend an entire afternoon exploring.

From her prior visit to the center, Anna remembered a group of offices off a hallway to the left of the entrance. Turning in that direction, she headed for the largest one first. A thin blond-haired woman, in her early twenties, Anna judged, sat at the first desk, talking on the phone. As Anna walked in, she looked up and smiled a greeting, holding up one forefinger in a universal silent request for a moment's wait.

"Hi. Thanks for hanging out," the woman said as she replaced the receiver. "What can I do for you?"

"I was wondering if you had a director or coordinator for volunteers. I find myself with some free time and wanted to see if I could be of help here."

"Oh, how wonderful," she exclaimed. "Yes, we're always happy to have more help. Just a minute, I'll see if Jill is free."

Anna chose one of the hard plastic chairs that were lined up against the wall and sat down to wait. The room was quiet and the ticking of the clock seemed abnormally loud. In the distance, she heard the clacking of keyboards, the distant ringing of a telephone, and the droning of various copiers and printers. Another young woman appeared.

"Hi, I'm Jill. I hear you want to help us out."

"Hi, I'm Anna Miller. I'd like to if I can."

"I'd love to talk to you. Come on back to my office." Jill continued talking as they walked a short distance down the hallway to her door. "So, I thought I knew everyone in town, but we've never met. Have you recently moved here?"

"In a way, I suppose. I've been here almost a month now, and I'm renting a cottage about a mile from here. I came here to do some research, but my progress has been slower than I expected, so I have some free time. But I'm not really sure how long I will be staying," Anna explained.

"Well, we don't require any long-term commitment, so we would be happy to have you for as long as you would like." Jill nodded emphatically. Anna was getting the impression they didn't get too many volunteers walking in off the street.

"Let me give you a brief introduction to us. The Senior Center is a place for meeting and socializing. Many of our seniors are very active. They live on their own but come here to play cards or talk with their friends. We keep in touch with them and if one is sick or recovering from an injury, we'll take meals over and help around the house. Some can no longer drive and may need rides to run errands, go to doctor's appointments, and that sort of thing." Anna nodded as Jill continued.

"Here at the center, we have volunteers that socialize, play cards or games, and give our seniors someone to talk to if they need. We had a volunteer last year put together a cookbook with recipes that each of our members contributed to. Everyone really enjoyed that. After that, everyone had ideas for a book on county history, instruction on crafts, and a collection of stories or songs. We've talked about sponsoring the cost if we had a volunteer interested in taking the lead. Getting the members to share their old hobbies and encouraging them to teach others is a great way to help keep their minds sharp. I've never believed a person has to get feeble-minded and stagnant in their old age. I think with a place like this to come to where they can stay active and even have a project to contribute to, they can stay vibrant well past their work retirement. As a matter of fact, all the free time a person has after retirement, why I think that could be the time of their life where they have the most accomplishments."

"That all sounds wonderful for the seniors you have here, and there's several areas I can assist in," Anna said. "I'm thinking I would be able to be here two or three afternoons a week, if that's something that would be all right."

"That would really be a blessing, Anna." Jill seemed grateful for the few hours of time Anna suggested. "Naturally, we like to know who we are working with, so I have some paperwork for you. General information, permission for a background check, and that sort of thing."

"Of course, no problem." Anna watched as Jill turned and rummaged through several drawers in a filing cabinet against the wall. She muttered a few times, running through a mental checklist as she pulled several pages from various files. She straightened the pile by tapping them on her desk, long ways then sideways, before handing them to Anna.

"That's fine, then. You fill these out and it will take a couple of days to get everything together. Why don't we say you come back by next Tuesday and we'll get everything started? Feel free to use one of the tables out front and fill those out," Jill said, waving toward the paperwork. "Just give them to Sandy at the front and she'll make sure I get them."

Anna's stomach growled as she slid onto a stool at the counter in the cafe. She waved at Kim, who was handling the lunch crowd with her usual breezy competence. Kim waved back, flashing her customary grin.

A second waitress approached her, one she had not met before, and quickly took her order. Anna looked around the cafe and realized most of the faces in the room were now at least vaguely familiar. She didn't know all the names and had not spoken to most of them, but she was beginning to recognize them by sight and a friendly nod. Somehow, this temporary waypoint in her life was becoming more of a home.

As if in confirmation, Kim walked behind her, patting her shoulder as she passed. "Hey, girlfriend."

Strange how two words could encapsulate such a feeling of belonging - of acceptance, and of friendship. Somehow, they did. Anna felt like she fit in here. No longer an outsider, but one of the family.

CHAPTER FOURTEEN

Intent on stocking groceries for her new home, Anna pushed a cart down the narrow aisle, stopping in front of the potato chip display.

"Hello, beautiful." The rumbling timbre of the voice was instantly familiar and sent shivers down Anna's spine.

"Hey, stranger," she said, looking up. "Accosting women in the grocery store now?"

"I do whatever it takes."

"Smart, you wouldn't want your moves to get stale or anything," she retorted. "So, are you shopping or stalking?"

"Shopping. Running into you was completely a happy accident."

"I see. You know, you could have picked up the phone and called," she chided. She couldn't help the feeling of excitement his presence always seemed to bring, but she was still annoyed with him about being ignored. She hadn't heard from him, and while she knew it was childish, her feelings were hurt.

"Well, it took longer than I had planned, but I got back yesterday and planned on calling, but I saw you over here and had to come see you in person." He reached over and touched her elbow. "I got your message a few days ago about Harold Jones. I'm sorry that didn't work out, but do you want to grab dinner and talk about it?"

Staring at his earnest, handsome face and raised eyebrow, Anna's annoyance at him lessened considerably. He was irresistible to her, it seemed. "Sure. I'd like that."

"Okay then. Is tomorrow good? Around seven?"

"Sounds perfect. I'll even let you pick me up," she said loftily. "I'll text you my new address."

"Wait, what?"

"We'll talk over dinner and I'll explain everything, but right now I have to hurry or I'll be late." Anna leaned over and gave him a peck on the cheek before pushing her cart toward to checkout line.

"Late for what?" Logan wondered aloud.

Anna looked around, pleased with the results of the last few days she had spent settling into the tiny summerhouse. She had only moved in four days ago, but felt an odd sense of pride in the small place and couldn't wait to show Logan. He didn't keep her waiting and knocked on her door moments before seven. Anna opened the door with one hand and used her free arm in a grand sweeping gesture.

"Welcome to my castle." Anna stood back and spun around in a circle. She enjoyed Logan's clear admiration of her shapely legs revealed by the short skater's skirt on her dress. She knew the vivid green complimented her dark hair and lightly tanned skin.

"This is nice," he said, tearing his gaze away from her and looking around. "Compact, efficient, and not a hotel room. I bet you're loving that part."

"Definitely," she said. "And I appreciate the compact part too since I have to clean it myself now that I don't have daily maid service."

He nodded and walked over, wrapping her up in a warm hug. She returned the embrace and leaned her head back, accepting his kiss.

"I missed you."

"Missed you too. I'm glad you're back."

He held her tightly and kissed her again, longer this time. She leaned into him, savoring his closeness. He pulled back and met her eyes, resting his palm against the side of her face.

"I'm glad you've decided to stick around for a while. I guess you're finding Lander is a pretty nice place to be."

"It certainly has its appeal," she replied, grinning at him. "So, are you hungry? I had a plan, but now I'm not sure it's a good idea."

"What's not a good idea?"

"I was hoping you'd want to stay here and order a pizza. I thought it might be more comfortable to talk here. Plus, I would be able to get at my research notes if you have any bright ideas. But now I'm not sure it's a good idea," she said playfully. "Can I trust you being here alone with me?"

Logan looked around at the room, with its cozy arrangement of loveseat and overstuffed chair near a small table and galley-style kitchenette and his eyes fell on the queen-sized bed that seemed to dominate the room. He nodded his head in the direction of the bed and raised his eyebrows. "Hmmm, I see. Well, I'll try to behave, but no promises. Pizza is a great incentive, though."

Anna hesitated, and Logan laughed at her expression, pulling out his phone to look up the pizzeria phone number.

"It's sure not a compliment that you can behave in exchange for pizza," she mumbled under her breath.

After a brief debate on the merits of thin-crust versus thick and a haggling negotiation over toppings, they came to an agreement of pepperoni and green pepper on a thin crust. Anna felt she had won a small victory because never in her life had anyone given in to her pizza preferences. Logan smiled indulgently, and she triumphantly dialed the number he provided and placed their order. When she had finished, she threw her cell phone on the counter and flopped into the easy chair, curling her legs under her and motioning for Logan to sit on the loveseat.

"Girl, it's good to see you, and you look beautiful tonight."

"Thank you, but you stay over there and behave," she grinned.

"Okay, fine. I'm sorry. Bring me up to date. Your voicemail sounded troubled," he said, leaning forward to take her hand. "I'm sorry I wasn't able to be there for you. The area I was in didn't have service and I didn't get your message for several days."

Anna shook her head. "It was fine, really. I needed some time to process. I got ahead of myself and caught up in a fantasy of finding this whole new family. I'm not really sure why it became so important. It was almost like I was obsessed."

"Family is important, to know your roots and where you came from. That's a basic desire that many people have. To find out your grandparents were your adoptive grandparents had to be a shock to you. I get that you felt like the history, or your ancestry and heritage from them was all of a sudden in question. I understand why you would want to find out why that happened and even find relatives you never knew you had. Family is important, but remember it's not just biological relatives that matter, it's the ones who are always there for you, the ones that stand by you," Logan said.

"I'm starting to see that." Anna nodded. "When your father showed me the family history on the wall there at the ranch, my first thought was how odd it was to have a room with another family's history. But, the more he talked about Wyatt and his family, I understood that to him, to you even, family is who you choose, not just who's connected to you by blood. The grandparents I grew up knowing, they were my family. I don't think I could have loved them any more if they had been blood. I always thought they were, and now knowing they weren't actually biological relatives doesn't change my love for them. It changed my idea of heritage, I think. I know I really grabbed onto the idea of having more family somewhere. I lost what I had but thought I could replace them. But that doesn't work, does it? You can't replace family with some substitution. A bloodline doesn't automatically make you connected by anything more than genetics. I guess the more I have thought about it, it doesn't change anything for me. Seeing how much your dad loved the Hamilton family, I get that I may not have to find my blood family, I can make one on my own with the friends and people I care about."

"So, you're giving up the search?" Logan asked, sitting back in surprise.

"No, I think I've come too far for that," Anna said, shaking her head emphatically. "I still want the answers, but I'm not sure that I should expect it to be life-changing. Or maybe I'm trying to convince myself of that so I won't set myself up for that kind of disappointment again."

"So, where are you as far as investigating?"

"Well, I suppose you could say I'm halfway. I've eliminated Harold Jones, obviously, and I've talked to and eliminated Frank Johnson, Leo, and Donald Brown. That leaves Eugene Morris, Clarence Williams, Marvin Smythe, and your friend, Wyatt Hamilton."

"Well, excluding Wyatt for a minute, what do you know about the other three? Have you been able to research them?" Logan asked.

"I know that Eugene Morris was severely injured. He spent months recovering in a military hospital overseas, and when he was sent home, he was unable to walk. I think he may have lost one or more limbs. From what I read, it seems like he never left the house once he came back. He lived there until he died in 1962."

"But he was here in town during the right time period?"

"Maybe. It would be close, but not knowing exactly who my grandmother was it's tough to be sure. Although, unless she was a nurse or something, I can't imagine how she would meet him or how they would have the opportunity to, well, you know…" She finished awkwardly.

Logan laughed at her discomfiture. "Hook up?"

She joined his laughter, throwing a pillow at him. "Yeah, that. It's not something I want to think about grandparents doing."

"Okay; I agree with your logic on that one, hah, and your opinion of that image! We'll put him at the bottom of the pile. How about Clarence Williams? I don't know that name – what happened to him?"

"He joined the air force and made a career of it. He actually never moved back to Lander. From what I could find in the society pages, there were only a couple of mentions over the years of him visiting his mother. She died in 1956 and I couldn't find him after that. I suppose I could go through military records and see where he was stationed and try to track him down."

"Well, he seems to be an unlikely candidate, unless your grandmother met him during a brief encounter while he was in town. If that were true, you need to re-think a couple of the original assumptions."

"Exactly," she said, pleased he remembered. "I based this on a star-crossed lovers assumption, that the war brought them together in a chance meeting that would have never otherwise happened, and then the war separated them."

"You have to admit it's a reach," he said doubtfully.

"Yes, but what about my father's research from the Port of New York? I still don't know why he had that, but I have to assume he knew something that led him to that immigration record. And it doesn't make sense in that time period that she would be from Wyoming and he would be from a foreign county."

"What if she had been a nurse and worked with the military?"

"Possible. But then why wasn't there a scandal of a local, pregnant, unmarried woman? If she were a local, there would have been gossip, right? So far, the only gossip I've uncovered was the girl Sunny that was a seamstress. She left town, but there didn't seem to be much scandal there."

"True, but I don't think you would find that in the papers," he said, laughing. "You should ask Bo's grandmother and her friend again."

"They were the ones that told me about Sunny," she said. "Maybe since then, they've remembered something else. It would be pretty easy to sit and talk with them again. I started volunteering there; I forgot to tell you about that."

"Just like that? One visit and they roped you in?"

"Well, not exactly. After I came back from Idaho Falls, I realized I needed to do something with my time if the research was going this slow. If I'm not going to have anything to do all day, I need to get involved, or get a job, or decide to go back to Iowa. I wasn't ready to let the grandparent search go yet, so I found this place and a few things to do," she explained.

"A few things?" he questioned. "Do tell, what else have you gotten yourself into?"

A quick rapping came from the door.

"Saved by the bell," she cried. "Or by the knock anyway."

As Anna answered the door, Logan rummaged through the sparse kitchen to come up with two plates, a couple of forks, and a roll of paper towels.

Anna returned with the cardboard box, setting it on the coffee table with a flourish. "Dinner is served." They dug into their dinner, discussing Anna's research and posing scenarios about Anna's grandparents, each one more outlandish than the last. Anna fell into fits of laughter at Logan's elaborate storytelling and had to beg him to stop so she could eat in peace. He promised to behave and turned his attention to the pizza.

"You still haven't told me what you've found to keep yourself busy. Did you find a job?" Logan asked, snagging another slice from the box.

"Well, the Senior Center has an outreach program, so I'm doing errands for some of the members who can't get out themselves. I think I will do a day here and there of office temp work if somebody needs. And, I got, I think the word is 'volun-told' that I needed to work on the Pioneer Days committee. That's where I had to go yesterday after I saw you. They have me checking lights on floats for the parade and I think I have to do some set up work for the rodeo."

"Yes, the rodeo," Logan said knowingly. "You have to go to the rodeo with me. Have you ever been to one?"

"No, there were some back in Iowa, but not many, so I never had the opportunity to go to one. We did have a lot of parades, so I'm pretty comfortable there," she said, wriggling her eyebrows.

"Well, good," he replied, laughing. "So you've been around some floats, decorated a few or built one from the ground-up on a flatbed, have you?"

"Hey, now, don't be bashing my parade float building abilities. I've got that down cold, baby. The rodeo, not so much." She grinned and shrugged.

"You'll love it, I promise," he said confidently. "Pioneer Days is the biggest event of the year around here, and not only because it's the Fourth of July."

"I'm beginning to understand that."

"Well, we're pretty proud of it. You know it's the oldest paid rodeo in the world."

"That's a pretty big distinction for a small town," Anna said.

"Well, we have all the traditional rodeo events: bull riding, saddle bronc, bareback, team roping, steer wrestling, and calf roping. The all-Indian relay is a crazy fast and a great race. Native American riders come from the Wind River Indian Reservation and they ride bareback around the track, grabbing a new horse every lap. You'll love it. Then, of course, barrel racing, breakaway, ribbon roping, and mini bull riding."

"So it's really the oldest?"

"Yup. Ours is three years older than Cheyenne's Frontier Days. Of course, theirs is bigger and really well known. We started in 1894 on Bill O'Neil's ranch, just south of town. In the beginning, they had a ten-mile relay race.

There were three teams with five horses each and they would alternate horses every two miles. In time, they switched locations, added grandstands, starting printing out paper programs, and added events. Nowadays, pretty much any rodeo you go to will have the six basic events." Seeing Anna's glazed deer-in-the-headlights blank stare accompanied by vague head nodding, Logan laughed. "Bull riding, saddle bronc, bareback, team roping, steer wrestling, and calf roping."

Anna would not have been able to repeat those six if her life depended on it. She was overwhelmed by the details but couldn't help but be swept up at Logan's obvious excitement. Most of what he had shared was completely foreign to her, and she wasn't sure she understood enough to even ask intelligent questions, but she she looked forward to the events. "You make it sound so exciting. Really, really complicated, and probably intense, but a lot of fun."

Logan reached over and grabbed her playfully, pulling her onto the loveseat next to him. "I will be there to show you everything. I will explain it to you and promise to protect you from crazed cattle and cowboys."

Anna grinned and leaned over to kiss him. "Well," she breathed, her voice barely above a whisper, "when you put it like that, how could I say no?"

She looked up and locked eyes with him. The air seemed to vanish from the room. He tipped his head to one side, studying her. Slowly, as if to ensure the magic of the moment, he brushed the back of his fingers against her cheek.

Anna leaned into his touch and closed her eyes. "Look at me," Logan whispered.

Anna opened her eyes slowly, gazing into his deep blue eyes. She leaned forward to taste his lips.

He readily returned her kiss, moving slowly and deliberately. He let his lips trail over hers as his hand slid across her neck. He buried his fingers in her hair, pulling her closer. He opened his mouth slightly and she could feel the slight whisper of his breath across her tongue. The warm taste of him lingered. Gently, he shifted and slid a line of slow, warm kisses from the side of her mouth up the line of her jaw to the soft sensitive spot below her ear.

Anna shivered.

She buried her face in his shoulder, breathing in his scent. They both lost interest in discussing research and rodeos.

CHAPTER FIFTEEN

Anna had a hard time keeping the smile off her face. Life was good. The past month had flown by, and she had loved every minute. Logan had been attentive, despite several trips to deliver horses, a couple of out of town auctions, and another week in Colorado on business. The day after their pizza date, Anna had come home to find a flower delivery next to her door with a handwritten card:

Roses are red
Violets are blue
There isn't an hour today
I haven't thought about you.

It was cheesy and sweet. Anna couldn't help but smile. The flowers sat in water until they wilted and dried out, but each time she saw them, she smiled.

They had been out to dinner twice more, and managed to spend an entire afternoon fishing. She recalled that day with a smile. Not too much time had been spent focused on the fishing but it had been a memorable afternoon.

Logan made time to talk or text several times a week. Anna loved curling up on the patio chair, enjoying the warm evenings outside while she listened as Logan shared the details of his business. They talked about favorite movies, music, and their "someday" dreams. Anna had never felt closer to a man, even her near-fiancée she had spent close to two years with. Logan was different. He looked at the world the same way she did, and they easily laughed at each other's silly humor.

She had spent time with Kim, had made a few more friends, and put in quite a few hours at the community center and on the Pioneer Days tasks. Anna realized now how much she had drifted from her girlfriends in Iowa. After high school, one had moved away to Minneapolis for college and stayed after graduation. Her two closest friends had both gotten married, and Anna felt awkward as a third wheel and avoided the couples when she was single. They had trouble finding time for girls' nights, juggling husbands, children, and babysitters. Anna admitted to herself now she hadn't made much of an effort to stay in touch. After the disastrous relationship and breakup with David, she was the only single one in her crowd. Shortly after, Mom had gotten sick and time just slipped away. Anna regretted now losing touch. Getting to know Kim had reminded her how great it was to have chick nights.

She looked around the busy tent and felt like she belonged. Lander Pioneer Days had officially kicked off the days of celebration, activities, and events leading up to the Fourth of July. The volunteers had their hands full keeping up with the details. Anna found that Logan had not overestimated the importance of the two-day rodeo. Competitors traveled from miles around, and every aspect of each event was planned to the smallest detail. Anna wished she could have worked on more of the rodeo preparation, but her lack of experience with horses, livestock, or any rodeo event left her with very little to offer in the way of assistance.

The event organizers kept Anna busy in other areas. She worked with the teams setting up the 5k marathon, the BBQ dinner, the pancake breakfast, and the pageant parade. She erected tents for water stations along the marathon route, helped set up the first aid station and worked on creating signs. Today, her office and organizational skills were in high demand for list-making and last-minute detail-checking.

Anna felt like she was among friends. As she looked around, the name of each person was familiar to her and she had gotten to know each one, at least in a small way. She was anxious for the preparations to be done and the fun to start. Logan was a large part of the reason she could not keep the smile off her face. As she thought of him, he appeared.

"Logan," she called, waving her hand so that he could find her in the teeming crowd. She watched as he made his way through the maze of tables, bags, boxes, and people.

"Hey, are you ready to get sprung from this joint?" he said, jerking his head in the direction of the exit.

"Yes," Anna said, giddy with excitement. "I hear the governor called and I got early release from work camp, so let's go play."

"Time to educate you on what a real rodeo's all about."

They crossed toward the grandstands, stopping along the way at vendor tents and occasionally exchanging greetings with friends passing by. Anna was surprised by how many people she knew, which made her feel like part of the community. Nearly thirty minutes later after several stops, they had made their way to the grandstands. They found seats, which led to another round of introductions to a group of older men sporting cowboy hats, hiding sun-wrinkled eyes. Logan's father Roy was there, deep in conversations with several other local ranchers. She sat next to Logan, feeling a keen awareness of deep-seated happiness and the thrill of excitement at being close to him.

She looked over as he glanced at her and winked. The level of attraction and passion in their relationship constantly surprised her, and she loved the feeling it was mutual.

"Here," he said, handing her an event flyer detailing the activities. "Here's a rodeo schedule if you'd like to take a look."

She studied the program which seemed to be a complicated layout of events, codes, and divisions. In a short time, she gave up on trying to interpret the complex sport on her own. She touched Logan's knee to get his attention.

"Okay, I have some questions. What's the difference between these sections – the ones that say roughstock and timed? What does that mean?"

"Basically, timed events are where you try and get the fastest time and roughstock is where you have to meet a minimum time and get an overall point score. In the timed events, you try to get the fastest time and in roughstock you try and get the highest score," he explained.

Anna looked at the page and back to Logan and shook her head, still confused.

"Roughstock events are the saddle bronc, the bareback, and the bull riding. Those are the ones where they have to make the eight-second mark for any points. If they're bucked off before eight seconds, there's no score. The judges score each ride, based on points for the rider and the mount. The rider's points are based on the skill level he displays during the ride, and the mount's points are based on how difficult the ride was. The combined total is the score for the ride. Before the event, the rider draws his mount – it's basically a random lottery system." Logan paused to make sure Anna was following. She nodded, and he continued. "For the timed ones, like the calf roping, team roping, steer wrestling, barrels, and the rest of the events, the winners are the ones with the fastest times. Each event has different rules that can result in disqualification or penalties that add to the time, but in general it's speed. Some have a one-shot round and others may have several rounds that are added together or averaged for the overall time."

"Whew. That's a lot, but I think I get the idea. I'm sure I'll have a lot of questions for each event so don't plan on going anywhere."

Logan's eyes swept over her with a look of intensity that raised her temperature several degrees. "Oh, I didn't plan on going anywhere for quite some time, darlin'."

The announcer's voice echoed over the rodeo grounds, and the opening ceremonies began, rescuing Anna from a reply. The event kicked off with a fanfare, a greeting, a moving rendition of the national anthem, and a prayer by a local minister. The competitors were introduced, riding into the arena with parade-like showmanship, followed by rhinestone-encrusted rodeo-glam female riders proudly displaying sponsor flags, riding in at full gallop, dashing around the arena one after another, and then leaving the arena with a cloud of dust in their wake.

The frenzied excitement was evident in the crowd as the arena cleared and the first event got underway. The seasoned announcer provided event and participant details, answering many of Anna's questions as they formed.

"Folks, welcome again to the Lander Pioneer Days Rodeo. We're kicking things off with the ever-popular and hugely exciting bronc riding. These cowboys are in for a wild ride and just about anything can happen. We're looking down here at

chute three, where this young cowboy drew a bronc named Razzmatazz."

Anna was caught up in the crowd's anticipation, eagerly awaiting the action. The chute seemed to be surrounded by cowboys, and she could see one sitting on the horse, his attention occupied with ropes and focused on the horse beneath him. Two other cowboys, in large hats and traditional-looking chaps, stood outside the gate, on the arena side, ready to pull it open. The mounted cowboy suddenly nodded and the gate flew open, the two on the arena side running and jumping up on the fence.

The bronc erupted into action, jumping and twisting, tossing his head and kicking up his back legs. Anna watched the powerful athletic motion of the mid-jump thrusting kick and marveled at the cowboy's ability to stay on the beast's back. She realized that as the man's body was thrown back, up, and sideways, he managed to maintain a seat on the horse's back and one hand firmly attached to the rope. The other hand was high in the air, attached to the flailing free arm. She remembered reading that the cowboy's free arm was not allowed to touch the animal in any way during the eight seconds or the rider would be disqualified. She never realized how long eight seconds could feel and could only imagine what it was like to the cowboy being thrown around.

After what seemed like an eternity, the buzzer sounded.

"And let's give a round of appreciation for our pickup men today, Lyle and Bo. These boys are gonna keep our riders safe out there today."

Anna looked at Logan. "Is that Bo from the ranch? Hazel's grandson? The horse looks familiar."

"Yup. Bo spends more time training horses than working the cattle. He's one of the best."

"What exactly is a pickup man?" Anna asked.

"The cowboys on horseback off to the side, see them there?" Logan pointed. "They'll be there for the bronc, saddle bronc, and bull riding events. They help the riders dismount safely, make sure they don't get hung up. They're also there to make sure that the bronc or bull gets out of the arena quickly to keep the people and animals safe."

Anna watched breathless as the ride ended, and the pickup man rode in alongside the bronc. The cowboy seemed to easily jump off his animal, using the pickup man's arm as balance, then sliding unceremoniously to the ground. The crowd murmured until the announcer's voice blasted again.

"We're off to a solid start here. The first ride of the day gets an 81.5. We'll see if that can hold it as we get ready for the next ride. Our next cowboy is here in chute number one. He's going up against Locomotion. Let's see what this boy brought with him to work today."

Just as Anna felt like she understood the bronc riding, the rodeo moved on to steer wrestling event, which Logan explained was also called "bulldogging." That event moved very fast. All of the action was between three and ten seconds for each competitor and it was difficult for her to catch all the movements. Anna watched as a steer was released, then a mounted cowboy galloped after it, and when he was close, he launched himself off the horse toward the steer. Several cowboys missed entirely and ended up face-first in the dirt. One managed to land where he intended, grabbing the steer to wrestle it to the ground. Anna resisted the urge to laugh when the steer shook its head slightly and took off running again, dragging the hapless cowboy along with him. Two successfully brought their animals to the ground.

"Does that hurt them?" Anna asked, worried about the animals.

"Nah. You can see it's a pretty high risk for the cowboy. All kinds of things can go wrong where they can get injured. The cattle are very strong and injury to one of them is rare. The statistics on injury to the cattle is around five-hundredths of one percent. The guys are a lot more likely to get hurt."

"Is this something you would do in real life, working with the cattle?" she asked, hoping Logan wasn't tiring of her incessant questions.

"It's not really something we would have to do in modern ranching operations, but back in the day, there might have been a use for subduing cattle if you needed to treat an injury or something. Team roping and calf roping are really more the thing we would use today."

"How is calf roping different than steer wrestling?"

"The cowboy ropes the calf, and the horse is trained to hold tension on the rope while the cowboy dismounts, and gets the calf on its side—he 'flanks' the calf—then ties three legs together. The cowboy backs off and the tie has to hold for six seconds."

"So if it comes untied, is it a penalty of extra seconds or do they lose their turn?" Anna asked.

Logan laughed. "It's not really losing their turn, they get a 'no time'. But, yes, it has to stay tied."

"And you actually do this stuff out at the ranch?" she asked, incredulous that Logan would be so casual about something that sounded so complicated and dangerous.

"Sure. We need to give calves medicine, treat injuries, and tag them."

"So how is this calf roping different from team roping? Is it the same thing but with full-grown cattle?"

"No, it's a different process. Team roping involves two riders, working as a team. One ropes the head of the steer, usually the horns, and the other ropes the back legs. They are called a 'header' and a 'heeler'. It takes two because while a calf, depending on how old it is, will weigh two hundred to five hundred pounds, a steer will easily be a thousand to fifteen hundred. A bull will get over two thousand."

Suddenly, Anna's attention was drawn back to the arena, where the saddle bronc riding competition was beginning. She quickly saw it was nearly the same as bronc riding, but included a small saddle. She wondered why they bothered to have two different events, but for once decided not to ask the question. The saddle bronc was followed by calf roping, then the team roping. Both events were exciting to watch and made more sense after Logan's explanations. Each event had more rules, penalties, and details than she expected and raised more questions, but Logan continued to be patient in explaining.

They took a break for hot dogs and nachos, washed them down with soda, then watched the barrel racing and an event that turned out to be one of the crowd favorites, the ribbon roping. Anna cheered along with everyone else as a cowboy on a horse roped a calf and a hapless individual representing a local business ran to the animal to pull a ribbon off its tail then ran back to a starting line, all in less than a minute. Anna was sure this wasn't a skill needed on a ranch and didn't bother to ask. She was glad it was included because it was a lot of fun to watch.

"Logan, thank you so much for being here with me today. It's been so much fun and you've been great explaining it all to me," she said, throwing her arm around his shoulder and leaning in to kiss his cheek.

"If you liked that, you'll love the next event. This is one you're not going to see at every rodeo and it's really something."

Anna could hear the echo from the speaker blaring the announcer's voice as he explained the events. His ease and expertise were apparent and the crowd listened intently. Anna could feel the excitement gathering as he built the tension like a seasoned carnival barker.

"If you have never seen this one, folks, you're in for a real treat. The Indian Relay is one of the wildest, most colorful events in all of equine sports. This is one of the oldest events you'll see, included at powwows and Indian rodeos. We'll get underway here in a minute and what you'll see requires expert horsemanship, teamwork, and pageantry. But make no mistake, these are one-thousand-pound horses and there is the potential for disaster at every turn.

"As a reminder, the first team to complete the full relay of all three horses wins. A team is automatically disqualified for the use of lead ropes, if they have a loose horse on the track, or they have more than two false starts. And no unsportsmanlike behavior or arguing with the officials. We want the horses and riders out there to stay safe and we'll do all we can on that, so be sure we don't allow any animal cruelty. Okay, it looks like they're getting things set up and we'll be ready to go here in just a minute. You folks ready?"

Anna could see the teams gathered in small groups, wearing similar colors. She could see four teams, based on the colors of green, blue, red, and yellow. Most weren't wearing shirts but signified their team color with feathered headbands, pants, or even huge hand-painted emblems on their chest. Even the horses matched with leg wraps or painted symbols. Each color-coded group had four men and three horses. Anna watched as the teams lined up at the starting line. She was surprised by the lack of saddles.

"They ride bareback?" she asked, elbowing Logan in the ribs.

"Yeah, they do," he said, elbowing her back as he laughed.

"Oh, sorry, I got caught up," she shrugged, cocking her head and twisting her mouth into an apologetic grin.

He threw his arm around her in a half bear hug. "Touch me anytime," he said suggestively, wriggling his eyebrows until she pushed him away in mock disgust.

Looking back at the track, Anna watched as the riders stood ready next to the first horse while other team members stood holding the second and third horses. The air was tense with excitement, and Anna jumped when the gun was fired.

The riders vaulted onto their horses' backs, riding furiously down the track. The horses were beautiful creatures, and for each, the full gallop was so smooth, it was like poetry in motion. Anna had heard that cliché many times, but until this moment when it popped into her head, she never really grasped the meaning. She couldn't help but lean forward as the four pounded past, blazing toward their teammates. Anna looked over to the relay point and realized the waiting horses had picked up on the excitement and were prancing anxiously, tossing their heads. She watched as one raised up majestically on its back legs, pawing the air while the man holding its reins tried to control it.

The action peaked at the exchange, where to Anna's eye, everything happened at once. The rider didn't seem to slow down at all but threw the reins into the waiting hands of his teammate. The rider jumped to the ground and immediately vaulted on the back of the next horse, tearing off down the track again. In seconds, the race was on again. Anna was torn between watching the horses fighting for the lead and the skill being demonstrated by the ones readying the next horse and the one that had finished the lap.

Even now, knowing what to watch for, Anna again held her breath as the exciting exchange took place from the second to the third horse. She watched as they completed the last lap, unconsciously grabbing onto Logan's arm, shaking it as she leaned toward the track, completely absorbed in the final seconds.

"Whoop! Whoop!"

"Yes!"

"Go, Grady! Go!"

Shouts and cheers erupted all around them as the blue team crossed the finish line a nose ahead of team yellow. Red and green were right behind. Anna jumped with the rest of the crowd and turned toward Logan, her eyes glittering with excitement. "I have never seen anything like that before. It was unbelievable. I didn't know anyone could jump off a horse at that speed or jump on one bareback like that."

"I knew you would enjoy it," he said. "A few more of these and we'll make a cowgirl out of you yet."

Anna laughed. "I have enjoyed this so much, but it was even better having you here to explain it all to me. I'd love to go to another one with you."

"It would be my pleasure," he said, grabbing her hand and lifting it to kiss her fingertips.

Anna knew she was grinning like a fool, but couldn't help herself.

CHAPTER SIXTEEN

Stormy Adams looked across the arena to the grandstands. From her vantage point on horseback, she could scan the crowd effortlessly.

She spotted Roy and several of her father's friends first. Two rows down, Logan was head to head, deep in conversation with a vaguely familiar brunette. Stormy's temper flared when she saw him smile and brush his lips against the brunette's temple. Her grip tightened on the flagpole she held and her feet unconsciously bounced in the stirrups. Sitting here portraying an outward calm was a tremendous effort when she wanted to bolt across the arena and tear Logan's hand away from that tramp. He had been increasingly distant for the past month, and now she knew why. Stormy's horse pranced and sidestepped, agitated by Stormy's emotional state. She forced her attention away from the scene. She would take care of that later. Right now, she and the other flag carriers were waiting for the signal to make the circuit of the arena. As one of the veterans, she was expected to perform flawlessly, and losing control of her mount was not in that definition.

The calf roping event was completed, and Stormy led the flag carriers on the blindingly fast gallop around the arena. Each carried a corporate flag representing one of the rodeo sponsors. The flag carriers were decked out in their rodeo finest, glittering with rhinestones, bright colors, and stiff cowboy hats. The horses matched the riders in finery, rhinestones, and colors. She was in her element. In the lead, sparkling and beautiful. Stormy was accustomed to being the center of attention. She was young, hot, and rich. Her face was flushed with anger and exertion by the time they completed the circuit. She had carefully averted her eyes as she rode past the section where Logan was seated. She didn't want to risk him seeing the daggers she would undoubtedly be shooting at him. No, she needed to keep her anger directed at the slut horning in on her man.

Coming to a halt at the corral, Stormy threw her reins over the post and gracefully slid off her mount.

"Stormy, sweetie, dish. What's up with you and Logan?" The question posed made Stormy stop and grit her teeth. She bit back a scathing reply and turned to face the owner of the thinly-veiled taunt.

"Sara, good to see you. Some of that baby weight is finally coming off. Good for you, girlfriend." Stormy delivered the observation with a syrupy smile.

"Bless your heart," Sara replied with a glitter in her eye that contradicted any shred of warmth or genuine gratitude. "It's so sweet of you to notice that about me when you seem to be overlooking your man's new preoccupation."

"Logan and I are fine. We occasionally see other people, but we have an understanding. You may not be secure enough in your relationship to comprehend, but I have no concerns. It's just a casual flirtation."

"Well, I guess you may be right, sugar. If it were my man, I wouldn't be so understanding about him publicly humiliating me like that. I would feel mortified he did that in front of everyone, but you're a stronger woman than I am," Sara said sweetly. "Maybe one day I can be more like you."

"You can try, but today's not that day," Stormy said sharply, then spun on her heel and used every bit of her self-control to amble leisurely toward the concession tents. She would maintain her image at all costs and vowed to handle this situation with Logan before it got out of hand.

Stormy calmly ordered dinner and a beer from the barbeque tent while she waited. She edged in with a few girlfriends who had a spot at a picnic table with a direct view of the rodeo grounds. She watched the events and looked to the entire world like nothing was wrong.

Inside she was seething. There was no way she was going to let all her plans fall apart. She was on the edge of achieving the dream first envisioned by her great-grandmother more than seventy years ago. She had come so far and was so close to her goal she refused to allow anything to get in her way. Especially some nobody that blew into town a few weeks ago.

This is my town, my legacy. She had heard the stories from before the time she could remember. Gram taught her to love the land, and how hard Gram's parents had worked to make this ranch. When they settled here, they were among the first residents of the county. Stormy did love the land and the ranch. She hated the cattle and the dirt but loved the status her family had here and the legacy that was hers. She often wished Gram had married Wyatt Hamilton when she had the chance. Their ranch would be twice the size it was currently and they would be the most prosperous in the county. But instead, Bessie Bellamy's daughter Grace married Herbert and not Wyatt. Stormy had the opportunity to join the ranches now by marrying Logan.

Stormy's grandfather, Herbert Adams, and Wyatt Hamilton had been close friends. Stormy's father, Jack, and later Stormy herself practically grew up there on Wyatt's ranch. Stormy didn't know why Wyatt never married, but that didn't affect his friendship with Herbert, or Grace for that matter. Grace's mother, Bessie, and Wyatt's mother, Alice Ann, remained friends their entire lives, so they were as close as if they were one family. When Wyatt hired Roy to work on the ranch, Roy was still a teenager and he easily fit into the Hamilton clan. When he married Beth, she was welcomed. Stormy knew that her mother, Alma, had been close friends with Beth. Because of that friendship, Stormy and Logan pretty much grew up together. They had all mourned Beth when she died in a car accident when Logan was ten years old. By that time, Herbert, Bessie, and Alice Ann were gone too, and it was only Wyatt, Roy, and Logan on the Hamilton Ranch.

Wyatt maintained a close friendship with Herbert's widow, and they often accompanied each other to social events and business functions. Grace Adams had been a fixture in Wyatt's life for years, and the two insisted it was not a romantic involvement, but Stormy always wondered. She thought it was strange that Wyatt never married or had children and grandchildren of his own. Wyatt had allowed Logan to follow him everywhere and treated him like the grandson he never had. However, other than time with Grace, Wyatt didn't date at all.

When he died, he left the ranch to Roy in his will, knowing it would go one day to Logan. It was past time that the two families were joined together. Stormy knew it, Roy knew it, and soon Logan would accept it.

Stormy turned her attention to the identity of the brunette. By casually asking a few questions, she was amazed to learn how ingrained in the community this girl had become in only a few weeks. That worked to Stormy's advantage because she realized it was going to be surprisingly easy to handle this problem.

Standing at the large plate-glass window of the real estate office, Stormy Adams looked at the sparse traffic. It seemed the first workday after the holiday was not well-attended. There were only two days left in the week, so many had taken advantage and extended the holiday. Stormy smirked. She knew of one helpful little office temp that would have a full plate today. As if conjured by her will, Stormy saw a mousy-looking brown-haired figure scurrying along the sidewalk. The door opened quietly and the brunette walked in. Stormy's eyes swept over her, taking in the trim figure, unblemished skin, and engaging smile. The girl was the very definition of wholesome. And pretty too, she had to admit.

"Good morning, I'm Anna Miller. You must be Stormy Adams." She seemed friendly and confident as she stepped forward, shaking hands with a firm grip.

"Oh, hon, I am so glad you were able to come on such short notice," Stormy gushed.

"I was happy to get the call. I'm glad you were able to get my name from someone. I only recently decided to look for temp work."

"Well, that is the beauty of a small town. We're all friends here and look out for each other." Stormy reached out and patted Anna's hand like an indulgent grandmother.

"I am really starting to feel that. It is so nice," Anna said sincerely.

"Well, let's get you settled in," Stormy said as she headed toward the back of the room. The real estate office was housed in a narrow section of an original downtown building.

Anna followed Stormy towards the storage area. It was a space only twenty feet wide but extended back nearly eighty feet, mostly due to an extension that had been added sometime in the building's history. The front area they had walked through contained several forest green, comfortable-looking chairs, artfully arranged plants, a pewter-colored lantern-turned-lamp, a decorative display saddle, and a table topped with several listing magazines. The area behind that held two small desks, facing in opposite directions. One was piled with paperwork and personal items, and the other looked stark with only the computer terminal and was devoid of any sign it was ever used. Stormy breezed by those work areas, opened a door on the center of the back wall, and entered a room beyond.

Anna let out an unconscious sigh as she looked at her temporary workspace. The room should have its photo in the dictionary under multipurpose. It was the epitome of an organizational nightmare. Three four-drawer filing cabinets stood against the wall to her left. A large wooden worktable stood in front of them, near the middle of the room, and was topped with piles of manila folders, loose papers, photographs, and bound reports. On her right, a counter had been created using two-by-sixes and plywood, creating a kitchenette that housed a dorm-size refrigerator, coffeemaker, toaster oven, and microwave. A small white table with two plastic chairs was near the back of the room, next to a large metal storage unit with locking doors, two four-tier bookshelves, and at least three smaller bookshelves and a credenza. The room was bursting with furniture and the overall effect was cramped and claustrophobic. Anna's eyes watered from the overpowering smell emanating from the direction of the kitchenette.

Stormy saw her expression and laughed lightly. "Oh, yes, let's prop open this back door, shall we? If someone asks you to taste-test a breakfast burrito with fish, just say no. Lesson learned on that one."

Clicking her tongue, Stormy walked briskly to the back door, opening it and propping it with a brick from the alleyway. "I'll leave the other open as well and that should clear this out."

"Thanks, I'm sure it won't take long. Fish burrito, huh?" Anna smiled wanly.

"Maybe a scented candle as well," she said fishing under the counter for a wax-filled jar. Anna squinted at the label. Tangerine lilac? The fish burrito might be preferable.

"So, it's a basic filing catch-up project. Most everything is labeled with the client name or the property ID, although some might have the address and you will need to cross-reference. That won't be a problem will it?" She lit the candle and the sickeningly-sweet scent started to fill the area, somehow blending with rather than disguising the odious fish.

Anna sighed inwardly, afraid to take another deep breath in the rancid-smelling room. "No, it's fine. I'm sure I can get this straightened out. I'll start on the ones labeled and put any questions off to the side and we can go through those as a second step."

"That sounds brilliant, hon, thank you so much. You're just a dear," Stormy said, kissing her fingers and laying them on top of Anna's head. "My fiancée's father will be here shortly, so I'll be tied up for a while, but I'll come back and check on you later."

Anna felt a sense of peace and a flood of relief as Stormy glided back to the front. The woman's presence lived up to her name. Anna felt like she had survived a tornado. Although, Anna thought, she might not be aware how overwhelming her personality truly was. It seemed like women who were that beautiful and elegant were always poised and in control. Anna felt insignificant and awkward next to women like that.

Fortunately, she felt very much at ease and in control when it came to office organization. Turning, she assessed the project. There seemed to be no organization, as if each item had been tossed on the top of the pile in the order it had been received. She took a moment to look in the file drawers. The first contained client folders, alphabetized by last name. The second was filled with property folders, arranged numerically by MLS, and the third contained office records, which seemed to be arranged by color for categories and then alphabetically by vendor. Anna eyed the open drawer warily. It seemed like an unnecessarily complicated system. Unfortunately, she had been hired to file, not reorganize. She thought the best approach would be to separate the filing into the sections then file each cabinet's contents separately. She turned toward the table and began the arduous task of sorting.

A short time later, she heard voices in the front. She recognized the loud voice of Roy, Logan's father, and moved toward the door, intending to pop her head out and say hello.

"Stormy, darlin', you get prettier every day."

"Mr. Harris, Roy, if I didn't know better, I'd call you a flirt." Anna heard Stormy respond with a girlish-like giggle. "Is that any way to talk to your future daughter-in-law?"

Anna's stomach dropped. Surely she heard wrong. She held her breath, waiting for Roy's response.

"Ah, Stormy-girl, you couldn't feel any more like my daughter than you do right now," he said fondly.

"Yes, we do have the most wonderful family," Stormy said. Anna watched through the partially opened door as Stormy motioned for Roy to join her at the desk. "Logan and I finished up the paperwork for the land purchase. After we're married and fully join the ranches, he is going to have an operation that we will pass on for generations."

Anna could not believe what she was hearing. Logan didn't act like an engaged man. Anna had met Roy, and he never said a word. Thinking back to the dinner at the ranch, Logan had introduced her as a friend. They had not sat next to each other at dinner, and it was possible no one had seen them later. It had been dark by her car and they could have easily blended into the shadows. *What about the rodeo?* she thought. *There was no way anyone could have thought that was just innocent friends horsing around, could they?*

Her head spun, and the tight quarters and cloying smell in the room made it hard to breathe. She felt a deep stabbing pain in her chest and couldn't listen to any more. Grabbing her purse, she stumbled out the back door and rushed to the safety of her summerhouse.

CHAPTER SEVENTEEN

Anna paced the room, unable to stop shaking. She had barely gotten her footing back and the world was finally beginning to make sense. Now it felt like everything was falling apart again. But this wasn't the pain of loss; this was different. This was betrayal. This pain was sharp and ragged. Each breath she tried to draw was like shards of glass shredding her lungs. Her heart ached like it was wrapped in red-hot barbed wire and every breath brought new agony. Her hands shook and angry tears flowed from her eyes. She sobbed, giving in to the emotional turmoil of the past few months and losing all track of time. Everything had been under control and she had come to terms with her loss. This new wave of loneliness and utter desolation was unexpected and devastating. The new life she had begun to build, a new understanding of herself, and a new love with Logan felt like it had all been swept away in a moment. The new loss reignited and intensified the original. She had lost something before, but so much more now.

She relived every moment with Logan. *What did I miss?* She realized now she had fallen in love with him. He had seemed so genuine, so kind and caring. His quick wit, ready laugh, and easy company were a combination she had never experienced with anyone else. It had been so easy to spend time with him. *Am I just a fling to him? When he went to Denver, did he go alone? Had Stormy had been with him and that's why he didn't respond to my message?* Anna knew he had explained that he had been in an area without a phone signal, but now she wondered if that was the truth.

She wanted to believe him, but how else could she interpret the conversation between Stormy and Roy? From what Anna had overheard, Roy had not acted like Stormy had said anything odd. He had responded as if a marriage between Stormy and Logan were a foregone conclusion. But if that were true, why would he act so welcoming when Anna had been to dinner at the ranch? She pondered that and realized she had been treated like everyone else at the table. She had been simply another friend, a welcomed guest of no special significance. She desperately wanted to know the truth, but at this moment she had no desire to talk to Logan. All the time they had spent together, the hours of talking and texting. How could he be such a liar? *What was the point of talking to him now?* she wondered. *It's not like I would believe anything he said anyway.*

In time, the stream of tears stopped and the gut-wrenching sobs subsided. She no longer had the energy to cry. She hiccupped and laid her head back against the pillows on the loveseat. She remembered the night when she and Logan had sat here, talking and touching. A deep longing and sadness seemed to settle over her, adding to the empty loneliness. She forced herself momentarily in the direction of anger. The all-too-familiar humiliation of a man's rejection. *Why does this keep happening to me? What is so wrong with me that I'm always somebody's second choice? No, I'm not going to be second choice. It's his loss. I'm not going to keep crying over him.* For a moment, she felt the pull of melancholy but fought the urge to give in.

"No," she said aloud as she stood. "He's just a man. The most amazing, tender, caring, wonderful man I have ever met, but still just a man. Two months ago, you didn't even know he existed and now you are letting him almost destroy you. What would Dad say right now?"

She willed herself to resurrect her father's spirit and seek his guidance. Throughout her life, he always had pearls of wisdom to help her navigate difficult situations. *Where is that Viking heart Dad said I had?* she thought. *I need to take the pain and learn from it, use it for something more productive than pity.* She needed to find some kind of peace, an emotional balance. Swallowing hard over the lump in her throat, she ignored the nausea and buzzing in her head. Resolutely, she headed for the shower.

Standing under the stinging spray, Anna felt her energy return. She allowed the pain to turn into defiance and a little anger. Spending far more time than she normally would, she scrubbed her hair, loofahed every inch of skin, and used a pumice stone on her rough heels. She sought rejuvenation. When she stepped out of the shower, the agonizing emptiness in her chest had subsided to a lesser throbbing ache, and she felt a small spark of energy. She used vigorous strokes with the towel to fan the energy as she dried off. Pulling her still-damp hair into a ponytail, she donned her leotard and padded into the living room. Anna selected her favorite selection of calming but upbeat music, took a deep cleansing breath, and began her yoga routine.

She focused on the deep relaxation poses, concentrating on slow and steady breathing. Anna allowed the stress to drift away, focusing on integrating her body, mind, and breath. She felt her spirit calm and her peace return. The clarity of mind didn't take away the pain she felt and the emptiness was still present but manageable. To her disappointment, no wisdom came to her in her father's voice as guidance or advice. She had gained a greater understanding of herself over the past few weeks and was not about to lose the tenuous hold she had on her new awareness. She felt like she was at a crossroads; as trite as the cliché was, it felt right. The search for the truth in the past would give her an understanding of her history, but definite decision-making put her in control of the future. Should she concentrate on the past or the future? It was a decision that would have to be made soon.

Anna felt more in control and tried to focus on the positive points of her life. She decided a visit to the Senior Center would be both sufficiently distracting and be a constructive use of time. She quickly dressed in jeans and a T-shirt and headed to her car, deciding to forego the walk through town.

As she walked into the activity room, a familiar sense of welcome came over her. Anna paused to say hello to several people she had become acquainted with, as she made her way over to the corner where Hazel and Gladys were engaged in a card game with two others.

"Anna, dear, how good to see you," Gladys said, looking up as Anna approached.

"Sugar, I didn't know you were coming by today," Hazel stood up and pulled Anna into a grandmotherly embrace.

"How are you, Hazel? You are looking beautiful," Anna said, holding onto the hug as long as possible.

Gladys stood up, patting Anna's shoulder until Hazel relinquished control and then Gladys pulled Anna into a bear hug of her own.

"Sit, sit, talk as we play," Hazel insisted, nodding at the other two occupants. "Anna, this is Buddy and Les. Boys, this is Anna."

"Ahhh, I know Anna. She's been coming around for weeks now, working in the office and doing meals." Buddy turned and looked at Anna. "Haven't had a chance to sit and talk with you yet."

Anna pulled up a chair and watched as Les shuffled and dealt the cards.

"So, Anna, I am sorry I haven't seen you recently. I went to visit my daughter in Tulsa – that's Bo's mamma. Gladys did tell me you've been volunteering here," Hazel said. Anna held back a smile as Hazel talked, but her eyes never left Les.

"Yes, I'll probably be here in the center more often, but the past couple of weeks I've been doing errands for home-bounds."

"Oh, Anna, that is nice of you."

"Well, I enjoy it, and it's keeping me busy now."

"How is your project coming along? Les, Buddy, Anna here is doing research on the history of Lander," Hazel explained.

"I am trying to decide the next step in that. I got off track and pretty much stopped. A guy…but that's something else," Anna said wanly. "Anyway, after the story you shared, I thought what I was looking for might be in Idaho Falls. I went there for a couple of days, but it didn't pan out. I took a break and did some other things, but now I want to finish what I started. Picking it up again, I guess."

"What was it you thought you were gonna find over there?" Les asked.

"Lester, don't be rude," Gladys chided. "That is her personal business."

Anna sighed. "No, I suppose it couldn't do any harm telling you the whole story. I actually came here, to Lander I mean, to find my grandparents."

"Who are they?" Buddy asked, his interested piqued.

"That's the problem, I don't exactly know. I'm not even certain that either of them were from Lander. I'm following clues."

All four set their cards down and stared at her. "I think there is a lot you didn't share with us on your last visit, Anna," Hazel said slowly. "Why don't you start at the beginning and tell us everything?"

Anna twisted her lips into a wry grin, shook her head, and snorted in an unladylike fashion. "Okay, this may sound crazy, or offend somebody, but here goes," she said, shrugging. "My mother passed away a little more than a year ago, and my father was killed in an accident a few months back. When I was packing up their house, I came across a strange file among my father's possessions. It seems that after my mother died, he decided to do some traveling and applied for a passport. The passport was denied due to a problem with his birth certificate. He started to research and found out that he was adopted when he was a baby. Before that moment, he had no idea. And he never mentioned anything to me. The first inkling I ever had was when I found that box. One of the notes in the file was that the birth mother requested the child's middle name be Lander. Lander was my father's middle name. That was really my only solid clue. There were other papers, other references and notes, but I started here."

She took a breath and looked around the table. "Hazel, one item was the reason I was so excited when you mentioned Idaho Falls. That was where my father's adoption was finalized, from what I understand. Unfortunately, I don't have enough solid evidence to prove my relationship with him and get the original birth certificate. He must have made it that far in his research before he died because he had paperwork about the Idaho voluntary adoption registry. All I have to really go on is a few slivers of information and his date of birth, April 25, 1948."

Anna looked over at Hazel, who had a shocked expression on her face. Anna thought she even looked a little pale.

"Hazel, what's wrong, is it your heart? Do you feel sick?" Anna felt a deep panic at the sight of her new friend's face. She was suddenly terrified of losing another person dear to her.

Hazel blew out the breath she had been holding, shaking her head. "No, dear, I am fine. But, Anna, honey, part of your search is over. I know who your grandmother is."

Anna stared, unable to formulate any thought. This day was testing the limits of her ability to cope.

Anna walked into the cafe feeling shell-shocked. Her day had started off happy, then taken a turn toward anguish, and now something that was of paramount importance to her had fallen in her lap and she should be elated. It was difficult for her to be happy because the pain of Logan's betrayal was still twisting in her gut. Annoyed, she pushed the thought aside and tried to focus on the amazing discovery she had made.

It was after two, and the lunch rush had tapered off. As Anna looked around, the restaurant was nearly empty, and she was thankful. She needed to talk to Kim about several things, but one question was burning more than the others.

"Hey girl," Kim said as she breezed out of the kitchen, then stopped when she saw Anna face. "Jeez, girlfriend, what's wrong?"

Anna fought to keep control as her eyes immediately welled up with unshed tears at her friend's concern. She took a deep breath and looked at the ceiling, blinking rapidly. She clenched her jaw and her fists, then shook her head as she exhaled sharply.

"Whew. We have some things to talk about. Can you take a break? Do you have a few minutes?" Anna's eyes begged Kim.

Kim looked at the clock and nodded. "You know what, chick? I'm gonna clock out. They can handle this without me and I was about done for the day anyhow." Kim reached over the counter and rubbed Anna's shoulder. "You hang on. Gimme a minute and we'll sit."

As Kim disappeared to the kitchen, Anna selected a booth in the back where they could talk in relative privacy. She grabbed a cup of coffee and waited for Kim.

A moment later, her friend slid in across from her and set down two glasses of water. "Spill it," she demanded without preamble.

Anna studied her for a moment. "Are Logan and Stormy Adams involved?"

Kim looked confused.

"Before you answer that, this morning Stormy was talking to Roy about her engagement to Logan. Not that they were engaged but that they would be. I don't understand."

"Logan and Stormy have a long history."

Anna sighed. "I can't believe this. I am so stupid."

"I am not sure I understand," Kim said.

"I thought that Logan and I were dating, like a normal dating relationship," Anna said, shaking her head. "We have been out to dinner, I went to the ranch, he came to my place for dinner right after I moved in, we've been out a couple of times since, and he took me to the rodeo. We talk all the time, we text, he calls me. I shared so much personal stuff with him. And all that time he had a girlfriend. Really a fiancée, I guess." Anna blinked, fighting back the tears that threatened to spill. She grit her teeth and dug deep to find anger to overcome the hurt.

"You just happened to overhear this? How did that happen exactly?" Kim sounded skeptical.

"I took a temp job at the office where she works. I overheard her and Roy talking." Anna laughed bitterly. "I can't believe I did it, but I walked out. I didn't say a word, I sort of bolted out the back door." She took a deep breath, working to maintain control.

"I am so sorry." Kim looked ready to cry herself. "I don't even know what to say, girlfriend. This sucks. It really sucks."

"I've never walked out on a job, but I couldn't believe it. No one said anything and I had never even seen the two of them together. But, then, I guess not too many people have seen him with me, like an actual date setting."

"They have been so on-again, off-again I don't think anyone around here even pays attention to which they are. I really had no idea you and Logan were anything more than friends."

"I thought we had something," Anna said softly, staring out of the window.

"Oh, Anna, I am so sorry. I don't even know what to say. I can't believe Logan would be serious about Stormy and seeing you too. It's not like him."

"Do you think I misunderstood friendship for something more?"

"I don't know. Do you think that's possible?"

Anna fought the lump building in her throat. "It seemed like so much more. I thought we really had something. We have great chemistry, but we've talked, shared, so much."

"Anna, girl, if you think so, then you have to talk to him. You have to know what's going on."

"Honestly, the thought of that makes me sick to my stomach. I think I need a break. Some distance and time to think."

"Are you thinking about going back to Iowa?" Kim asked, surprised. "Are you giving up your search for your grandparents?"

Anna chuckled, shaking her head, "You know, Kim, it has been one crazy day."

"I gather," Kim said wryly.

"About that research thing, well, I have part of my answer on that. I know who my grandmother is."

"What!" Kim shrieked. "And you didn't lead with that? Yes, let's focus on something good for a minute. Who? Who? How did you find out? Details, I need details."

"It was Hazel. If I had talked to her longer the first time we met, I would have known then."

"Hazel is your grandmother?" Kim whistled softly. "I did not see that coming."

Anna laughed. "No, but that would be fun, wouldn't it? Today, I was at the center and brought Hazel up to speed on what happened in Idaho."

"Yeah," Kim nodded, anxious to hear the story.

"So, today, Hazel was playing cards with a few other people, and they wanted to know the full story. Specifically, what I was researching and why. I explained finding my dad's research and everything that had happened up to this point. Finally, I told her really the only thing I know for certain is that he was born in Idaho and his date of birth. That's what did it."

"What was?"

"Just the date and the adoption."

"I don't understand." Kim looked at Anna, shaking her head in confusion.

"Hazel knew who my grandmother was because she knew her. The story she had told me before about the girl from the boarding house, the one that was her friend, the part she didn't tell me was the secret she kept. She had promised Sunny that she would never tell anyone, and she kept that promise until today."

"A secret about her pregnancy?" Kim said slowly.

"Exactly. When Sunny found out she was pregnant, she went to the baby's father. I guess things didn't go well because Hazel said Sunny was upset and then asked for help."

"So who was the father?"

"Sunny never told Hazel who it was. She asked Hazel to help her get to Idaho Falls and Hazel made sure some of the church folks got her set up. Hazel said it was the closest large town out of Wyoming where Sunny could have the baby and arrange for an adoption. She didn't want the scandal of having the baby here."

"That is unbelievable." Kim sat back, digesting the story, with dozens of questions forming in her mind. "So, now what?"

"I try to find her, I guess," Anna said.

"How?"

"Hazel stayed in touch with her for a while, a few years anyway. The last she knew, Sunny had gotten married to a man named Art Rogers and they lived in Mesa, Arizona."

"That's pretty specific."

"Yeah," Anna replied. "If I can find her in Mesa, I think I'll drive down there and work up the courage to see her. I need some distance from this Logan thing anyway."

"Jeez, Anna you're right. What an unbelievable day."

CHAPTER EIGHTEEN

Anna sat on the small patio at her summerhouse and stared at her laptop. The light breeze kept her comfortably cool and scented the air with the blended aroma of lilac and pine. It was pleasant, and the lilac reminded her of Iowa. Her mother had loved the scent and had planted a lilac bush outside her kitchen window. Condensation collected on her glass of lemonade, droplets rolling down the sides, and making a small pool on the glass tabletop.

Her cell phone buzzed. She saw the name on the screen. Logan.

She ignored him.

Her heart was torn. She desperately wanted to see Logan, to talk with him, but she was afraid he would confirm what she already knew. She felt like a coward for not facing him. She was also angry. She should be happy and excited right now, but she felt like he'd stolen that from her. Logan and Stormy. The thought of it sickened her to her stomach again. But that wasn't fair. It was just Logan really. And she wouldn't give in to the temptation again. Like Kim said, focus on the positive. She had found the first part of what she had been searching for – her grandmother. A quick Internet search had found several listings around Mesa that were possibilities. At this point, based on what Hazel had said, it was the right name in the right area. It was more information than she had before she came to Lander. This was more than a clue; it was a solid lead. She wanted to share her excitement with Logan. He had been so supportive and so helpful in her efforts that it seemed natural to tell him. Unfortunately, he was the very reason that she could not enjoy this moment. Her heart ached from his betrayal, and it was hard to think of anything else. Except how much she missed her father. She would love to talk to him about all this right now.

Feeling very much alone, she closed the laptop. She had to finish what she started. Meeting Logan was not something she had planned on, but she would not have chosen to have it any other way. She would cherish the times with him and keep those memories close. She didn't think she would ever stop loving him, even though he had been a part of her life for such a short amount of time. He was a part of her now. The pain she could do without, however, and a distraction was exactly what she needed right now. She picked up the patio area and headed inside. She needed to pack for a trip to Arizona.

Anna considered her route options. Either way, she would be on the road for fifteen hours or more and would stop for the night somewhere along the way. The fastest route would take her on Interstate 15 through Utah from Salt Lake and Provo down to Flagstaff. The other route was along the eastern side of Utah and western Colorado, using several smaller highways. She was no stranger to road trips, but in the past had always stuck to the Interstates. Her recent trip to Idaho Falls had introduced her to the beauty of this part of the country. She had heard how scenic and breathtaking the Colorado Mountains were and this was her opportunity to experience part of it. Since she was in no hurry, taking the slightly longer, more scenic route would be an opportunity she could not pass up. It would be more interesting than the monotony of a four-lane interstate, and the lack of regular exits populated with the standard fare of fast-food chain restaurants might allow her to sample some of the local flavor.

As she prepared for the trip, Anna could not help but think she might never see Lander or the summerhouse again. She had friends here and loved the area, but she hesitated to consider a permanent move. Seeing Logan, even on occasion, would be too deep a pain to tolerate. Even now, she could not bring herself to contact him and let him know she was leaving. To satisfy the urge, she left brief messages with Kim and Margaret, promising to provide more detail later.

When she picked up her phone, she saw the notice that Logan had left a voicemail several hours before. She angrily punched the digits to access the message and deleted it without listening. She wasn't going to get pulled back into the attraction for him, the relationship she already missed. Maybe when the hurt eased and her anger cooled she could be more rational, but right now all she wanted to do was be as far from him as possible. She wasn't sure if she was moving toward the answer of her grandparents by going to Arizona or using it as a convenient way to avoid Logan. She admitted to herself it was probably a bit of both.

It was only a week into July, but she had paid her rent through the end of the month. Her agreement with the owner had been a verbal renewal month-to-month. If she was not here to make the request, the owner would assume she was finished with the rental. Anna had packed all her belongings and loaded everything into her old Civic, including a cooler full of items from the refrigerator. She didn't have much, but the water, fruit, and cheese would come in handy on the road. She hesitated, but at the last minute, decided to retain the key. If she found her grandmother and decided to stay in Arizona, or return to Iowa, she would mail the key back. If she ended up returning to Lander before the end of the month, she would have a place to stay. It would be embarrassing to leave the key then have to call for a spare if she decided to come back.

When she left town, Anna opted for the road less traveled, as she thought of it, and headed south for Highway 28, then took 191 into Utah. The route took her through Flaming Gorge National Recreation Area, which she reached after about three hours of driving. She reasoned it was a good time to stop and stretch her legs.

The scenic drive was gorgeous, from the multi-colored rock walls, the thick forest, deep canyons, to the sparkling water of the reservoir. Anna found a parking area and a marked trail. Growing up in Iowa, the area around Lander, in Wyoming, was spectacular to her, but this area was stunning. The late morning sun shimmered off the water and the shadows cast from the cliffs and overhead clouds were fluid and ever-changing.

She checked her phone and saw a text message.

Hey babe, I left you a voicemail. Free for dinner?

She ignored it and threw the phone back in the passenger seat. After checking the large billboard of trails, Anna chose a wide, moderate incline path that the sign indicated was beginner level. Knowing she would be getting back in the car for many more hours of driving, she had no desire for heavy exercise or to work up a sweat and be left craving a shower for the next six hours. The easy trail afforded an outstanding view.

She worked off her anger and frustration as she walked. How could she have been so stupid to trust her heart to another man? This time she was the other woman. *That part is really disgusting*, she thought. *All the time I thought he was with me, he was with her and sneaking around with me. What kind of idiot does that make me?* She worked the hurt into anger and attempted to burn off the anger with physical exertion. She knew it was working when the weight lifted, and the twisting knot in her gut eased. *I've done this before*, she thought, *getting over a guy, it's old hat. No problem.* Anna knew that Logan wasn't like any other guy, and nothing about this was old hat. She worked the mantra over in her head anyway.

The air was clear and fresh, without the typical Midwestern mugginess of mid-July. Anna was beginning to appreciate summer in this part of the country. She was not certain she wanted to test out the winters, but that decision was a long way off. She kept climbing. As she reached the end of the trail, she topped the hill. Her romantic troubles seemed far away from this vantage point. In this moment, she enjoyed the timeless beauty of nature and listened to the uncomplicated chirps and whistles of birdsong and the hum of insects. It was somehow alive with activity yet calming and peaceful.

Anna finished the slow hike in just over an hour. She was soon back in the Honda and motivated for the next leg of the drive. She deliberately ignored looking at her cell phone. The route along 191 was officially designated as the Flaming Gorge Scenic Byway. The brochure indicated it was nearly one hundred and fifty miles long, taking her all the way to Vernal before she would veer east into Colorado. Cutting back to the west before Grand Junction, she would be back in Utah until she crossed into Arizona. By late afternoon, she stopped for fuel in Loma, Colorado, and followed Interstate 70 back into Utah before turning on to Highway 191 again. She found she enjoyed the break from the smaller, winding roads as she traveled the smooth interstate for fifty miles.

From studying the map, Anna determined Moab, Utah, was about halfway along her route and would be about the time she would be ready to stop for the day. It was a little after six o'clock when she came near and was happy to see that there were a number of hotels in the Moab area. She had arbitrarily chosen it as the halfway point, but it had not looked very big on the map, so she was worried there may not be many options for accommodations. Once she arrived, Anna realized she should have been more diligent in her research. Moab was a popular tourist destination with fantastic national parks and amazing rock formations. After securing a room at the third hotel she tried, she was thankful to be out of the car for the day.

The temptation to stay and explore the area was strong. She was almost tempted to change her original plan of an early start and limited-stop drive the next day. She had no idea this area was so beautiful. But, now that she was getting close, she was anxious for the opportunity to meet her grandmother. She needed to know the answers to her questions and to understand why her grandmother had made the choices she had made. Perhaps finding those answers would help Anna make the decisions in her own life and start to feel more settled. She wanted to ask her grandmother why she given up her own child. Who was the father? Why did the father not want his child, or did he even know? Anna was not sure at this point whether she would even be able to ask the questions when face-to-face with her grandmother.

In the end, the pull of her family's history was too strong. She had lived with the mystery for weeks and the answer seemed so close. Anna had little trouble sleeping and woke around dawn. She sipped coffee and watched the early morning rays of the sunrise over the mountains. She again thought of how calming the scene was and how far away her life in Lander seemed. The empty ache of missing her father and the blinding pain of losing Logan eased. It was strange that she thought in those terms. She missed her father because he was not physically here, yet he was still with her. Anna felt his presence, comforting her when she remembered his words of advice or recalled memories of their family time together. The thought of him was accompanied by a bittersweet ache that he was no longer there. When she remembered her time with Logan, the pain was keen. Her love for him was still there, she could feel it, but it was overwhelmed by a sense of loss for the future they could have had, that had dissipated without warning. Anna focused again on the mountains and the sunrise. This was the promise of a fresh start each new day. She vowed as she put miles between herself and Lander that she would distance the longing of her heart.

Focused on her goal and reenergized to make progress, Anna packed up the car and again headed south. Her GPS indicated it would be seven to eight hours, so after mentally adding in additional time for stops along the way, she estimated she would arrive in Mesa around four-thirty or so. Anna was able to resist the urge to pull off and explore the many natural wonders, monuments, and tourist attractions along the way. She stopped for fuel, food, and a few short walks to stretch her legs. The drive was easy and the miles passed quickly through Utah and into Arizona, past Flagstaff, Sedona, and south toward Phoenix. By the time Anna arrived in Mesa, the sun was still strong. She found a hotel and checked in for a three-day stay, confirming that it could be extended if necessary. The Arizona heat was oppressive. Her phone gauged it at 105. Anna wondered how anyone could voluntarily endure such temperatures day after day. She felt like she could melt into a puddle of sweat at any moment. There was an uncomfortable slickness on the backs of her legs as she realized a glaze of sweat clung to her like a coating of cooking oil. It was not nearly as humid as many summer days in Iowa, but the lack of moisture in the air didn't make it any more tolerable for her.

Heaving her bag from the car, the effort felt monumental. She was relieved to duck inside the air-conditioned lobby and make her way to her assigned room. Anna threw her bag on the queen-sized bed and looked around. The room was predictably plain for the low-budget chain hotel, but it was clean and seemed comfortable enough for her purposes. One bed, a small couch facing a cheap coffee table, a floor lamp next to a small reading chair, and a desk with a chair up against the wall.

Anna dug through her bag, pulling out the shower essentials. The water pressure was excellent, so she indulged in the alternating relaxing hot and invigorating cold spray for much longer than her normal routine. Suitably refreshed, she pulled on cotton shorts and a tank top. She flopped down on one of the chairs, kicked her feet over the arm, and opened the contact list on her phone. She hit Kim's name and her friend answered on the second ring.

"I'm here," she said without preamble.

"Girlfriend, I was a little worried about you," Kim said, the sigh in her voice reflecting her relief. "Thank you for calling me. How are you doing?"

"It's beautiful here. It was a great drive. Lots to see, a little hot," Anna said, ticking things off on her fingers, the gestures unappreciated in the empty room. "I'm great as long as I keep my mind on other things. Anything."

"Are you sure leaving was a good idea?"

"Yeah. I came to Lander to find my grandparents, and I did that. The next step was to talk to one of them. The only one I can be sure of is here, so I'm here to talk to her," Anna said as she looked toward the ceiling and squeezed her eyes closed tightly.

"You don't think you should have talked to Logan?" Kim asked pointedly.

"I'm sure I will at some point; I'm not ready yet. He keeps calling and texting," Anna admitted.

"Why don't you talk to him? Just hear what he has to say."

"And hear him say he's getting married but he doesn't love her? That she doesn't understand him? Or maybe it's a family obligation and a marriage in name only so he wants to keep dating me?" Anna couldn't keep the bitter edge out of her voice.

"Well…"

"I don't see how this works out, really," Anna said, interrupting Kim. "And I need to know how I feel and what I really want before I talk to him. I came out there to find my family, my history, and with Logan, I lost sight of that. What if I stay in Arizona? What if I want to go back to Iowa? How does a rancher from Wyoming fit into that?"

"You're probably right about that," Kim admitted.

"Stormy may be better for him, but if I want to fight for him, I think I should be sure it's a battle I want to win."

"All right, girlfriend, I'll run interference for you to give you some time. No promises on how long, though." Kim laughed. "I think you guys would be good together, and if he convinces you to come back here, I wouldn't be upset to have my friend back."

"You're a sweetheart, Kim. Thank you for everything. I'll call you in a few days and let you know how things are going." Anna ended the call then dialed another number from memory. She spent twenty minutes on the phone with Margaret, updating her on the grandparent search and deliberately leaving out any details of her romantic life. Once her honorary aunt was satisfied she was still safe and healthy, that no marauders or serial killers had claimed her as a victim, Anna promised to call the following weekend and talk more. Responding to the hunger pangs that now plagued her, Anna rummaged through the drawers in the desk for the hotel's courtesy binder, hoping to find some local food options. She was pleased to find a list of restaurants that included ones nearby that delivered. Placing a quick call, she secured a dinner order.

Basic creature comforts attended to, Anna turned her attention to her main goal. She organized a space on the table-style desk for her laptop and notepad. Pulling up a chair, she opened the massive local phone book. She should feel like the dry research was old hat by now, but Anna felt a tingle of excitement. This time she was not randomly searching through old newspapers. This time, she was starting the local search for her grandmother. Her grandmother, Sunny Rogers.

By the time dinner arrived, Anna had short-listed only three names and addresses. The fragrant lasagna and crisp Italian bread tasted better than any she had eaten in months. As she savored the meal, she considered her approach.

The area had several senior communities, and two of the names had addresses in different ones. A third name Anna had found was "S. Rogers" but she decided to wait for follow-up until she explored the first two. The most direct approach would be to simply introduce herself and explain her research.

Anna considered the potential responses, and most were not good. It was possible that memory loss would be a factor. If she found the right Sunny, she might not remember. Or if she did remember, she might deny she had given a child up for adoption. If whatever reason had led her grandmother to that action was still important in her mind, she might be in denial. It might be some terrible secret that Sunny believed buried, and Anna might end up traumatizing a total stranger. Anna wondered if she talked to each woman and each denied having a child she gave up, how could she be sure they were telling the truth? What if one of the women admitted she was the birth mother but refused to talk about it? Anna would be no further along in solving the mystery than she was now.

It was so much easier talking with Gladys and Hazel. They had been open with her, enjoying the company of a new friend. The old gossip had seemed irrelevant to them. Anna knew that was the answer. She needed to meet Sunny in the same way she had met Gladys and Hazel. An uncomplicated friendship to establish trust would take longer, but honestly, she thought to herself, where else do I have to be?

CHAPTER NINETEEN

"Miss Miller, please come into my office." The administrator of SunVilla Village smiled and gestured.

Anna smiled and dutifully followed the gray-haired figure. This was her second stop today, filling out paperwork and completing the process to become a volunteer at the senior community center. Anna had found a Sunshine Rodgers and a Sunny Rogers, each living in different communities. She applied to work at both, hoping that she could befriend each one and, in time, feel comfortable enough to launch a personal conversation about children. Although she had no idea how that would ever be comfortable. It was probably a crazy plan and would never work, but she could not think of anything else. If she had stayed in Lander, she would have spent much of her time volunteering at a senior center anyway, so this really wasn't that much different. She would still be helping, but she might find her family in the process. After a brief interview process and confirming details, the administrator seemed thankful. "We never have enough volunteers, and you will be so welcome."

"Thank you. I am looking forward to spending time here," Anna said truthfully.

"Come back the day after tomorrow at one o'clock and I'll have Iris give you the tour." Anna was thrilled she wouldn't have excess time to fill up. Apparently, here in Arizona, the background check and verification was much faster. Her first stop at Prairie Sun Valley had been equally successful. They had requested she spend two hours a day helping in the office until she cleared the background check.

For two days, Anna explored the area, indulging in shopping and a trip to the movie theatre when she wasn't in the Prairie Sun Valley office. She had not realized the culture shock she would have to arrive in a sprawling major metropolitan area after spending weeks in a small Wyoming town. She started to feel a little homesick for the quiet pace of life in Lander. She missed her friends but staunchly refused to think about Logan.

It was better when she spent time at the senior centers, even though she was assigned to the office for the first few days. She was able to check the resident list and quickly found Sunny's name. She was one step closer. Spending time with the residents was even more rewarding and, thankfully, distracting. She enjoyed hearing their stories and memories from their lives, and she encouraged them to share while they played games or worked on other projects. The centers understood that staying active played a vital role in mental sharpness and overall energy.

Anna shadowed several other volunteers during her training, working alongside them, but Anna considered the use of the term "working" to be a stretch. She sat and played cards, relying on several of the seniors to teach her the basics of Euchre, Hearts, Gin Rummy, and Pinochle. One sharp resident had eyed her suspiciously when she insisted she had never played and needed the game explained in detail. "Balderdash," he scoffed. Anna smiled demurely and winked.

In addition to playing games, she helped with errands, pet walking, and chauffeuring residents to doctor's appointments. After nearly a week, Anna was becoming familiar with the grounds. Nearly every day was hot and sunny, and her routine settled into a comfortable balance of three mornings a week at Prairie Sun Valley and three afternoons a week at SunVilla Village. She enjoyed the variety and each day had a full morning or afternoon to herself. Sundays, she had decided, would be a day to herself. She had created a life for herself in Lander, and she could do it again here in Mesa. Well, she could make friends, anyway. She had no desire to dip her toe into the dating pool. She would rather be bitten by a rattlesnake then rescued by a scorpion-toting coyote than have a man in her life again. Rattlesnakes and scorpions in the same thought made Anna realize how worried she had been after reading the flyers for hiking trails in the area. There were a surprising number of warnings. She thought the bears and mountain lions were worrisome in Wyoming, but the dangers in the desert might be worse.

She contemplated the next day's hiking destination as the pulled into the lot at SunVilla Village for her afternoon shift. She eased into what had become her favorite parking spot, near the back of the lot under a large shade tree. She exited and started toward the main building when she noticed a woman struggling to pull a wheeled cart, her arms loaded with books.

Chuckling, Anna rushed to rescue the books before they spilled to the ground.

"Aren't you just an angel, appearing out of nowhere to come to my aid," the woman exclaimed happily.

"I'm a volunteer here, so I'm happy to help. It would be a shame to lose all these books. You must be an avid reader."

"Well, I have the time and might as well keep busy, you know," she quipped with a bright smile.

"I'm Anna Miller," she replied, shifting the pile of books to one arm, so she could extend her other to shake hands.

"Hello, sweetheart. I'm Sunny Rogers." The word sounded like "sveethart," and the accent of the melodious voice instantly reminded Anna of the glamorous actress Zsa Zsa Gabor. Anna resisted the sudden urge to ask her to say "dahling." The old woman's grip was firm at the fingertips but without pressure from the palm. Anna supported the thin hand, cupping it with her own. Her heart pounded and she felt her palms grow damp. She looked into eyes that were a replica of her father's, a smoky gray that never took on a blue hue. This was her grandmother. She was alive, and Anna had found her. Her heart leapt to her throat and her mouth went dry. For a moment, she swore she felt lightheaded. In that instant, the world was surreal.

"Here, let me carry these and we can walk together. Do you have a unit nearby?" Anna asked, shifting the books again, trying to act nonchalant.

"Thank you, dahling. You are sweet. They are not that heavy, but the walk in the heat wears me out."

"Of course, it's my pleasure." Anna resisted the urge to laugh out loud from sheer happiness. The woman's accent was adorable.

"I suppose it doesn't do me much good to have this little cart; when I bring back so much it doesn't fit. Why is it we always want to take more than we can carry?" Sunny asked philosophically. Sunny continued to chat without noticing Anna's long silences and curious glances.

They reached Sunny's unit, and Anna waited as the older lady unlocked the door and stepped inside. It was a small but well-furnished one-bedroom unit. Stepping inside to the living room, Anna could see the doors to the bathroom and single bedroom. In front of her, the living room continued on to a small eat-in kitchen that was marked by the change from carpet to tile. The walls were filled with a mix of landscape paintings, family portraits, collages of snapshots, and obvious souvenirs from a long life well-lived.

"You can just set those books over on the table. Thank you, sweetie."

"Oh my, Sunny, is this your family?" Anna looked at the grouping of photos on the table. "They are lovely. Your sons or daughters?"

"My, yes, that is quite a group, now isn't it? We had that taken, oh, probably ten, twelve years ago now, I think," Sunny said, shuffling slightly over the carpeted floor. "My, ye ow."

Anna noticed the odd phrase but said nothing.

"Yes, now, this is my family. My husband, Art, the tall one in the back. He's passed away now. My son, Charles, and my daughter Pamela, with her husband Dean. The girl there is Ashley, my granddaughter."

Anna looked at a photograph of her aunt, her uncle, and a cousin while she stood next to her grandmother. But she couldn't acknowledge it yet. Not yet. "They're beautiful. Do they live around here?" Anna's voice caught in her throat, and she coughed to cover her emotion.

"Pamela and Dean do."

"That's nice. And they visit?"

"I see Pam every Sunday when they take me to dinner. Ashley is married now and has two boys, a set of twins as cute as they can be. They live down in Tucson. I see them a few times a year. Pamela takes me down to see them. Charles lives in Denver and travels quite a bit, but he calls me every week."

"It sounds like you are all very close. That is so nice, Sunny." Anna cleared her throat and abruptly changed the subject. "So, what can I do here?"

"I would welcome a bit of help putting those groceries away, thank you," Sunny said.

Anna put the few items away, then wrote her number on a piece of paper, handing it to Sunny. "I need to go back to the community room this afternoon, but if you need anything, give me a call and I can lend a hand. I can do errands, help with housework, read to you, or just sit in on a card game if you would like."

"Thank you. You are an angel."

Anna impulsively hugged Sunny gently, hiding the emotional tears by turning and leaving quickly. She walked slowly to the main building, blinking rapidly and breathing deep to control her emotions. Try as she might, the butterfly flutter would not still.

Sunny called Anna every few days over the next week. Anna was happy for the distraction from Logan and wanted to get to know Sunny. Anna helped with the housework and kept Sunny company. She shared little of herself, but Sunny kept up a steady stream of jabber that filled in what would have been silence. It was clear to Anna that more than anything, Sunny craved company. Her small apartment had the keepsakes of a long life filled with family and happy memories. The walls were filled with photos, and Anna soon heard many of the stories behind each one.

Sunny also had a number of unusual landscapes displayed. Anna stopped and studied one, drawn to the depiction of a surreal landscape with brilliant colors. There was a wide expanse of green, like a large pasture, but broken up by a huge crevasse, a fissure in the ground exposing brown and black rock that looked almost volcanic. Incongruously set in the middle was a lovely two-story white frame house with a peaceful-looking blue river in front that wound around in a meandering sort of way. The background was dominated by large, mist-shrouded mountains.

"This is an amazing painting. The artist's imagination has really brought the image to life. It's so vivid," she said, captivated.

"Thank you. It's one of my favorites. I love it there."

"There?" Anna asked, surprised. "It's a real place?"

"Yes, that's Þingvellir, a national park in Iceland."

"It's beautiful. Is this your work?"

"Oh, no. A cousin of mine in Iceland did those for me."

"That's Iceland? How fascinating. How did your cousin end up in Iceland?"

"It's home for me. I grew up there. My cousin, Karl, always lived there," Sunny said, smiling.

"I could tell you had an accent but couldn't place it. Let's see, if my geography is right, that's up near Greenland, right?"

Sunny laughed and continued proudly, "Yes, it's one of the Scandinavian countries, originally founded by Vikings from Norway they say."

"Real Vikings? That's quite a claim. So, you're a descendant of Vikings then?" Anna bit back a chuckle. All this time, her dad had been right. They really did have Viking blood. She felt a rush of sadness that she would never be able to tell him.

"Well, yes, I suppose I am."

"Sometime you will have to tell me the story about how you came to America."

"Oh, I'm not sure how interesting that would be. My, so many years ago, I would barely remember anything." Sunny laughed, waving.

"You know, studies have shown that recalling memories is good for your mental agility. So it would be good for you, and I would be a very good listener. I don't know much about Iceland and it would be fascinating."

"You are quite a little salesperson, aren't you?"

"History is important. Ancient history, world history, and personal history." Anna shrugged. "It's all the same, and all of it is important."

"I'm sure it would be very dull, what I could remember," Sunny said, hesitating.

"Please. I would like to hear your story." Anna knew from the look in Sunny's eye she was ready to give in. Anna smiled.

CHAPTER TWENTY

Kim looked across the cafe and the table where Logan and Stormy sat, obviously deep in a heated exchange. She watched as Logan pushed back from the table with the heels of his hand in a gesture of disgust. Kim could see the tic of his jaw muscle as he stared out of the window, looking like he was trying to overcome a desire to throttle the blonde sitting across from him.

After a moment, he sighed, drained his coffee cup, and pushed it to the edge of the table. With an elbow on the table, he rested his chin on his knuckles and stared at Stormy.

Stormy reached out to touch his hand, but he jerked back, pulling away. Her face reflected a carefully crafted look of hurt, which was a thinly-veiled disguise of the contempt and anger that was evident.

Kim reluctantly approached the table to refill the cup. Predictably, she could hear the conversation clearly as she approached.

"I can't believe you could say that to me!" Stormy fumed.

"It's true, Storm," Logan said heavily. "You are like a sister to me and always will be. You and I both know that even when we dated, we never had a spark."

"Logan, we were meant to be together." Stormy's voice had a sharp edge, almost daring him to disagree with her.

"We were more of a habit than anything. That doesn't mean we were meant to be together."

"But our families have history, and we have a legacy to build."

"Stormy, I will not be told how to live my own life. Anna is the one I want in my life, and I am going to go find her. You need to accept that."

"I made sure you won't be leaving Lander anytime soon. You're short by three ranch hands," she said firmly, with an air of confidence. "And if your father manages to track them down, that transmission will make the trip back pretty slow."

Logan stared at her, disbelieving.

"Oh, stop, I'm not psychotic. I didn't do anything to your men; they think that you sent them to Cheyenne for a couple of days. You and I needed some time together. I will help you at the ranch. I couldn't have you chasing after her until you and I have time."

"Stormy, you will not stand in my way."

"I need a little more from you," Stormy said, in a calm and soft voice that gave Logan a queasy feeling in the pit of his stomach.

"No."

"Every woman knows the best way to get a man's attention is to tell him you don't want him," Stormy explained. "You think you want her now because you can't have her. That's all it is. I need you to realize that you are wrong."

"Stormy, if someone wants you in their life, they will put you there. You cannot force, sneak, or bully your way in. You and I are friends, but you cannot make it more than that just because you want to."

Logan stood up suddenly and whirled, nearly running into Kim, who stood frozen, unable to stop herself from blatantly eavesdropping.

"You," Logan said accusingly. "Let's talk over here." Without waiting, Logan stomped to the counter, digging into his pocket for a wad of bills.

A flicker of anger flashed over Stormy's face before assuming a look of calm. Kim knew Stormy hid her emotions well and had never seen her lose control like that before. She almost felt sorry for the woman who had never before been denied anything she wanted. But, honestly, she didn't know why Logan hadn't done it sooner.

Turning away, Kim followed Logan slowly, wishing with her entire being that she could be anywhere else in the world at this moment. Wishing that she had been anywhere else in the world when Anna had come in that day, devastated by Stormy's lie.

Kim nearly slunk to the cash register, where she stood silently.

There was way no way she was going to start the conversation.

"Anna is important to me. It has been more than two weeks since she has talked to me, Kim. It's killing me."

"Logan, I didn't mean to come between you two. I would never deliberately hurt either one of you," Kim said earnestly.

"What did you say to her?" he asked.

"Logan, I am so sorry—" Kim began, but Logan quickly interrupted.

"S'ok. Stormy set her up good. I didn't put it together until after Dad told me about a strange meeting with Stormy at her office. He couldn't figure out why she had called him there."

"So, you already know then?"

"I know enough, based on what Dad said. I found out she had a bogus temp job Stormy called her on for the sole purpose of witnessing her little stage production. I went to Anna's summerhouse when she stopped taking my calls and didn't return messages. The place is cleaned out, Kim." Logan choked on the last words. "She's gone."

"I know."

Logan's eyes flashed. "You know? How is it you know? What did you say to her?"

"She asked about you and Stormy. I only told her you two had a history, I swear."

"Really? So, why did she leave before she talked to me?" Logan asked accusingly. "And where is she?"

"Logan," Kim said, her temper rising. "Not everything in this world is about you. She found her grandmother."

It took Logan hours to unravel the mess that Stormy had made. His first call had been to his father, to warn him about the impending engine trouble. Logan was able to contact each of the ranch hands, and they all promised to return from Cheyenne the following day. He called in favors and helped get the day's chores done without his normal crew. Logan had helped out many neighbors and counted most as close friends. He had not even needed to explain the situation for friends to come help him out.

He knew Anna was his next priority. Kim had told him what Anna had learned from Hazel. Taking no chances that any critical information was overlooked, Logan stopped by the center to talk with Hazel himself.

"It's about time you came here to talk to me," Hazel said with a knowing smile.

"Were you expecting me?"

"You're Anna's young man, aren't you?"

Logan nodded. "Yes, ma'am, Anna's my girl. I think I might need your help to find her so I can convince her of that though. She is the most important thing in the world to me and I need to do whatever I can to make sure she understands that."

Hazel winked and patted the seat beside her. "You just sit right down and we'll work this all out. We have a lot to talk about."

As the sun was setting, Logan pulled a duffle bag from the closet and started packing. He pulled a couple shirts from the closet when he heard the back door slam and various thumping and banging sounds coming from the vicinity of the kitchen.

Logan walked down the hall and leaned on the doorframe, watching his father move about the room, muttering. "Hey, Dad, rough day?"

Roy snorted. "Yeah, something like that. Thanks for the heads up."

"Glad we caught it in time."

"Little miss smarty-pants drained just enough of the fluid to make that tranny a mess. Would have been better if she had drained it all together, then it wouldn't have started a'tall."

"Yes, but her plan was for you to get stranded somewhere, not conveniently stuck right here on the ranch."

"I still don't understand why." Roy assembled a sandwich and settled on one of the barstools at the island.

"Because of the ranch. Or because of Anna, or me, or something along those lines."

"Still lost," Roy said sarcastically.

"Well, I'll give you the highlights and then I'm taking off. Now that I know where Anna is, I'm going there and I'm not going to leave until we talk this out. It's been too long already and she needs to know I never lied to her."

"That girl is something special, Logan. You do what you gotta do. I can wait to hear what started this."

"Short version – Stormy wants to join the ranches, to marry me. After I met Anna, Stormy saw her as a threat and used you to get rid of her. That's what the conversation at the realty office was all about. Anna was doing the filing in the back room and heard everything."

Roy stared at Logan, the realization hitting him as he recalled the conversation, "Jeez, Logan, she musta' been tore up. I am so sorry. I had no idea."

"Stormy planned it that way, Dad. It's not your fault," Logan said, walking over to settle on a stool across the island. "But can we agree this Stormy marriage topic is off the table, permanently?"

"Yeah, yeah," Roy said thoughtfully.

Logan watched as Roy seemed to struggle with an internal thought process.

"Son, there's something else I have to tell you," he said.

At dawn, Logan headed south to Mesa, his head still working to grasp the enormity of what his father had shared.

CHAPTER TWENTY-ONE

Sunny sat in the shade under the large table umbrella. Anna joined her, setting down a tray between them on the table. She had arranged a small plate filled with apple slices, a square of brown bread, butter, a few cookies, a glass of lemonade and a carafe of coffee.

"I have been looking forward to this story," Anna said with a slight laugh. "I did a little research to make sure I knew some basic facts so I didn't look uneducated."

"Did you now? Do tell, what have you learned so far?"

"Iceland is a small island in the Atlantic, south of Greenland and sort of northwest of Ireland. It's a part of Scandinavia, used to be owned by Denmark, but originally settled by Norwegians."

Sunny laughed, clapping her hands delightedly. "Very, very good. Yes, some of Iceland's first settlers came from Norway around 875. But, dear, that was way before my time."

"Of course, but tell me your story. How does someone from Iceland end up in America – in Arizona of all places?"

"My hometown is Dalvik, in northern Iceland. It is a beautiful little village, a harbor on the west shore of Eyjafjörður."

Anna listened to the exotic language roll off Sunny's tongue. The town name sounded like Aye-ya-f'yore-thur. It was very musical listening to Sunny's pronunciation but complicated enough Anna knew she would be never be able to recreate the sounds.

"There are days that I miss it so much," Sunny continued. "I can close my eyes and hear the ocean and the call of the seagulls. The sight of the sun sparkling on the water when the clouds part. The sun is much stronger here, you know. I remember as a little girl running for the sunshine. The clouds are so common in the Icelandic sky. The little patches of sun would make a bright spot on the ground and we would run to stand in the sunshine until the clouds would move and then we would run to the next sunny spot."

Anna poured coffee for Sunny and shook her head at how the woman could drink the hot liquid outdoors in the summer heat.

"I remember the earthquake of 1934. I was just seven years old. It was right after our noon meal on a Saturday in early June. Oh, the ground shook and rumbled something awful. There were whole houses torn top to bottom. Jóhann lived down the street from us and he came to help. Everyone was running around and checking to see who was injured or needed help. Mama was caught under a dresser that had fallen. Jóhann barely even fit in the house but he was so strong he lifted it right off her without any help. I remember he left the village not too long after that. He was unusually big, you know. He was over seven feet tall, he was. He was too big for the fishing boats so he moved to Denmark for work, I think. I heard after the war, he traveled with that Barnum & Bailey show. He was quite famous. Have you ever heard of him? Well, probably not. Anyway, Jóhann K. Pétursson his name was. Such a nice man."

Anna smiled indulgently as Sunny prattled on as the memories assailed her. "Goodness, I haven't thought about that in years. That really had nothing to do with how I came to America, but I got a little homesick there."

Sunny sighed, then continued. "I suppose my story started the summer I was seventeen. Pabbi sent me to Reykjavik to stay with his sister, my Aunt Sunna. I had always been very good in school and was especially good with languages. By the time I was sixteen, I spoke Icelandic, Danish, English, and some Italian. There were more and more troops in Reykjavik and many English-speaking soldiers were coming into the grocery. Pabbi sent me to help them since my English was good and at that time, many Icelanders did not speak English. I was very excited to go."

"Who was Pabbi?" Anna asked.

"Oh, Pabbi, my father. Pabbi is the Icelandic word for father. I guess my mind switched languages on me there. So, Pabbi decided to send me to Reykjavik. I had often gone from our village down to Akureyri on my bike. I remember it was only forty kilometers or so and was a nice ride when the weather was good to take the trip. This time, I packed all my things and went to Akureyri to say goodbye to my friends. I knew I would be gone at least through the next spring. If I had known then it would be so many years before I saw that country again, I think I may have ridden slower." Sunny's voice trailed off and a faraway look came over her face. Anna could see she was lost in the memories.

"Tell me about it," she encouraged. "It must be beautiful there."

"It is, like no other place on earth I think," Sunny said. "It is rugged and beautiful and breathtaking, my homeland. This was before they had what they call now the 'ring road' when I traveled. We would ride horses or our bicycles on the gravel roads and paths. After generations of sheep and horses, the paths are as well-worn as any trails you would find here in America's national parks. I remember that for the first part of the trip I was sad to be leaving my friends, but excited. I can close my eyes and still see the mountains. They are so tall and beautiful there. The sharp cliffs with patches of green everywhere. The white dots of sheep grazing all along the ridges and waterfalls everywhere. The snow is at the very top of the mountains and there are little glaciers where the water comes from every year. The little streams running along the gullies where you look up and see water falling from what seems like a hundred feet above you." She stopped and broke off some of the bread, covered it with the sweet butter, then poured a cup of coffee and sipped.

"That part of Iceland is called Tröllaskagi, you know. That means 'Troll Peninsula,' and it is magical. You need only to look around at all the trolls that were caught in the sunlight and turned to stone to understand that name. I will show you pictures sometime and you will believe. You know, I have not seen those mountains since that summer. I have been back to visit a few times, but never to my village. That first day, I remember the weather was so beautiful. It was not too cold and didn't rain, so I biked all the way to Blönduós. It took all day, but in the summer the midnight sun really does shine until midnight."

Anna grinned, "I've heard the term midnight sun. I never thought about it being a real thing. They don't just call it that for nothing, huh?"

Sunny winked. "No, they don't. I stayed with family for the night and then went on the next day to a friend's farm down Grábrók."

"And how far was that?"

"It was all day. I stopped and rested some, but, oh my, eight hours perhaps?"

"You biked for eight hours? I can't imagine doing that," Anna said, impressed but a little doubtful that Sunny remembered the events accurately.

"Well, times were different then. We biked everywhere. And I grew up on a farm where I was used to working every day and we would after spend hours riding bareback on our horses. Our legs were pretty strong. And I was used to milking the cows, sometimes herding the sheep, and climbing the cliffs to collect bird's eggs and berries. I think the bike ride was a bit of a vacation for me."

Anna laughed.

"From there, the terrain is much flatter. It is closer to the western coastline and there are many small farms with horses and many sheep. The ride was easy then, and I arrived in Reykjavik. I had been there many times before, but this was the first time in several years. I couldn't believe there was so much more activity. My aunt's store was so busy, and I didn't have time to miss the countryside so much. I worked many days with my cousin, Arna."

Sunny paused and nibbled on her snacks, taking another sip of coffee.

"There was so much military there then, in the city. We weren't touched too much by the war, but the servicemen were everywhere. We were encouraged to keep a distance, but they were so exotic compared to Icelandic men. Their courtesies and gallantry were so different. Icelandic men treated women as equals and didn't have any of the courting rituals like flowers or holding the door open. We giggled and simpered like American girls when the military men were around and the Icelandic men would walk away in disgust," she said laughing.

"My, I had forgotten that. So, one day, my cousin begged me to go to the USO dance with her. They were having a famous American singer, Marlene

Dietrich. She wanted to hear the music and dance with one of the dashing soldiers."

Anna smiled at the nostalgic tone in Sunny's voice.

"It was late in the summer, maybe early fall. That time when the Midnight Sun doesn't shine anymore but sometimes the early Northern Lights fly overhead." Sunny's eyes closed and a sad smile played on her thin lips.

"I remember a slight chill in the air as we hurried down the street. We could hear the music from at least a block away. As we got closer, there were all sorts of military men milling about on the street, coming and going. I don't think the door ever stayed closed. When we got inside, it was heavy and warm from so many people. We left our coats and made it through the crowd to get a drink. There were a few people there I knew, girlfriends from town, but mostly it was men in uniform."

"Was that the first time you had been to the USO?"

"Oh, yes. I hadn't been in town long, but Arna knew my English was good enough I could help her talk to any young man there." Sunny laughed. "I am certain to this day that was her intention."

Anna grinned, and silently encouraged Sunny to continue.

"I don't remember the songs, really, but I remember the feeling. It was exciting and new. I wasn't watching where I was going. I was looking all over the room. I ran right into the back of a soldier, and not just a little bump. I nearly soaked his shirt with my drink." Sunny laughed in memory. "He turned around like he was ready to defend himself against an attack and had to look down to find the threat, I was so much shorter than he was. And then he smiled. Oh my, what a smile."

Anna watched as Sunny's face softened, the memory of the love evident on her face.

"We danced and danced and then we talked and talked. It was the first night he started calling me Sunny."

"Started calling you Sunny?" Anna said, confused. "That wasn't your name?" Seeing Sunny's negative shake of her head, Anna asked, "What was your given name?"

"It is Solveig. He didn't have any trouble pronouncing it, but said that

Sol, with an o, meant sun and my smile was like the sun. He was quite the charmer. We…well, we just clicked. After that first night, we wanted to be together. I had to work many days, and he had his duties in the army, but whenever we could we snuck away. We spent every moment we could together over the next few weeks." She looked at Anna with a deep sadness in her eyes. Anna smiled and touched Sunny's shoulder.

"How sweet. It sounds like you had a wonderful connection. What was his name?" Anna held her breath in anticipation.

"Yes, he was quite a man, my Sam." She laughed at a memory. Anna felt a pang of disappointment. Sam? There was no man named Sam in any of her research that she could recall. Samuel, Sampson, what else could Sam be short for?

"I remember once we went to Þingvellir. The place in the painting you admired. Another of his friends was driving," Sunny paused, thinking. "Motor pool, I think you call it." Anna nodded and Sunny continued.

"I remember an old ugly truck, it had a big canvas on the back and it was very noisy. Sam's friend was driving, and there was another couple with us. We went to Þingvellir for the day. I don't remember anything about the other people there that day. I guess we all went our separate ways. I remember Sam was homesick and talked about the beautiful forest near his home. There was a waterfall he liked to go to when he needed to think and there was a little waterfall there at Þingvellir I showed him. We had a little picnic there. We hiked around the area and spent the day talking. I told him the stories of the old Viking encampments held there every year and the history of the park. The fragile moss and how you can't walk on it or the Hidden will punish you."

"The Hidden?" Anna said, interrupting.

Sunny smiled wryly. "Oh, yes. The Hidden Folk are quite real in Iceland. You won't see them unless they want you to, but they are the protectors of the land. If you destroy anything or move a rock that might be their home, misfortune will surely follow. Oh, no, you don't mess with the Hidden."

Anna laughed and shook her head. "All right then. I really can't believe you weren't kidding about the Vikings. That is so cool. I'm sorry, continue your story."

"I told Sam all about the Hidden and he said he understood. The Indians in America had many legends about nature and the consequences of angering the spirits. He made me laugh when he told me he rode his horse through the Popo Agie trail. I thought he was making that up but he told me it was from the language of the Indians there. In the Crow language, the word 'Popo' means 'Head' and 'Agie' means 'River'. He taught me Crow words and I taught him Icelandic ones."

Anna recognized the name of the trail. She had been hiking there a few weeks ago. Sunny did have a connection with Lander; the Popo Agie trail was right outside of town, in Sinks Canyon. She felt relief that she had been on the right track, a sense of anticipation that she was near the truth, and frustration she still didn't know who her grandfather was.

"We had a few wonderful months together," Sunny said wistfully, a slight smile on her lips and a far-away look in her eyes. "We took long walks around the Tjörnin, the pond in Reykjavik. I told him of Icelandic history and he told me about life in America. I cooked Icelandic food for him and we went fishing together. He had many duties for the military but we found time."

"Did he die in the war?" Anna asked softly.

"What? Oh, my no. No, no. We had a wonderful romance and then he had orders to leave Iceland. The US military sent him to another base."

"Oh, so you never saw him again?" Anna said sadly.

Sunny's eyes glinted with mischief. "We were young and adventurous and in love. He was the reason I came to America. We made plans to be together and he helped me make all the arrangements. He said he wanted me to come to America to be with him. After he was sent away, it took months of waiting, but finally in October 1946, I left Iceland and sailed to America."

"What an adventure that must have been," Anna said.

"When the ship came into New York harbor, I saw the Lady Liberty. I was excited, but for the first time, I was really scared and so homesick I wanted to change my mind. I looked at the city across the harbor and everything was so big. Such tall skyscrapers and so many buildings they seemed to go on forever. Just looking at it nearly terrified me."

"I can only imagine what that must have been like for you. I think I would have been bawling like a baby."

Sunny smiled. "Oh, no, not cry. We Icelanders were raised that we could howl or scream or holler, but not cry. A Viking never cries."

"A Viking?" Anna questioned, raising one eyebrow. "Oh, come now, you're not that old," Anna said with a laugh.

"Yes, all Icelanders, most Scandinavian really, but all Icelanders are descendants of Vikings. Yes, the Viking had a reputation for cold-blooded violence and marauding, but there's a greater legacy we still honor. We tend to approach life with an attitude of adventure, self-reliance, tenacity, and tolerance. And contentment of course. We endeavor and we survive." Sunny winked. "And we make sure to enjoy ourselves doing it."

"That is quite a legacy," Anna said. "No wonder you have led such an amazing life. But, I'm sorry, please continue. This story is fascinating."

"Where was I? Oh, yes, the building we came to was immense. There wasn't anything like that in Iceland. In that day, not even a three-story building that I recall. I never knew buildings could be so big or that they would even need to be. After we docked and we went inside, I was disappointed at how…how should I put this? How utilitarian it all was. So little furniture, only a few benches and all very basic. But full of people. Oh, so many, many people. I remember there was so much noise. There were people everywhere and they all looked so poor. There were so many different languages that I didn't understand and such confusion. Some children crying, some children playing. It seemed to me like utter chaos." Sunny shook her head, making a tsk-ing sound with her tongue. "But in the middle of it, the Red Cross workers were bustling about, carrying their clipboards and looking for all the world like they had everything under control. They all were in plain black uniforms I think, but I remember the Red Cross emblem on their hats and they all had armbands with the same emblem. They each had a manifest of passengers from different ships. Somehow they found everyone they were looking for and organized the immigrants, making sure everyone went where they should. I remember they were so nice, so helpful. I felt better as soon as I realized they were in charge of everything. I did feel bad for all those people who didn't speak any English. I thought my English was good but even I had a hard time following some of the very fast talking and some of the words were new to me."

Anna was awed and desperately wished she could pause this moment in time to absorb it all. This was someone who had experienced Ellis Island as an immigrant, one of the key historical elements of American history. She also realized that this was her own grandmother, telling her this personal story. What if she had never found her? Never had the opportunity to hear this? She suddenly felt the desire to share her identity, to let Sunny know she wasn't just sharing this story to an interested person, but she was sharing it with her long-lost granddaughter, her own flesh and blood. But now was not the time. Not yet. Not until she heard the entire story.

She encouraged Sunny to continue. "So where did you go from there? That was Ellis Island, right? That is amazing, what a piece of American history and to experience that firsthand…"

"Yes, I went from there to Grand Central Station, you know. Now that was a beautiful building; very ornate and fancy. It was very large also and so full of people. My; New York had more people I think than the whole of Iceland. Once on the train and away from the bustle of New York, I began to relax and calm down. I slept for hours at a time and each time I woke up, the landscape outside the window changed. At first, there were many towns and so many buildings, then we went through mountains, and then rolling hills of green grass. Later, the land became flat and there were fields of grain as far as I could see. It seemed strange for the land to be so flat, without a hill or mountain in sight. This new country was so big.

"After two days on the train, I finally arrived in Wyoming. In Casper, I had to change trains to get to Lander but it only ran three days a week. I had to stay in Casper for two days waiting for the next train. I remember finding a pretty waterfall. And one night over dinner, an older man told me a story about Ernest Hemingway being in town earlier that year. I had no idea who that was then, but I remembered the name, and over the years, I became quite a fan.

"Finally, after weeks of travel, I made it to the little town of Lander. Anna, my word, it was so beautiful, like a little piece of heaven. And sometimes if I squinted or looked at the mountains just right, it looked a little like Iceland. I wasn't as homesick then. But, then also I had my Sam." Sunny smiled but Anna saw a sadness in her eyes.

The alarm on her wrist beeped softly.

"Is that a medical reminder or an appointment?" Anna asked.

"What? Oh, I'm sorry, I suppose I was woolgathering there for a moment."

"Your alarm is going off," Anna said, pointing.

"Thank you, dear. I didn't hear that. It must be four o'clock. I set that to get ready for our monthly potluck tonight. We like to get together once a month and celebrate birthdays. Isn't that fun?"

"That does sound like fun, yes," Anna said, trying to keep her voice steady. Inside her head she felt like screaming, or at least unleashing an agonizing moan. How could Sunny stop the story here? Anna had no idea how to encourage her to continue. She grit her teeth in frustration and pasted on what she hoped was a convincing nonchalant smile. "I'll head out. The schedule has me back here on Monday, but you call me in the meantime if you need anything."

"Thank you, Anna."

After a quick hug, Anna headed out the door and across the parking lot, her head full of decades-old memories. She could not help being frustrated with where the story had ended. Who was Sam, and what had happened after Sunny arrived in Wyoming?

CHAPTER TWENTY-TWO

Anna parked under the trees to keep her car shaded for the afternoon, and the nervous butterflies in her stomach once again took full flight. It was a beautiful Sunday morning, the sky was clear and the light breeze made the Arizona summer heat tolerable. It was the perfect day for a hike and Anna thought of the trail map she had picked up for Superstition Mountain. There were forty separate trails, and Anna wished she had decided to explore one of those instead of agreeing to the uncomfortable position she faced today.

She had come to terms with getting to know her grandmother incognito, as it were. Sunny thought of her only as "Anna, the helpful volunteer" and nothing more. More than anything, Anna wanted to introduce herself and be able to ask specific questions. She wanted to share photos of her dad so that Sunny could see how her son James turned out. Anna wanted Sunny to recognize her as her granddaughter but didn't want to risk the tenuous relationship they had by admitting the truth. She still didn't know the reason Sunny had given her child up for adoption, and more than anything, Anna still wanted that answer. Even if it meant never telling Sunny the truth about her own identity. She hoped it never came to that.

But today, the situation was going to get much more difficult.

Sunny had called yesterday and asked Anna to help prepare a Sunday barbecue for her family – Sunny's daughter, granddaughter, and their husbands, along with the twins, Sunny's great-grandchildren. Anna sighed. *My aunt, my uncle, my cousins, but total strangers. I will be meeting them and will know who they are, but they are going to treat me like the hired help. If I'm lucky, I'll be invisible, if not, I'll be run ragged. Why did I agree to this?* Anna knew when Sunny asked, there was no way she could refuse.

"It's just that they worry over me, Anna. They fuss so," Sunny had explained.

"A barbecue sounds pretty easy, Sunny. What would you need me to do?"

"Would you do the shopping for me and come by on Sunday? You could help me with setting it up."

"Sure, it doesn't even sound like that would take too long,"

"Thank you, dear. If Pamela sees me do too much, or if I have to rest at all, she starts in on me moving to the assisted living wing in the main complex." Sunny huffed. "I am not that old."

Anna laughed. "Of course you aren't. You have more energy than most seventy-year-olds around here."

"Well, some of that can be our little secret, my dear," Sunny said conspiratorially. "What Pamela does not know can't hurt her."

Anna had nodded solemnly and used her forefinger to make an "X" sign across her heart.

As she walked toward Sunny's unit, she hefted the three small grocery bags that held the mealtime supplies. Her mind went in circles with pointless worry. She might not have to pretend anything. It was likely she would finish the setup and not even meet the family. *There may be no reason for me to stay until they arrive*, she thought. *I might never meet them.*

Anna resolved to take it one moment at a time. She needed to stop thinking of Sunny as her grandmother; otherwise she would be likely to slip. How could she possibly explain? Unless she started calling all the residents Gram and Pops. She smiled at the thought. How lovely it would be to adopt them all as grandparents. Pushing the worries to the back of her mind, Anna rapped firmly on Sunny's door. Hearing a shouted greeting from inside, Anna slipped her arm through the handles of the plastic grocery bag to free up a hand and turn the knob. Entering, she kicked off her shoes and padded to the kitchen with the bags.

"You're all set here, a feast fit for kings."

"Anna, you are an angel." Sunny beamed.

Laughing, Anna nodded. "Aw, you're so sweet for noticing. Now, let's get this all unpacked and organized."

They worked together, washing the fruit and vegetables and patting them dry with paper towels. They sliced tomatoes and tore the lettuce for the burgers and then diced up apples and grapes for a simple fruit salad. Sunny had made a jello mold that she brought out and added whipped cream, the diced fruit, and some walnuts to make the summer side dish. Anna worked spices and chopped onion into burgers, which she separated with wax paper and stored in the refrigerator. Next, they prepared foil packages of peppers, zucchini, and squash tossed in olive oil and spices. Folding and crimping six packages, they lined them up on the counter until they would be put on the grill.

Anna had Sunny sit and entertain her with stories of her friends while she arranged seating for the extra guests and set the table. She grouped condiments with salt and pepper, along with extra napkins in a green floral motif metal holder at the center of the table.

"Plates and flatware," Anna said, nodding. "Do you want glasses on the table now or wait to fill them first?"

"Let's wait," Sunny said. "So, then Leta told me her granddaughter lost custody of her puppy in the divorce. Leta said the girl felt guilty and admitted she missed her dog more than she missed her ex-husband. Leta said 'That's okay, sweetheart, the dog was a lot nicer than he was.' And that's the honest truth, too. I met the man once."

Anna laughed and grouped the glasses on the kitchen counter, ready to be filled when the guests were ready.

"I think that's about it," Anna began when a small ruckus erupted at the front door with the murmur of voices, accompanied with thumps and culminating in a flurry of knocks at the door.

"They're here." Sunny beamed, getting up and hurrying to the door. Throwing it open, she greeted the family with wide hugs, resounding cheek-kissing, and exclamations of welcome. Anna unconsciously took a few steps back, retreating into the dim recesses of the kitchen. She puttered around, nervously cleaning and checking the preparations they had made, wondering how to gracefully exit. She was still not sure if she had wanted to meet her unknown relatives or avoid the discomfort. At this point, that decision was now out of her hands.

"Anna, come meet my Pamela." Sunny's voice was surprisingly strong for her age, but quivered slightly at the effort of the volume necessary to overcome the din in the living room.

Anna sighed, plastered a smile on her face, and stepped out of the kitchen.

"Anna, this is my daughter Pamela, and her husband Dean. Pam, Dean, this is Anna, a volunteer here that has become a dear friend." Sunny nodded emphatically. "My granddaughter Ashley and her husband are parking the car. These two noisemakers are Mason and Noah. And, yes, they are twins."

Pamela glided forward, extending both of her hands to wrap around Anna's. "It is very nice to meet you, Anna. Mom mentioned what help you have been to her. From the family, we all thank you so much." Anna felt Pamela slip a folded bill into her hand. With a shock, she realized it was a twenty-dollar bill. Her own aunt had just tipped her for spending time with her grandmother. She was thankful later for her dumbfounded speechlessness when she realized her unemotional response of a nod and intelligible mumble was completely appropriate for a stranger.

Pamela wrapped her arm around Anna's shoulder, pulling her into the kitchen. "I have been so worried about her living here by herself. I know the community is filled with her friends, and the staff here are very attentive. It is a wonderful arrangement for her, but I still worry about when she is here alone."

"I haven't known her all that long, but she seems very capable and competent to me," Anna observed.

"Oh, she is for her age, but she is getting older. She could fall and break a bone, have a heart attack or stroke, oh, any number of things," Pamela said, furtively looking toward the living room as if she didn't want her mother to overhear. "I am glad she's taken with you and that she seems comfortable calling to have you here."

"I am glad I can help, it's what we're here for and I do enjoy her company."

"Just watch her, look out for her. I don't want her doing anything where she might overtax or strain herself. I think she does too much and it is not good for her. Like this cookout, such a silly idea and far too much work. I only agreed to it because she said you would be here to do the work. I can't imagine her putting together something like this by herself," Pamela said, aghast at the idea.

"I had no idea she tried to take on too much. I'll keep an eye out and help whenever I can."

"Thank goodness she finally gave up driving. I was terrified every time she said she was going somewhere. Although, it was never more than a few miles. The poor dear is too nervous to travel more than an hour by car and petrified to fly. That's why I have to have Ashley come here for visits. Mom simply can't travel anymore, but then she was always a homebody."

Anna looked at Pamela strangely but wisely bit her tongue. This description didn't fit into the story of the woman who had traveled thousands of miles across the world for a man she had known only a few months. The breathless excitement Anna had heard in Sunny's voice as she described New York and the cross-country train ride hardly coincided with the meek wallflower Pamela described.

"That's interesting. It seems from some of the pictures and the stories she's told, I thought she traveled quite a bit." Anna could not resist the comment, if for no other reason than to provoke Pamela's response.

"Well, she had a grand adventure when she emigrated from Iceland. That's where she's from, you know. She came to New York and was completely overwhelmed by the strange and busy city. Who knows what would have happened if she hadn't met my father. Her first day there, he rescued her from certain death by saving her from stepping in front of a speeding taxicab. He could see right off that she was completely incapable of traversing the city by herself, so he took her under his wing. Within a week, they were married."

"Wow," Anna breathed, not having to pretend her speechless amazement at the story.

"Such a wonderful love story isn't it? My father was only there for two weeks on a business trip. He lived here in Mesa, and brought her back here to live. She didn't speak much English and he took care of everything. They were like that right up until he died."

"That is the most amazing story I have ever heard," Anna said blandly.

"Look at me, going on and on when you probably want to get on home. Dean and Brandon have started the grill, so we're all set here. Thank you again so much," Pamela said dismissively.

Anna nodded numbly. She grabbed her bag, and quickly waved to Sunny, and then snuck out the door. Once outside, Anna took a deep breath and struggled with her shock. Either Sunny had spun an elaborate fairy tale for Anna's benefit or Pamela's version of Sunny's life story was a complete fabrication.

CHAPTER TWENTY-THREE

Anna was tempted to switch with another volunteer to avoid Sunny. She felt like she needed some time. Time for what, she wasn't sure, but she needed to figure it out. Her default solution for mental detangling was outdoor therapy, so she headed for one of the longer trails on Superstition Mountain. Pamela's dismissal had hurt. It was unreasonable; Pamela had no idea Anna was her niece, but Anna had hoped for an instant family connection. She wasn't even sure she liked Pamela all that much, but it hurt to be excluded from the family gathering. *Which is completely stupid,* she thought. *It may be my family by blood, but it's not my family.* We have no history, no memories, and it was difficult to conjure up feelings of love for total strangers.

The experience at Superstition Mountain was vastly different from hiking the trails in Wyoming. Here, the air was drier and the sun much hotter. The trails were hard-packed and filled with small stones and pebbles. Instead of tall trees shading the area, the surrounding growth was mostly scrub brush and cactus. Some areas had a layer of ground cover that back home in Iowa she would have considered to be weeds, but here she appreciated the touch of green. Grass was rare and grew in sparse clusters, except after periods of rain. Anna missed the green, but could appreciate the rugged beauty of the land. All the vegetation had a hearty tenacity for life, no matter what the odds, and each plant took root where ever it could and adapted to the inhospitable environment. Some of the vegetation had adapted so much, Anna realized, that from the plant's point of view, the desert wasn't even inhospitable anymore.

It was the way of nature, and the way of life. Fighting change was an exhausting and often bloody battle, many times futile in the end. Understanding and adapting was far more successful. Anna looked around at the desert vegetation. She suddenly realized adapting to change was not the same as giving up. These plants had not given up or given in – they found a different way to succeed and to thrive. She knew that she would as well. Anna had no idea where this journey was taking her, but she was still committed to knowing the truth. She needed to hear the rest of Sunny's story.

She needed to talk to Logan. After finally reading a few texts, she knew her stubborn refusal to communicate was verging on adolescent behavior. He meant too much to her and something was off because he kept reaching out. She needed closure one way or another. Her heart still hurt, but she was beginning to feel the urge to call him. Maybe text. She'd nearly reached out to him this morning. She toyed with the dollar bill sticking out of the cell phone pocket. The memory of the day he had given her the flowers was as vivid as it was sweet. Her feelings for him were still strong and she couldn't deny she loved him. Perhaps she had made a mistake. It might be good to hear Logan's side of the story. She wanted desperately to talk to him but was afraid of what he might say. She had to do it sooner or later. *Soon*, she thought; *I'll definitely talk to him soon.*

Resolutely, she took the next two hours to finish hiking the trail. Her timing was perfect and she caught the vibrant show of colors at sunset as the brilliant hues of blue, pink, and orange mixed together like celestial sherbet. Her vantage point from the rocky trail was clear of any city buildings or signs of civilization. As she watched the sun slink down to the horizon in the burst of color, she felt an inner peace and a renewed sense of purpose. She looked forward to another chat with her grandmother.

"As soon as I arrived in Wyoming, I realized how different things were there. Since the war, American patriotism was very high. There were American flags everywhere and blue flag plaques were common in front windows. I was very aware of being an immigrant. Everyone was very nice, mind you, but I felt pressured to fit in."

"What do you mean?" Anna asked. They were again ensconced on the small shaded terrace, a cool glass of lemonade and a small pile of cookies on the table between them. Anna had convinced Sunny to try an iced coffee, which Sunny immediately proclaimed excellent after the first sip. She had settled in to continue her story.

"I had been in town for a short time. Sam helped me arrange for a room at the boarding house. I made friends with a lady there who was so very nice. She introduced me to a dressmaker who needed a seamstress so I could have an income. I was homesick but it was easier getting to know a few people and starting a life."

"So you and Sam were courting?" Anna prodded.

Sunny sighed, the far-away look returning to her eyes. "Well, yes, by my thought we were. He had asked me to leave my family and my country after all. We talked about a life together. It was all so romantic and I was young and naive. In my country, the promise of a commitment is as accepted as the marriage commitment. I did not understand that American men sometimes thought differently."

Anna's stomach tightened. She realized her grandmother's most guarded secret was her deepest shame and it was unlikely Sunny would share that disgrace. She held her breath and waited.

"In the end, I found out he was promised to another. We were not to have the future he promised." Sunny laughed wryly. "It was his mother that told me about his deception. At first, I could not believe it. I left messages and wrote him letters begging him to explain, but he never did."

"You never spoke to him after that?" Anna asked, incredulous. "His mother told you he was basically engaged and that's how you found out?" Sunny's story sounded eerily familiar. "What did you do then?"

"I was humiliated and could not bear to stay in the same community. My friend had a car and drove me to a large town nearby. It was there I met my husband, Art. He was a very good man. He was gentle and dependable."

Anna realized how much Sunny was glossing over in her story. Driven by the need to know the truth, she phrased her words carefully. "Pam told me you met Art in New York when you first arrived. They don't know about Sam?"

Sunny exhaled. "My, no, he was a learning experience in my life, sort of a personal embarrassment I never wanted to relive. Honestly, Anna, I'm not sure why I told you all of this." She paused for a moment, contemplating. "I suppose you're a good listener, and perhaps at my age, there are things I need to get out in the open."

"I don't think there is anything wrong with that," Anna said. "That's part of why I am here, to give you someone to talk to, and you can think of me like a priest. What you tell me won't go any further than the two of us." As she looked, Anna could see the emotional strain in the older woman's eyes, which looked tired and drawn.

"Why don't you let me help you inside? I think you might like to lie down for a little while. It's been quite hot out here today and I know that tends to sap your energy."

"Maybe not a nap, but I'll relax in the chair. The air-conditioned coolness will feel good, I think." Anna was not surprised at how quickly Sunny acquiesced.

Anna gathered their dishes and opened the door, carefully watching as her grandmother navigated the small step. Sunny settled into the plush recliner as Anna continued into the kitchen to put away the few dishes. She returned with a glass of water, setting it on the small table next to her charge.

"My, I have not thought about Sam in years," Sunny said. Anna thought she saw a shadow cross Sunny's face, a hint that the statement might not quite be true.

CHAPTER TWENTY-FOUR

Anna sat in a chair by the window, staring out over the ugly parking lot behind her hotel. But she was not focused on the scenery; her mind was busy replaying the story Sunny had shared. What a devastating blow that must have been for her. Having recently gone through an emotional trauma with Logan, she could only imagine how much worse her grandmother felt having her dreams torn away. She had left her country, her homeland, and everything familiar, friends, family to follow her heart, only to have it shattered. Anna tried to image the day Sunny went to see Sam and his mother intervened. To be carrying his child and be faced with that betrayal, it was little wonder she felt she had no choice but to give the baby up. In those days, how would a single young woman alone survive, especially a recent immigrant?

Anna was unaware of the time passing as she mulled over her newly-discovered family history. A knock at the door pulled her out of her reflection, the blinding flash running through her neck making her painfully aware she had been immobile for too long.

She wondered if housekeeping had forgotten something. She quickly looked around the room, but everything seemed to be in order.

Feeling uneasy, she peered through the peephole before deciding whether to open the door.

Her heart plummeted to somewhere below her stomach before catapulting into her throat. Logan. She shook her head in disbelief. Logan?

Clearing her throat, she focused on keeping her voice from quaking. "Yes?"

"Anna, it's Logan. I need to talk to you."

"Now is really not a good time."

"Seriously? You're not even going to open the door?" He sounded incredulous and the moment felt surreal. She had dreamed of him back in her life and now he was here - standing on the other side of her hotel room door. She laid her forehead against the peephole, marveling at the happiness she felt. What happened to all that hurt and anger? In a moment, his voice and the glimpse of his worried face she caught through the peephole brought a flood of emotion to her.

Anna couldn't keep a nervous giggle from erupting. "No."

"Anna…"

"How did you even find me?" she demanded. She tried to recover her anger or at least annoyance. Her heart was racing and she was finding it hard to think straight. She wanted to talk to him, sure, but on her terms.

"Kim. Anna, she's your friend and she knew this was important."

"I don't think she's my friend anymore," Anna said, petulantly. "Why would it be important for me to talk to you?"

"Anna, if you won't listen to me, please listen to my dad."

"What?" Anna thought she heard him wrong. Accidentally eavesdropping on Roy was what started this.

"I know you are angry at me and we need to talk about that, but not right now. Do you hear me? This is not about us; it is about you. Who you really are and who your grandfather is."

"Logan, what are you talking about?"

"Open the door."

Anna threw open the door and looked at him warily. He returned her stare, cocking his head.

With a dramatically noisy exhale, Anna stepped back, gesturing with her hand and deliberately turning her face away from Logan.

He grinned and stepped inside, knowing he'd just won a major battle.

Anna took a deep breath, clenching her teeth as she felt a tightening in her stomach. Closing her eyes, she felt him walk into the room, filling up the small space with his presence. He walked to the small desk and placed the bag on the surface. Opening it, he took out a laptop and quickly set it up.

"I know now why you left Lander. I know why you didn't stop to talk to me about it. I get it. You know what? You still don't have to talk to me. Just listen, please."

"What is this?" Anna asked, watching his laptop as a program loaded.

"It's a video chat. I set it up with Dad so he could talk to you. I knew you wouldn't want to talk to me. But, Anna, you need to listen because he has something you need to hear."

She should have been hurt and angry, but being in the same room with Logan was having the opposite effect on her. She felt calm. The knot in her chest that had been a constant companion for several weeks was slowly loosening. It felt right to have him near. She nodded, and Logan smiled gratefully.

Connecting the link, Logan tested the audio. "Dad? Can you hear me?" The screen suddenly filled with the face of Roy Harris.

"Yup. This end is working fine. You hear me okay? I see you both there, too," Roy confirmed.

"Perfect. I'm going to step back and let you talk to Anna."

Anna watched him as he crossed the room, commandeering the reading chair she had just vacated. He nodded, motioning for her to sit in front of the computer.

She sat down and looked at the screen, uncertain of the protocol in a situation like this. She didn't harbor any anger toward Logan's father, but she was far from comfortable. Basic courtesy won out. "Roy, good to see you. How are you?"

"I'm doing fine, Anna. How are you?"

"I'm good, thank you. It's been very nice down here. I have enjoyed it."

"I only want to say I that am really sorry about any hurt I may have caused you. I had no idea what that girl was up to."

"It's fine. I understand, and we really don't have to talk about it," Anna said, wanting to forget the entire conversation as the memory of it flashed through her mind.

"I understand. Well, I'll get right to what I wanted to tell you – why Logan thought it was important to come down there and make sure you heard."

Anna nodded as a sudden burst of emotion formed as a lump in her throat, making any response impossible.

"I told you about the family history of the Hamiltons, and the Bellamy-Adams family next door," Roy began.

"Yes," Anna said guardedly.

"Anna, I understand this may be important," Roy said, "but it was a long, long time ago, and when you first came 'round I didn't know what you were really researching. I didn't put it all together until, well, until Logan and I sat down and talked this Stormy thing out. He told me what you had been looking into and what you had found out and then it all made sense."

"Really?" Anna said, thinking this might be an elaborate ruse to get her and Logan into the same room.

"You have to know, Anna. I think it's the missing part of the story. I think I know who your grandfather was."

Anna was instantly attentive. "Yes, please, tell me the story."

"Well, like I told you before, there was some history with Wyatt and Grace Bellamy, the daughter at the neighboring ranch. After Wyatt came back from the war, the families expected him and Grace to get married. The mothers pushed them together for a while but nothing really sparked it seems. Turns out, neither of them fancied that idea much, and after a year or so, Grace met Herbert Adams. They didn't have children for a long time, but I remember they had just had Jack, and Herbert was busting with pride over finally having a boy to take over the legacy. I think that day, Wyatt's daddy was wondering when Wyatt would settle down and have babies. I guess that's what it was, but I hadn't thought about it in years until Logan and I were talking."

"Okay," Anna said anxiously.

"I walked in one day, into the main house to get Mr. Hamilton from his office. But I heard voices and figured out real quick that it was a private conversation. I didn't want to interrupt, but I couldn't help overhearing. It was Mr. Hamilton talking to his wife, Alice Ann."

"I haven't seen Wyatt take to any girl since he got back from the war. I do remember that sweet foreign girl he kept company with for a while, but seems to me she moved away."

"Yes, well I nipped that in the bud," Alice Ann said firmly.

"You nipped what?"

"I saw how Wyatt looked at her, he was smitten. And when that little hussy came here looking for him one day, well, that look of guilt and desperation in her eyes told me the whole story."

"Alice Ann…" he said, a warning tone in his voice. "Did you meddle in our son's life?"

"No, I did not," she snapped. "I saw her for the tramp she was and she had gotten herself into trouble and was looking to blame our boy for it. I wasn't having any part of a foreigner coming in and trapping our Wyatt into marriage. I doubt he was the one, what with Grace next door looking to marry him. He wouldn't have, he just wouldn't," she insisted.

"Are you saying that girl was carrying our grandchild and you sent her away?"

Alice Ann glared at him, notching her chin in the air and refusing to answer.

"Alice Ann, did you even tell Wyatt?"

She shook her head. "Why would I spread such lies? You know our boy, he would have taken responsibility."

"Yes, he would have married her."

"And we would have lost our son. Think of the shame, him married to a foreigner and an early baby to boot." Alice Ann's calm was broken as her voice nearly raised to a shriek.

"How could you? How could you deny our son his child and deny us our grandchild?"

"No," she bit out stubbornly. "It wasn't…It couldn't have been."

"Woman, what have you done?"

Roy paused in his recollection and explained, "I had only been working for the family for a few months. I was fresh out of school and not even eighteen. That was the first time I heard him raise his voice and I didn't stick around to hear the rest of what went on."

"What?" Anna felt cheated.

Roy said, "I always wondered what happened, but I never heard Wyatt talk about it, so I don't know if he ever knew.

"You never told him about it?"

"Anna, I was only the hired help back then and an inexperienced young kid. It wasn't my place to say anything, and by then it had been probably ten years since what Alice Ann did." Roy shrugged. "It was a bad thing, but Mr. Hamilton died a couple years after that and I doubt Alice Ann ever would have told Wyatt then."

"So the whole thing stayed a secret?"

"As far as I know, yes. For ten years, Alice Ann kept that secret from her husband and after that, they both did."

"That's quite a secret. Why was this so important for you to tell me?" Anna said.

"Don't you see? Sunny was the immigrant that was friends with Hazel. They were talking about a lost grandchild, so it has to be your father. Anna, Wyatt was your grandfather."

Anna was quiet, absorbing the information and evaluating the details. "Roy," she said finally, "I'm not doubting what you heard, but he can't be my grandfather."

"Why not?"

"I have spent a lot of time with my grandmother now, and she hasn't told me every detail, but enough that I can be sure. The man she talked about being in love with and the one that brought her to Lander was named Sam."

"What?" Logan's sudden exclamation startled Anna. She had nearly forgotten he was there by the window, listening to every word. "Dad, who the devil is Sam?"

Roy's face registered shock for a moment, then he looked thoughtful and shrugged. "I can't think of anyone named Sam, but I can tell you Wyatt's middle name was Samuel."

Anna's heart sped up. The implications of this were overwhelming. If this were true, she had so many answers now. She couldn't wait to tell Sunny. If her Sam was Wyatt, he never left her, never knew about the baby. Anna wondered if Wyatt loved Sunny so much that he never married anyone else. She needed to make sure that Sam really was Wyatt. If they were the same, Sunny would be so happy that Sam had never betrayed her. *Unlike Logan*, Anna thought darkly.

"Roy, I can't thank you enough for sharing all this with me," Anna said sincerely.

"You're welcome, but Logan put this together," Roy said pointedly. "You should really thank him, Anna."

Logan got up and went to the computer. "Okay, Dad, thank you. I appreciate it but I'll take the link down now."

"Goodnight, Logan. Goodbye, Anna."

Anna heard a soft beep and click as Logan snapped the top of the laptop closed. He stood silently, and she could feel his eyes on her. Knowing she had to deal with the problem that was now literally in front of her, Anna looked at Logan directly for the first time since he arrived.

Squaring her shoulders, she wrenched a smile to her face, and with as much grace as she could muster said, "Thank you for this, Logan. I appreciate all the effort it took to arrange this. I apologize for being stubborn and for refusing to take your calls or return messages. You were a good friend to do this."

"I would do just about anything for you Anna," he said softly. "I nearly went out of my mind with worry when you disappeared."

"Why would you bother?"

"Sometimes someone comes into your life and they change everything. You connect with them in a way you never imagined possible. From then on, you can't imagine your life without them. And, I guess, like it or not, you won't live your life without them, not really. Even if they aren't with you, you carry them in your heart and they're a part of your very soul. You are that for me, Anna. You touched something in me. In a really short time, you changed how I see things and now I can't go back." He moved toward her but stopped when she folded her arms and stepped backward.

"Logan, you're not making any sense," Anna said. "You pretty much have to live without me since you're marrying Stormy."

"No, I am absolutely, positively, not now and not ever, marrying Stormy," Logan said slowly.

"Not ever, huh?" Anna whispered as her heart soared. Despite her best effort to control her emotions, a flood of relief and excitement coursed through her.

"I dated her casually, I will admit, probably more out of convenience and shared history, but that was it. She never made me feel the way that you do." He closed the distance between them and reached out to her. Pulling her against his chest, he kissed her deeply with all the passion and longing he felt. She melted into his embrace and returned his passionate kiss.

"I'm glad you're here," she whispered.

"I had to come, Anna. I could not lose you. I need you in my life," he said, looking at her intensely.

"How can you be so sure about how you feel?" Anna asked.

"How can you not? Can you really deny what's between us?"

"I'm afraid to trust it. What I feel for you is strong, intense, but I don't know if it's a physical passion or something deeper. It feels deeper. I know I think about you often and I want to share things with you, good or bad. I want to be where you are. Is that the same for you?"

"You make me feel like more than I am." Logan stopped, searching for the right words, "No, that's not right. You make me feel like I am somehow everything I always thought I could be."

Anna held her breath, not wanting to hear his words but desperate to know how he really felt.

"It's not really as if you complete me. I didn't really feel like anything was missing before I met you. But it's more that you encourage me and you challenge me to be more, to do better. I don't even have to be around you, but I want to be a better me because of you. I can't explain it – it's not that I'm trying to impress you, but somehow you give me such motivation. I have this certainty now that I can achieve so much."

Logan stood behind her, wrapping his arms around her shoulders. She could feel his breath against her hair, warm on her neck. Shivers erupted and traveled from her neck down her spine as he spoke softly.

"I remember from college, I think it was Plato who had the idea that humans were made with four arms, four legs, and one head with two faces. Those humans were very powerful, and the gods were afraid that one day the humans would be a threat so they decided to split them and divide their power. They made sure that each new half would survive on its own. But now when you meet someone that makes you feel stronger and better, that's you recognizing that you belong together."

"You think we belong together?" she asked softly.

"I think we owe it to ourselves to figure that out."

CHAPTER TWENTY-FIVE

Anna looked up at the pale blue Arizona sky, clear except for a small ridge of wispy clouds, feeling happier than she had in several weeks. It was impossible for her to keep the smile from her face. The evening with Logan had been beyond her wildest dreams, or would have been if she had ever allowed herself to create a wild dream that centered on him. He loved her. As much as she loved him, he loved her as well. She was still trying to adjust to the knowledge, just as she was trying to understand the fact that Wyatt Hamilton was her grandfather.

As she drove to SunVilla Village, Anna considered how she would share what she had learned about Wyatt and Alice Ann. She could only imagine Sunny's shock at the news. *If I can even tell her*, Anna thought suddenly. It occurred to her that in order to share the shocking news that Wyatt had always been faithful to her, Anna would have to deliver the even more shocking news that she was Sunny's granddaughter. She was at a loss to think of how to start that conversation. Anna's stomach was in knots by the time she pulled into the parking lot. She shifted the car into park. As she twisted the key from the ignition, Anna realized her hand was shaking. She giggled in anticipation and headed into the main building. Catching herself, she shook her head, giggling like a teenager. She knew it had more to do with Logan than her anticipation of sharing her secret with Sunny. But after so many weeks, months really, on this search, to be able to actually introduce herself confidentially to her grandmother made her almost giddy. Having Logan here with her was an added bonus.

She had several other tasks on her schedule today before she could visit with Sunny. As she bounced across the parking lot, the excitement bubbling inside her was almost unbearable.

It was after three when Anna knocked on Sunny's door. The older woman was waiting by the door, eager for Anna's company and chauffeur service.

"My goodness, dear, you look bright and chipper today," Sunny observed shrewdly.

Ann smiled innocently. "Thank you. Well, you look prepared for quite a mission." The floor around the door was piled with boxes, bags, a large purse, books, and a few books, with bits of paper stuck in the cover of the top.

"I thought as long as you could drive, I would like to get some of these errands done if that is all right. There wasn't anything else I needed today."

"Of course," Anna said warmly. "Let me go get the car and I'll bring it to the door. It will be easier to take this stuff out and less you have to walk in this heat."

Returning in a few minutes, Anna quickly stowed the packages in the back seat and helped Sunny settle into the front and buckle the safety belt.

"All right then, boss, where to?"

"There is a little shopping complex down off the parkway that has a post office and pharmacy. It's just right around the corner from where I need to return those," Sunny said, pointing to the store logo on the bags. Anna recognized the well-known department store and knew exactly where it was located. She had never been to the complex before but had driven by the area enough times she thought she could find the post office without any difficulty.

Anna pulled out of the complex and eased into the flow of traffic. "It was nice meeting some of your family on Sunday."

"Pamela seemed quite taken with you," Sunny said. "She told me how nice you were and that she was glad you were here to help me."

"She is very concerned about your well-being," Anna said and then laughed. "She was very specific when she told me to keep you out of trouble."

Sunny tittered. "I can be a real rabble-rouser, so you might have your hands full."

Anna looked sidelong at her and wagged her forefinger. "I've got my eye on you."

Sunny chuckled and looked out the window, watching the houses flash by as she nodded her head slightly, as older people often do when they are lost in memories. Anna decided to broach the subject foremost on her mind.

"So, uh, Pamela talked to me a little in the kitchen on Sunday, you know," she said.

"Uh-huh."

"She told me the story of how you and Art met," Anna continued, "in New York."

After a moment, she began to strum her fingers on her door's armrest. "Um, yes, well, that is one of her favorite stories."

"You didn't mention Art to me in your story yet. Did you go back to New York after Wyoming?" she asked.

"Oh, fiddle." Anna saw a blush creep up Sunny's neck and her hand seemed to shake.

"Oh, Sunny, I'm sorry, I didn't mean to upset you. It is honestly none of my business." Anna struggled to apologize, fearful now that the unexpected stress would impact the older woman's heath.

Sunny sighed. "In here, now, this is the turn."

The silence in the car was broken only by the soft hiss of the air conditioner as Anna parked the car. "Shall we do the post office first?" She got out of the car and reached into the back seat for the package. As she pushed aside the pile of books, she spied a paper sticking out from the book cover of one and she recognized the design. Reaching over, she snatched the prescription form and grabbed the box. She walked around to the front of the car and met Sunny. In an awkward silence, they crossed to the covered sidewalk.

"You can wait here, Anna, I'll only be a minute," Sunny said, motioning to the metal benches in the shade, the legs sunk in concrete as a theft deterrent. She took the box and the prescription paper and headed toward the entrances.

A gnawing guilt churned in Anna's stomach as a heavy weight settled in her chest. Regret and shame left a bitter taste in her mouth and she wished desperately she had been more tactful in pointing out Sunny's obvious lie. She was afraid now that she had lost her only chance to find out the truth. What bothered her more was the knowledge she had embarrassed her friend and caused emotional stress to an elderly woman. She closed her eyes and shook her head at her own eagerness. When she admitted it, it was selfish and it left her feeling mean. Should she apologize again or try to ignore it? She sat watching the traffic flow, cars constantly pulling in, people shuffling from one area to another, everyone intent on their life's errands and tasks. Anna sat and watched. She saw Sunny exit the post office and walk to the pharmacy two doors down, then go inside. She watched a stooped, gray-haired man walking a small dog, more cars coming and going, and the driver of a delivery truck park in the fire zone. She now sat in front of an ugly tire, breathing in exhaust fumes.

She got up and walked toward the pharmacy and fresh air.

Sunny exited as Anna neared the door. She pointed over her shoulder with a little laugh. "The air got a little toxic over there, so I was forced into action."

Sunny glanced in the direction Anna gestured and then wrinkled her nose. "I don't blame you. If you still have time, there are two more stops I would like to make." Sunny sounded hesitant, as if asking permission.

"No problem at all," Anna said, nodding.

"And then, I would like to take you to dinner and explain a few things."

"Only if you are comfortable. I don't want you to feel like you need to explain anything."

"I have already confided in you, so I might as well finish the story. Then one person will know."

"Sunny, I will keep every confidence you have entrusted to me," Anna said sincerely.

Sunny nodded briskly and walked off to the car. Anna followed her, somewhat confused at her rapid change in attitude.

After finishing the errands, Anna and Sunny chose a small family-style restaurant that offered comfortable seating with high-backed booths that afforded privacy and a feeling of intimacy. They were seated quickly and a server promptly appeared to take their drink orders. After a quick perusal of the menu, they both chose salad and iced tea.

"I am sorry for my abruptness earlier," Sunny said. "I have told that story for so long, and now reliving all these memories telling you, I was caught off guard. I had no idea Pamela would have shared the story of Art and I meeting in New York. The other, over time I suppose, has become almost like the memory of a book I read or a movie I watched. I could almost imagine it was not part of my life, my history."

"I never meant to cause any harm by asking you about it, and I am very sorry if I have caused pain with the memories."

"No, it has been good to remember some of those wonderful times. Simply because something ended badly doesn't mean there weren't good parts worth remembering. We should always keep the good and let some of the bad fade."

"That's a very nice sentiment, Sunny. I will try to remember that."

"So, I had told you my friend who lived at the boarding house had a car and she drove me to Idaho Falls. The pastor of the church in Lander, where I had been staying made arrangements for me to rent a room from a young widow. He thought we might become friends. But we didn't hit it off, the widow and I. I spent several months in Idaho Falls, working again as a seamstress. I kept to myself more. I think I was afraid to make friends, afraid of creating a life and losing it again."

Sunny stopped, cocked her head, and had a faraway look in her eye as if watching an old movie. Anna reached over and patted her hand.

"Time passed. I was so alone and some days were very sad. I had given up my only connection to a man I had loved deeply. Looking back, I believe I mourned him as surely as if I had lost him in the war. I met Art one day in the grocery store. It was so ordinary but he had a gentle way about him that was soothing."

Anna was nearly holding her breath, not wanting to break the spell of Sunny's memory. "I must have looked especially sad that day because he walked up to me there in the store and handed me this bright yellow daisy. He handed it to me and said, 'A girl as beautiful as you should have a flower.' He told me later he went outside to a street vendor to get it and was afraid I would be gone by the time he returned. He said the fact that I was still there was proof to him that we were meant to meet."

"That is such a sweet story," Anna said. "I think that is the most romantic thing I have ever heard." She was frustrated by the missing part of the story. What about her pregnancy, her child?

"He had such a good heart. You know, we were married a few months later and moved down here to Arizona. He started a business and we had a family."

"And you never looked back," Anna said.

"You know, I did send a letter to my friend from the boarding house. She had been so good to me and so supportive. I'm afraid I was not nearly as good a friend to her back then. I sent her a letter after Art and I moved here and told her everything that happened. She wrote back, but I found after that we didn't have much in common. I suppose, too, I simply wanted to forget Sam."

"Sunny and Sam just faded away," Anna said with a sad smile. "And you never went back to using Solveig? That is a beautiful name, by the way."

"No, Solveig was foreign-sounding and many in America had trouble pronouncing it. Languages are difficult if it's something that is not native." She laughed. "That's why I was the only one that called Sam by his middle name."

Anna felt her heart stop and her breath caught in her throat. "What do you mean?"

"The Icelandic language does not have the 'w' letter," Sunny said, pronouncing it slowly and deliberately. "I could not say 'Viot'. It always made him laugh."

"Wyatt? His name was Wyatt."

CHAPTER TWENTY-SIX

The rest of dinner passed in a blur, and later Anna hardly remembered anything after that moment. That moment the question was answered was the moment for her that everything was confirmed. After they finished eating, she took Sunny back to SunVilla Village and immediately called Logan with hands that shook so badly she had to try several times to punch the correct buttons.

"Hi, beautiful, how did it go?" Logan answered, the warmth in his voice bringing an unconscious smile to her lips.

"Logan, it started out awful, then ended up good," she said breathlessly. "I want to tell you all about it. Can you meet me? I should be there in about ten minutes."

"Of course, babe," he replied instantly.

"I'll let you know when I get there," Anna said and hung up, anxious to get back to the hotel and tell Logan the entire story.

They had not talked much after the call with Roy. Their physical passions had taken over and any thought of conversation had been sidelined. Anna had been unwilling to give in to her desires completely, so Logan had taken a room at the same hotel to be close to her. It had been after one o'clock in the morning before he made that decision, and he had loudly grumbled his complaints to her about waking up in bed alone when they met for breakfast in the morning. Anna was still unsure about many things in her life, but had started to believe that a future with Logan was worth pursuing.

Anna pulled into the parking lot of the hotel and saw Logan lounging on a bench by the front entrance. Feeling like a giddy teenager with her first crush, she couldn't keep the grin off her face as she crossed the pavement to where he waited. He crushed her in his embrace and kissed her breathless.

"I could get used to a greeting like that," she laughed.

"You should," he said meaningfully. "And there's a lot more where that came from."

"Down boy. I have a lot to tell you, but don't know whether I can trust being alone with you."

"I can behave for a while," he said, throwing his arm around her shoulder, then nuzzling her neck noisily. "As long as we can take some make-out breaks."

"Ugh," she said, in mock frustration, "really? 'make-out breaks?' What am I going to do with you?"

"I can make a list," he immediately responded, suggestively wiggling his eyebrows.

Laughing, she grabbed his hand and pulled him toward the hotel entrance and down the hall. "We'll talk in my room. Her story is really something, but with what you know about Wyatt's side, I'm sure you can fill in the blanks."

"Some, yes, but there are some questions still. How do you feel about all this?" he asked.

"It's a little overwhelming. Honestly, I try to think of my dad, and the grandparents I grew up knowing, and then think about this whole other history that happened to get to what I remember; it's sort of amazing." Anna shook her head.

Arriving at her room, she pulled the plastic key out of the back pocket of her jeans and opened the door. Logan followed her in and she dropped her bag by the door, crossing the room and settling into the chair. Logan draped himself on the bed. She looked at him with a stern warning, but he shrugged and looked at her innocently.

"Tell me the story of your grandparents," he said, leaning back against the pillows and folding his hands behind his head.

Anna grinned. "Once upon a time, a cowboy from a small ranch in

Wyoming joined the military. He was sent to Iceland, where at a USO dance he met a beautiful local girl who had come from her small village in the north to help at her aunt's store in Reykjavik. It was love at first sight and they spent several months together until the war ended and he was sent home. He begged her to follow him, so she set out on the grand adventure to move to America. She was overwhelmed by Ellis Island and New York, but her resilient Viking spirit rose to the challenge and she persevered. She made her way to his small Wyoming town, and they continued their passionate love affair."

Anna paused for a moment. "That's pretty much where the fairy tale ends. Solveig went to see Wyatt when she realized she was pregnant but talked to Alice Ann instead. Wyatt's mom decided there was no way she would accept a daughter-in-law that was a foreigner and denied the grandchild. Wyatt never knew."

"Did Solveig—Sunny —say why she never told Wyatt about the baby?"

"She was pretty emotional at that part of the story," Anna said. "I am not sure exactly what Alice Ann said, but it must have been convincing. She never questioned that he was engaged to Grace. I think all these years, Sunny has imaged that Wyatt was married and had his own family."

"How could she just leave and not talk to him first?" Logan wondered.

"She was devastated. Even after all these years, I could tell she was still hurt. I can imagine what she was going through, I think," Anna said softly.

"Oh jeez, Anna, I'm sorry. I didn't think," he said, sitting up and swinging his feet over the edge of the bed. "You felt the same way when you heard Stormy talking to Dad?"

"It's all right. Yes, it made me feel awful, and it was like I was all torn up inside. I was angry and hurt. I felt stupid for trusting and really felt used. If we had been seeing each other for months, like they had been, and I had been pregnant, like she was, I can't imagine how much worse it would have been. I know I didn't want to talk to you, so it really does make sense to me that she wouldn't want to talk to him."

"But to give up the baby and never tell him," Logan said. "That seems desperate."

"She felt like she had no choice, I guess. It had to have been so hard for her, and in the forties, things were different than today. I don't know."

"So how did she end up here, in Arizona?"

"She met someone after the adoption. He was good to her and they moved here and had a wonderful life it seems. Her daughter, my aunt—" Anna laughed. "That seems odd to say, but anyway, my aunt told me the story of how they met, Sunny and her husband Art. Apparently, their story is that they met in New York just days after Sunny came through Ellis Island. He saved her from stepping in front of a taxi and it was love at first sight. Everyone thinks they married right after that and moved out here. Sunny pretty much cut out the entire Wyoming and Idaho part of her life."

"That's quite a story, but it seems to have worked out for her," Logan said.

"Yes, it seems like she has been very happy in her life here," Anna said. "I'm glad because she is really such a nice person, and good."

"I'm glad you found out everything you needed to know. So, are you coming back to Wyoming now?"

"What? No, not yet, I'm not done here," Anna exclaimed, her face registering the shock she felt.

"What more do you need to do? You know the whole story now."

"But she doesn't."

"What? You can't think you're going to tell her anything, Anna."

"Why not? She deserves to know. She should know Wyatt loved her, and never stopped loving her. She should know that her baby boy grew up to be an amazing man, a great father, and she deserves to know she has another granddaughter. I deserve for her to know."

"Anna, you can't."

"This is my family, my choice."

"You're already a part of the legacy at the ranch. Even if I didn't love you so much, you belong at the ranch."

"That's only a place – I am talking about real people. People I want in my life. I want my grandmother to know who I am, and for her to acknowledge that I am her granddaughter, and for me to have a relationship with the rest of my family. They're my family, Logan. They just don't know it," Anna said fervently, her eyes filling up with tears threatening to spill over.

"Family are the ones you choose to have around you. Wyatt was as close as any grandfather could have been to me. I loved him and I know he loved me too. He left the ranch to Dad, knowing I would inherit it one day. We can be a family, you and I. We'll be a family because we choose it."

She shook her head, "That's not the point…"

"Anna, sweetheart, you have to think about this," Logan said softly, coming over and pulling her into his arms. She resisted, pushing him away.

"Don't," she said, holding her hand out. "What is there to think about?"

"Remember what you said, her family has no idea. How is she going to tell them? What are they going to think?" Logan folded his arms against his chest. "Think about what you might do to that family, what you might do to her."

"What about what she did to me?" Anna said defiantly.

"What? Are you kidding me?" he asked incredulously. "She did not do anything to you. She gave your father up for adoption to ensure he had a good life. From what you say, he did. And it seems you did too."

Anna glared at him, trying to formulate an argument, but she was unable to refute his logic.

He pressed the advantage and continued. "Fate, or destiny even, intervened, and right now you're alone. I know you're looking to replace your family or find where you belong, but pushing your way into Sunny's family isn't the way to do it. Come back to Wyoming with me," he finished gently.

"I think you should leave now," Anna said firmly. "I would really like to be alone."

"No, come here. Let's talk this out." Logan sighed with exaggerated patience.

Anna stood and stared at him, her eyes glittering angrily. "I wish you would let me make my own life decisions."

"I think maybe you need some help making the right ones," Logan said, his temper finally snapping.

"I can't believe you said that to me."

"Anna, please, you have to think about what you're doing."

"That's exactly it. I want to think about it and I can't do that with you here. Go back to Wyoming, Logan."

"Anna, don't do this." His voice clearly reflected his annoyance.

"I need to. I've come too far to back down now." She walked to the door and opened it, "Logan, go home."

"Fine," he said, starting to sweep by her before stopping. He grabbed her shoulders and brought his mouth down on hers, possessively. "But this isn't over," he said resolutely.

Logan left and Anna sat for a long while in the dark room, staring out of the window into the dimly-lit parking lot. What if Logan was right? How could she tell Sunny about Wyatt and admit she was her granddaughter without Sunny's family finding out about her lie? If they knew, would her family forgive her?

She thought about everything Solveig had been through on her way to becoming Sunny Rogers. The adventurous girl, hopeful and in love. The Viking spirit she spoke of had seemed very real. Anna thought about those words and realized that was her legacy. Her true bloodline was that of the Vikings and she could choose to embrace it. Sunny's words came back to her as she thought of the qualities. Adventure, self-reliance, tenacity, and tolerance. And contentment of course. We endeavor and we survive. At that moment, Anna felt she had earned the legacy. The first part, anyway, described the last few months of her life. It had been more of an adventure than the previous thirty years combined. She had never thought there was the remotest possibility she would pick up with only a few clothes and chase clues across—she'd lost count of how many—states in search of answers to questions she had never realized she needed to ask. It had taken tenacity, that was for sure, and self-reliance.

The remaining elements were her decision. What tolerance did she need to find contentment? She thought about Sunny's decisions and the years of deceit. Anna wondered if Alice Ann ever regretted her rash decision to choose prejudice and greed over family. In the end, her own son seemed to have suffered the most, the one person Alice Ann should have protected. Wyatt never married, and never had a family of his own. Sunny found love and had children and grandchildren. Grace had married someone else and had a son. Wyatt had a son he never knew. Anna felt a twinge of sorrow for the grandfather she never knew. She could imagine his loneliness, the last member of his family alone in that big house. She wondered if he ever thought of Sunny or if he imagined what life would have been like with her.

Suddenly, Anna was overwhelmed with the feeling of being loved and desired. She had left Logan just as Sunny had left Wyatt. Anna thought now it was strange Wyatt never tracked Sunny down. She wondered if he had tried and failed. When Logan had shown up at her hotel room door, she had been angry and annoyed, but her heart had leapt with happiness that he found her. She had wanted all along for him to choose her, to chase her down only to tell her how much he loved her. And he had. Anna wasn't sure now that it was enough.

CHAPTER TWENTY-SEVEN

After a fitful night's sleep, Anna watched the sun come up over the distant mountains. She had given up and left her hotel room while it was still dark to head for her favorite trail at Superstition Mountain. She had perched on a large rock, listening to the sounds of the desert. The forest in Wyoming had been teeming with the noise of life, but the desert was much more subdued. The sounds took concentration to catch, small chirps and buzzing, the telltale rattle of the underbrush as a rodent scurried or snake slithered through. As she sat watching the blushing pink on the horizon slowly turn to a vibrant yellow, she heard a dove's cooing song. Small patches of color brightened the otherwise dull desert landscape. The flowers seemed to bloom almost in defiance of their scrubby, prickly neighbors. The orange globe mallow and delicate-looking blue gilia brought life to the worn-looking dusty ground. Endeavor and survive. The vibrant-colored bloom defied all odds and flourished in the desert. They adapted to the dry conditions, used the resources available, and changed to make do and grow regardless. To live was a choice, just like quitting was a choice. Anna knew happiness was a choice as well. She could act and pursue her heart's desire, or react and never be in control. She could choose how to handle this moment of her life, and it might well define her entire future.

All this time, was she searching for her past, or trying to find her future?

Anna smiled as she stood up slowly, brushing off her backside as she trotted down the trail. The closer she came to the parking lot, the quicker her steps came, and as she neared the end she was jogging.

Anna pulled into the now-familiar parking lot that afternoon. A large bunch of yellow daisies sat on the seat next to her, her first real gift to her grandmother. Anna had decided that the confidence of the private club that the two of them had created would sustain a secret of her own as well as Sunny's. She knew Sunny would welcome her as a granddaughter, even if she chose not to tell the rest of the family she had created with Art. Anna was part of a history before that, and the clandestine nature of their true relationship could make it that much more special. In time, with some preparation and laying some verbal groundwork, Sunny might even share with Pamela the great love she had known before Art. Pamela didn't need to think any less of her mother simply because she had loved someone before her father, even if Sunny had loved Wyatt more. *Pamela didn't need to know that part*, Anna thought. The idea that if Sunny had stayed with Wyatt, Pamela might never have been born was a little disconcerting, even from Anna's perspective.

She grabbed the flowers and headed to Sunny's unit. After a quick knock, she opened the door and shouted a greeting. "Sunny, it's Anna."

"Yes, dear, come in. My, aren't those pretty flowers?" Sunny said as she stuck her head out from the kitchen, wiping her hands on a dishtowel.

"They are for you. I saw them and remembered your story about Art, so I thought you might like them."

"How sweet. Thank you so much. Let me find a vase in here."

"They are sort of a goodbye as well."

"Yes, well, I thought you were spending an awful lot of time here," Sunny said. "A pretty young thing like you shouldn't be spending all her time with old fogies like us. You go back and pursue that career or get a good man in your life." Sunny nodded meaningfully.

Anna laughed. "That's the plan."

"Good, then. Thank you for keeping an old lady company. I've enjoyed our talks. It was nice after all, taking a long walk through my memories."

"Do you ever wish you could go back and change anything?"

"Oh my, I'm not sure I would. We all have a path in life that we have to walk to learn the lessons we need to be taught."

"Knowing how everything turned out, you would still have left Iceland to follow Sam, then leave Wyoming and end up with a life here?"

Sunny smiled. "Yes, I think I would."

Anna frowned slightly. She had planned this conversation in her head and it was not going the way she had thought it would. Where was the longing for Wyatt, or Sam, as Sunny thought of him? Sunny should be rekindling her love for Sam and be thrilled to have Anna as a connection to her lost love. How could her grandmother welcome her if she thought of the love affair as a life lesson?

"I want to thank you, Anna, for prodding me to share my memories with you. Reliving it all has been difficult, some parts, but looking back on my life, it all worked out exactly the way it was supposed to."

"What do you mean?"

"I wouldn't have traded the years I had with Art for anything," Sunny said fondly. "He was truly the love of my life." Anna watched as Sunny touched flowers gently, obviously lost in memories of Art. Realization struck her then. Solveig and Sam didn't have the torrid love affair that Anna had imagined. Solveig had a Viking sense of adventure and traveled to America to pursue a new life. She had loved Sam, but not enough to fight for him. Anna realized that Sunny, as she was now, had found contentment in a life with Art, not in a love affair with Wyatt. Anna realized that after Alice Ann had her away, Sunny never considered fighting for Wyatt. Sunny felt her heart had been broken, but she accepted it and left. She had walked away from the life with Wyatt, her Sam, and had given their child up to have a life with two parents that could love him. But for Sunny, she had not felt the commitment to Sam in a love that would endeavor and survive. She walked away.

But Sunny had loved Art. Loved him deeply. She had enjoyed a good life with him, raised a family, and now still surrounded herself with memories of their time together. *She doesn't mourn the lost love with Sam*, Anna thought with a shock. *He was simply a chapter she lived through and closed the book when it was done.* Anna felt the tears gather in her eyes and blinked quickly to dissipate them.

Anna heard a knock at the door, followed by a loud, "Yoo-hoo!" She instantly recognized Pam's voice. Anna looked up and saw a wriggling gray form in Pam's arms. As she closed the door, the animal's whine turned into a howling insistence to be on the ground.

"They had an adoption day at the animal shelter today, and this guy just stole my heart. Mom, I thought you might like him as company here." Pam released the dog, and it proceeded to rush from Sunny to the corners of the room, then dart from room to room, furiously wagging his tail and licking any human he came in contact with.

Sunny laughed. "What a cute little guy."

Pam nodded. "He's had all his shots and the vet says he's healthy. He's about eight years old and his last owner died about four months ago. He's been from shelter to doggy foster care and they've been looking for a home like this for him. An elderly person in a quiet home."

Sunny raised her eyebrow and Anna hid a grin. She was going to miss being around Sunny and even might miss Pam a little. Anna knew she could not reveal to Sunny that she was her granddaughter, not with Pam there. Anna wasn't sure now that Sunny would welcome knowing her, even if Pam hadn't stopped by. Oddly, Anna didn't feel a renewed sting of loss as she would have expected. Sunny might never learn of Anna's true identity, but that didn't seem to be as important now as it had been a few hours ago. Anna realized her search had always been about finding her roots, her heritage. Anna's goal had been to find her grandparents and to learn about them, who they were and what lives they had lived.

It occurred to her that after all this time, all the searching, she had not thought about introducing herself or even about being a part of their lives. She never considered that they might want to be a part of hers. Her life had not been interesting enough for anyone to want to be a part of, at least not until the last few months. Anna's search had been to discover them, not to have them know her. If she were honest, she never considered much beyond the mysterious identity of her grandmother and grandfather. Early in the process, she considered that she might have aunts and uncles, or even cousins, but that idea hadn't crossed her mind in quite a while. But, now they were here, and they were real. Pamela and Charles had no reason to want her in their lives; they had no connection beyond blood history. Anna realized she had not even tried to get to know them. On the day of the cookout, Anna hadn't made an excuse to stay to meet her cousin Ashley and her husband Brandon. The couple's twins, Mason and Noah, had been there that day and Anna didn't recall a single detail about them. All the time she had convinced herself she was searching for family, but that had never been what she wanted. It was a final goodbye and tribute to her father. The closing of one chapter of her life to make way for the next.

"Well, I'll let you all get acquainted. Pam, it was good seeing you again. Sunny, thank you again for sharing your stories."

"Thank you for helping me remember them."

Anna picked up her bag and stopped next to Pam's chair. She laid her hand on Pam's shoulder and looked at Sunny.

"Adoption is a good thing. My grandparents opened their home to a little guy named Lander. They called him James though. He was a lucky devil and had a great life. I wouldn't be here if it weren't for him, but that's another story. I'm glad things worked out the way they did."

Pam's attention was on the small dog and didn't see the brief pained expression on Sunny's face before a smile spread across it.

"This little guy is Rufus and I guess it will be up to Mom to see if he gets a new name."

Sunny came over to Anna and hugged her tightly. "Thank you for the flowers, dear. As we say in Iceland, Bless Bless."

After she left Sunny and Pam, Anna headed to the hotel room and packed her belongings. She left the plastic key on the nightstand and toted her bag to the car. *She really should wait until morning*, she thought. *Fourteen hours is a long drive. Who starts such a long trip home in the middle of the afternoon?* But there was no reason to stay any longer. She had found everything she had set out to, and she was done here. She was anxious to get on the road.

There was nothing left in Iowa. She could admit that now. It was the dried husks of a long-stale life. It was time to begin a new life, one with purpose. The research and effort of the past few months had been worthwhile, to know where she had come from and the legacy of her grandparents. Her Viking heritage from her grandmother had given her the sense of adventure, the tenacity to endeavor, and the ability to recognize contentment. Her grandfather had left her the legacy of family and home she accepted as rightfully hers.

Wyatt had not loved Sunny enough to find her, not the way Logan had come after Anna. Anna had no doubt now of Logan's feelings. She trusted in their love and was ready to commit fully. She recalled the Icelandic Proverb she had seen on Sunny's wall: '*The Bold and the Generous have the best lives.*' Be bold and be generous – she thought that was excellent advice.

Two days later, Anna swung the Honda into the familiar driveway and drank in the view as she passed the white fencing. She eased to a stop under the shade tree and shifted into park, cutting the engine. She saw Logan step out from the dark interior of the barn. Before she even thought about what she was doing, she dashed from the car and jumped into his arms with perfect confidence he would catch her.

He did.

ABOUT THE AUTHOR

Heidi Herman is a women's fiction author, writing stories of strong women who face and overcome obstacles to live their best lives. Her passion and a common theme in her writing is her Icelandic heritage.

She started with children's books and folklore, and now enjoys adding a little taste of Iceland in her contemporary novels. In addition to writing, she loves cooking, photography, travel, and exploring the outdoors.

She spends her time writing, researching Iceland, attending Scandinavian events, and pursuing adventure all along the way.

Website: www.heidihermanauthor.com
Facebook: https://www.facebook.com/HeidiHermanAuthor
Twitter: https://twitter.com/StoriesbyHeidi
Instagram: https://www.instagram.com/heidihermanauthor/

OTHER BOOKS BY HEIDI HERMAN

The Guardians of Iceland and other Icelandic Folk Tales
Legend of the Icelandic Yule Lads
Icelandic Yule Lads Mayhem at the North Pole
Icelandic Yule Lads & Other Legends Coloring Book
Homestyle Icelandic Cooking for American Kitchens